MARK LUKENS

THE EXORCIST'S APPRENTICE

THE EXORCIST'S APPRENTICE

A novel by

MARK LUKENS

Please check out these other books by the Author:

ANCIENT ENEMY – www.amazon.com/dp/B00FD4SP8M

THE SUMMONING – www.amazon.com/dp/B00HNEOHKU

DESCENDANTS OF MAGIC – www.amazon.com/dp/B00FWYYYYC

GHOST TOWN: A NOVELLA – www.amazon.com/dp/B00LEZRF7G

NIGHT TERRORS – www.amazon.com/dp/B00M66IU3U

A DARK COLLECTION: 12 SCARY STORIES – www.amazon.com/dp/B00JENAGLC

SIGHTINGS – www.amazon.com/dp/B00VAI31KW

WHAT LIES BELOW – www.amazon.com/dp/B0143LADEY

DEVIL'S ISLAND – Coming Soon

THE SUPERHUMAN GENE – Coming Soon

For centuries the Roman Catholic Church has employed a select few to investigate extreme cases of demonic possession, miracles, and paranormal activity. Some of these Investigators possess Gifts of the Spirit and other strange talents. Often, the calling of an Investigator is passed down from father to son.

PART ONE

CHAPTER ONE

Western Massachusetts

Lightning split the night sky as Paul drove his 1978 Ford Bronco through the rutted back roads. The truck's motor roared with power as the large knobby tires spun in the mud and pulled the beast of a truck up a small hill through the dense trees.

Rain splashed the windshield as Paul clenched the steering wheel, trying to hold it steady is it bucked under his hands. The headlights and the string of fog lights on the truck's roof pierced the darkness of the woods only so far and left everything else in shadows.

Paul knew he was driving way too fast down the dirt road. He knew he should slow down. But he had to hurry.

They were waiting for him.

He wore a long black coat over a dark sweater and a dark pair of pants. A crucifix of pure silver dangled from a chain around his neck. He had rings on the middle and third finger of each hand, and each ring was forged from pure iron. His dark and deep-set eyes were fixed on the trail through the woods as he drove, his mouth set in a grim line, his jaw muscles clenched. His angular and knotted muscles bulged underneath the sleeves of his sweater and coat as he fought to control the steering wheel.

Three sets of rosary beads hung from the rearview mirror. They clicked and rattled as the truck bounced down the ruts in the road.

Paul stomped the brake pedal down as he took a turn a little too quickly. He felt the back end of the Bronco sliding, and he heard the screech of pine needles and branches scraping at the side of the truck.

He pulled the wheel sharply to the right, overcorrecting the turn just a bit. He couldn't crash—he had to get there before it was too late.

Father James was already at the house; he had told Father McFadden that he had things under control there. But it didn't matter. Paul was coming out on Father McFadden's orders. Whether Father James realized it or not, whether he wanted to believe it or not, this exorcism he was performing was beginning to spiral out of control.

Paul stomped on the gas pedal after his truck quit sliding in the mud. The back tires spun in the mud for a moment and then he felt the tires grab traction.

He glanced at the passenger seat where his dark, floppy hat sat on top of his black canvas duffel bag, and then he looked back at the dirt road in front of him.

Almost there. Maybe a few more minutes.

A streak of lightning lit up the night sky above the trees for a split second, illuminating the narrow road that cut through the dense woods. Everything was washed in a blue light for just a moment. Five seconds later thunder rumbled through the darkness like a growling beast from Hell.

Paul saw in that brief flash of lightning that the rutted and bumpy dirt road in front of him was a straight shot for as far as he could see. Even though the trail had been reduced to a mud-slicked ribbon from the torrential downpour, he risked pressing down on the accelerator a little more, pushing his Bronco a little faster.

As he drove, a sudden vision flashed in his mind like one of the bolts of lightning from the night sky. His body went rigid as he gripped the steering wheel, but he no longer saw the road. He was underwater for a moment, suspended and floating in the cold darkness, trapped inside a vehicle. He saw light from somewhere in the darkness, illumination from a dashboard that was flickering. He saw pale hands reaching for him …

Paul blinked his eyes just in time to hit the brakes and yank the steering wheel to the right. The truck slid around a sharp bend through the trees, the tail end almost colliding with the trunk of a tree.

His heart thudded in his chest. He didn't remember driving down the road this far. How long had he seen that vision in his mind? He glanced at the battery-powered clock on the dashboard and saw that at least a full minute had passed while he'd seen the vision.

What did the vision mean? He'd never had one that strong before, and never one that had incapacitated him as a driver, even if only for a minute. He had been underwater in the vision, maybe trapped inside a vehicle. He didn't know what it meant, but he couldn't push away the feeling of fear and dread that had suddenly washed over him—a sense of … helplessness … of loss.

But he had to force the memory of the vision and the overwhelming feeling of it away for now. He needed to concentrate on getting to the Whittier house before it was too late.

CHAPTER TWO

The Whittier House

Paul's Ford Bronco emerged from the dark woods into the large clearing where the Whittier house stood. He slammed on the brakes and his truck slid to a stop only a few feet away from the three other vehicles parked in front of the dark home. One of the vehicles was a 2012 Ford F150 with a metal toolbox in back and large tires that were more suited to this rural area. The other two vehicles were definitely city cars, not ideal for the conditions that the storm had turned the woods into. Paul figured the truck belonged to the homeowner and the two cars belonged to Father James and his assistant.

Paul slammed the shifter into park and shut the engine off, and then the lights. The darkness smothered him immediately, but every few seconds there was a flash of lightning snaking across the sky that illuminated the world for a moment.

He grabbed his hat and canvas bag from the passenger seat and got out of his truck into the rain. He ran from his truck to the small front porch of the house, avoiding the puddles along the way. Rainwater drained off the brim of his hat like a waterfall as he climbed the wood steps. His breaths were puffs of clouds in front of him in the chilly night air.

A priest waited on the front porch for Paul, holding the door open. The doorway was dark behind the priest and Paul wondered if the electricity was already out. He approached the priest, stomping across the floorboards of the porch, leaving behind muddy footprints.

A flash of lightning illuminated the priest in the doorway. He was a few inches shorter than Paul and very thin. His eyes were dinner plates of fear on his pale face above the bright white square of his priest's collar that seemed to float in the darkness against his black clothes.

Paul had seen Father James a few times before, and this man wasn't him.

"I'm Father O'Leary," the man said in a high and shaky voice. He offered a trembling white hand to Paul.

Paul grabbed the young priest's hand in greeting and his golden-tanned skin was a contrast with the young priest's pale flesh. Paul squeezed a little too hard and he felt the man's hand nearly crumple in his grip. He also felt the clammy perspiration oozing from the man's palm.

"I'm Paul Lambert," he said as he let the man's hand go. He set his canvas bag down on the floor of the porch and the items inside the bag clinked together lightly. He took off his coat and hat and shook the rainwater off of them and then folded the coat over one arm.

Father O'Leary stood still for a moment in the doorway like shock was still rooting his shoes to the threshold, like he was paralyzed with dread.

"You're … you're not a …" the priest stammered.

"No, I'm not a priest," Paul finished his sentence for him. He saw even more fear in the man's large blue eyes—if that was even possible. "But I can help," Paul added.

"I don't know …" Father O'Leary said. "I've never seen … never seen anything like what's in there …"

"Is this your first exorcism?" Paul asked.

"No. My third. But this one is … is …"

"I know. Your faith must be strong, Father O'Leary, stronger than it's ever been before. It must not waver tonight."

The young priest didn't answer, but he nodded quickly. Then he moved out of the way to allow Paul entrance to the dark house.

Paul picked up his canvas bag from the porch floor and stepped inside. His eyes adjusted quickly to the darkness inside the home as Father O'Leary closed the door. A light over the stove in the kitchen provided a soft yellowish light; it was enough to see by.

The living room was filled with bedroom furniture and possessions: boxes, stacks of books and papers, piles of clothes, a desk pushed up against one of the couches and piled with more papers and books, a dresser with a heap of clothes still on hangers draped over it. Two lamps were on the floor next to the bedroom furniture. An empty bookcase had been set near a recliner. Pictures and framed photographs were stacked up against the bookcase. The furniture and possessions looked like they had been hastily piled together.

"We took everything out of the bedroom that could be thrown at us," Father O'Leary explained.

Paul nodded. At least Father James had followed his instructions so far. But maybe only because they'd come from Father McFadden.

A door opened and closed in the hallway and Paul heard the sound of footsteps approaching the living room. Father James entered the living room and stared at Paul who still stood near the front door with his canvas bag in one hand and his soggy coat over his other arm.

"Thank you for coming here, Paul," Father James said, but it sounded insincere to Paul.

Paul nodded as he laid his coat over the arm of a couch and placed his hat on top of it. He kept his dark canvas bag gripped in his other hand the whole time.

"How old is she?" Paul asked.

Father James stood six foot four, only two inches taller than Paul. But where Paul was lean and muscled, Father James was narrow-shouldered and big-boned with wide hips and a slight pot-belly that pushed his black shirt out. His face was long and jowly, like a basset hound's. He had deep wrinkles in his face, and his cobalt-blue eyes were surrounded by smaller wrinkles. He had a full head of silver hair that was combed back. He wore a black long-sleeved shirt with a white collar in front. A purple stole was draped over his shoulders. He flicked his sharp eyes to Father O'Leary.

"Go back there with her," Father James told the younger priest.

Father O'Leary seemed to hesitate for just a moment, but then he nodded and hurried through the living room, making his way around the bedroom furniture and then down the dark hall. He walked to a closed door on the left side of the hallway that had a line of flickering light coming from underneath it. Again he hesitated a moment before opening the door. His lips moved in a quick, silent prayer, and then he entered the bedroom.

Paul stared down the hallway, watching Father O'Leary enter the room. There was no sound from the bedroom, just an eerie silence. The flickering light of candles illuminated Father O'Leary and the hallway for a moment, and then the young priest entered and closed the door behind him.

Paul turned his attention back to Father James.

"Father McFadden didn't need to send you," Father James said, making no attempt to mask his feelings. "We have this thoroughly under control."

Paul didn't answer. He thought of Father O'Leary's face in the doorway when he had first arrived—the young priest looked like a scared animal ready to bolt away in panic at any moment.

"How old is the girl?" Paul asked again. He wasn't going to waste time arguing with the old, egocentric priest about whether he should be here or not. It was too late for that now. Father McFadden had sent him and that was the end of it.

"She's seventeen years old," Father James finally answered Paul's question. "Her name is Julia."

"Who else is in the house?"

"Just us, Julia Whittier, and her father, Richard."

And the demon, Paul thought. But he didn't say anything. It didn't need to be said. He glanced around at Julia's possessions scattered around the living room. He walked over to the bookcase and looked through the pictures and framed photos. He found what he was looking for—a photo of Julia. He picked it up and turned to Father James.

"I'm ready," he told the old priest.

But Father James stood very still in the murky living room. "I don't approve of the methods you use," he said.

Paul nodded like he was noting Father James's objections even though they really didn't matter right now. He walked towards Father James without a word, his canvas bag still in one hand, the photograph of Julia in the other.

Lightning flashed and lit up the living room in a wash of light-blue light, and it gave Paul the sense of being underwater for a moment. And in that moment, his mind slipped back to the horrifying vision he'd seen while driving here. The images themselves hadn't been horrifying, but it was the feelings that had accompanied them: dread, helplessness, loss. He couldn't help feeling that something was terribly wrong here in this house.

Father James didn't bother expounding on his disapproval of Paul's "methods" as he called them. He'd had his say and that seemed like it was enough for him. He turned without another word or gesture and walked through the living room, past an archway that led into the kitchen, and then down the hall to the bedroom door.

Paul followed Father James. He knew that the old priest, like most Catholic priests, thought Paul's practices during exorcisms were esoteric and banal at best, and dangerous voodoo at worst. But Paul wasn't going to waste time defending his ways. He had learned his gifts and techniques from his father. And his father had learned them from his father. Paul came from a long line of Investigators for the Church, and he was only sent to the very worst cases of possessions.

And this was a bad one, he could already sense that.

Father McFadden told Paul on the phone that this exorcism had been going on now for over thirty-six hours with no sign of the demon letting Julia Whittier go. That was why Father McFadden needed to send Paul here.

Paul followed Father James down the dark hallway. The only sounds were their shoes clomping on the wood floor and the rain pelting the roof. Paul noticed photographs and portraits arranged neatly along the hallway wall—the story of the Whittier family through the years, a history of Julia from baby to teenager. A mother was in many of the photos but she wasn't here at the house.

Paul wondered why.

Father James didn't give Paul a second look as he twisted the door handle and entered the bedroom.

CHAPTER THREE

Paul felt the drop in temperature immediately as he walked through the doorway. It was a little chilly outside, especially with the rain, but nowhere near freezing. In the bedroom it had to be forty degrees at the most.

The bedroom was lit up by a collection of candles on a small table in the far corner of the nearly empty room. On the table with the candles were two worn bibles, three glass vessels of holy water, and two large crucifixes.

Father James closed the bedroom door and locked it as Paul walked towards the middle of the room. His breath clouded up in front of him as he exhaled.

Julia's father, Richard, stood against the far wall, only steps away from the corner where the small table was. He was a heavyset man in his early forties. His hair was thinning and he looked like he might have been a muscular man in his youth, but now fat was overtaking his muscle quickly. Paul guessed, just from the pickup truck he had seen parked outside, that the man was some kind of contractor now, but Paul supposed he had endured a lifetime of hard physical labor earlier in his life. He wore dark pants and a flannel shirt with the sleeves rolled up to his elbows revealing his meaty forearms and large hands. He looked like a strong and powerful man; he was probably normally a rock for his daughter, but right now he looked shocked and frightened. His eyes were puffy and red, his face swollen from crying. He had watched his teenaged daughter, nearly a woman now, but still his little girl, suffer through this demonic possession, and now the person strapped down to the bed was not someone he knew anymore.

Father O'Leary stood near the same wall as Richard. The young priest had his bible and rosary beads in his hands like he needed something to hold onto, some kind of defense from the monster that had overtaken this girl.

In the exact center of the bedroom was Julia's bed, every side of it away from a wall. The headboard and footboard were made out of metal and decorated with fancy scrolls and leafy designs. All of the metal was painted white with decorative knobs on top of all four posts. The mattress was bare and filthy with dark stains.

Julia was tied down to the bed, spread-eagle. She wore a pair of old gray sweatpants, white socks on her feet, and a faded yellow long-sleeved thermal shirt. Hospital issue, fur-lined leather cuffs were wrapped around her wrists and ankles, and the cuffs were attached to strong ropes pulled tight and tied to the legs of the bed at each corner. The bonds allowed Julia some movement, but they still restricted her enough so that she couldn't hurt herself—or anyone else.

But Julia wasn't thrashing or pulling against the ropes right now. She was totally still, her dark eyes on Paul as soon as he entered the room. Her mouth was frozen in a twisted half-smile with a severe upturn on one side. Her head was cocked at an odd and painful-looking angle. Her coal-black eyes followed Paul's every movement.

Richard rushed across the room to Paul, his work boots thundering on the floorboards. He grabbed Paul's shoulders as tears slipped from his red-rimmed eyes.

"You can help her, can't you?"

Paul didn't pull away from the man's grasp. He felt the man's fingers digging into his shoulder muscles with a frightened person's panicked strength.

"We will help her," Paul said. "*God* will help her."

"She's … that's not her anymore," Richard said. "She was never like this before. I … I don't know how this happened."

"We can worry about that later. Right now we need to cast that demon out of her." "Are you a priest?" Richard asked, seeming to suddenly notice the lack of a collar around Paul's neck—he only saw the silver crucifix laying there against his black sweater.

"No," Paul told him.

"What are you, then? What's in that bag?"

Richard looked like he was going to panic, like a caged animal about to erupt into a rampage. Paul needed to calm the man down quickly.

"We can help her," Paul told Richard. "But you must stay calm."

"Calm?" he barked and pointed at the thin, pale girl strapped down to the bare bed. "Look at her. Look at my baby!" He was crying now. "She's dying."

"You can't stay in here if you can't remain calm," Paul said in an emotionless voice. "The demon wants any distractions it can get. You can't let yourself be that distraction."

Richard seemed like he was going to explode with rage, but his face fell in sudden defeat and he only nodded.

Paul handed the photograph of Julia to Richard. "Take this and show it to her. Remind her of who she really is. Talk to her. She's still inside there somewhere. But don't get too close to the bed."

Richard nodded again, and he seemed more relaxed now that he had something to do. He walked over to the bed with the framed photograph clutched in his hands, facing it towards her. He stayed a few feet away from her bedside.

"Julia, baby," Richard whispered. "I know you're still inside. I know you can still hear me."

He took another step closer to the bed, but Julia still didn't acknowledge him; her eyes were still focused on Paul as he set his canvas bag down on the floor near the wall directly across from the foot of the bed. He unzipped his canvas bag.

Julia's dark eyes moved from Paul to her father, and the strange half-smile on her face disappeared. Her face crumbled into sorrow and fear, and she seemed to recognize that her father was standing beside her bed.

"Daddy?" she whispered.

"Yes," Richard breathed out in a cloud of mist. He moved closer to the bed with the framed photo still clutched in his hands.

"Not too close," Paul warned as he crouched down by his bag.

Richard stopped a foot and half away from Julia's bedside with tears in his eyes. "Baby, it's me."

Julia stared at her father for a moment, and then fear overtook her as she shook her head back and forth, her stringy black hair flying around. The mattress squeaked from her sudden thrashing.

"No, Daddy! Please. Don't do it again! Don't touch me there! Don't make me do those things!"

Richard looked horrified. He tightened his grip on the framed photograph and it looked ready to snap.

"What are you talking about? That's not true!"

Paul jumped to his feet and Father James was at the other side of the bed holding his crucifix over Julia, praying quickly in Latin.

"Please don't do it again, Daddy!" Julia said, still shaking her head back and forth, her hair whipping across her face. And then she broke out into high, squealing laughter that turned deep and guttural.

Richard looked at Father James helplessly, but the priest's eyes were nearly closed as he mumbled his constant prayers. Richard turned to Paul. "I never did those things to her. That's not true. She's my daughter … I loved her …"

"That's not your daughter talking right now," Paul said.

Julia's face changed from a scared girl to a malevolent creature. Her eyes darkened and that strange half-smile was back on her cracked lips. Her skin became mottled and veiny again.

"Come on down here, Papa," Julia said in a guttural voice. "Come down here and touch me. I'm so horny right now."

Julia writhed on the bed, moaning. The ropes creaked as she pulled at them. The mattress squeaked and shook as she thrust her hips up and down.

Richard backed away from the bed in horror, back to the wall by the end table.

Paul stood up and walked to the bedside.

"Shut up," Paul told Julia in a calm and even voice, but it had a quiet power and menace in it.

Father O'Leary hurried to the foot of the bed, joining Father James in muttered prayers in Latin.

Julia's dark eyes flicked back to Paul and she stared at him, her face frozen in an expressionless blank slate except for the upturned smile, a smile that was false, a smile that didn't touch her eyes.

"I know you … Paul Lambert," Julia said.

CHAPTER FOUR

Paul hurried back to far wall where his canvas bag was on the floor. He pulled out a small handheld tape recorder from his bag and turned it on. He set the recorder down right next to the bag on the floor. Next, he pulled out a long metal flashlight and set it down next to the recorder. It was only a matter of time before the electricity went out and he would need the flashlight.

The next items Paul took out of his canvas duffel bag were two large metal canisters.

"Back away from the bed, please," Paul told the two priests as he set the canisters on the floor next to the bag.

Father O'Leary backed away, but Father James hesitated for a moment like he was finishing the prayers he was reciting. But then he backed away, still waving his crucifix at Julia on the bed, still whispering prayers.

The next thing Paul pulled out of his bag was a small copper chafing dish with a paste of myrrh, incense, camphor, and cloves spread out on the inside of it. He lit a candle directly underneath the chafing dish with a lighter, heating up the paste, and the aroma drifted up from the shallow bowl.

Paul then took a small box out of his canvas bag. The box was about half the size of a loaf of bread. It was constructed of wood and painted black, and it had words in ancient languages carved into nearly every square inch of the surface—the words were the names of God. He also pulled out a roll of thin iron wire and set it down next to the box. He unclasped the tiny lock on the lid of the box and opened it. A pungent odor drifted out from the box. A piece of parchment and a stick of sharpened charcoal were tucked down inside the box. As soon as Paul could learn the demon's name, he would write it down on the parchment and stuff it down inside the box. Then he would lock the box and wrap the iron wire around it, sealing it shut and trapping the power of the demon inside.

"These pagan rituals won't help," Father James warned. "Only God can help. Only Jesus Christ."

Paul wasn't going to argue with Father James right now, but he knew that these rituals were going to work. He unscrewed the lids of the two metal canisters he had taken out of his bag and dropped the lids back down into the open mouth of his duffel bag. He stood up and walked around the bed in a quick circle, pouring out simultaneous lines of salt and iron fillings from the metal cans.

"Stay outside this circle," he told the other three men in the bedroom.

After the circle around the bed was complete, Paul brought the nearly empty canisters back to his duffel bag and put the lids back on.

Father James ignored Paul for now and approached the bed again, standing right outside the circle of salt and iron. "Name yourself, demon!" he shouted at Julia.

Julia lay lifeless on the bed, her body as still as the expression on her face, her eyes still fixed on Paul.

"I command you in the name of Jesus to name yourself, demon!"

There was still no reaction from Julia.

Father James inched closer to the line of salt and iron. "You will name yourself, demon!! And you will remove yourself from this woman's body!!"

Julia still didn't move a muscle. She looked dead except for the slight rise and fall of her chest underneath the pale yellow shirt, and the faint mist of breath from her nostrils.

Father James stepped inside the circle, right up next to the bed. He waved his crucifix over Julia's body.

"Father … the circle," Paul said.

Father James ignored his warning.

"Name yourself!" Father James yelled as he laid the crucifix down on Julia's forehead.

There was no reaction from Julia. She didn't pull away from the crucifix. Her skin didn't sizzle or smoke; she just lay there.

And then Julia's dark eyes slowly moved from Paul to Father James. Her eyes were the only thing that moved; the rest of her head, face, and body were frozen.

"Name yourself, demon! You cannot fight the power of Jesus Christ! You must obey!"

"Obey," Julia mocked. "Obey. Obey. Obey."

Julia lifted her head up from the bed, but Father James did not back away, he didn't pull the crucifix away from her forehead.

She raised her head up higher, her neck muscles straining, her arms pulling at her cuffs, the ropes stretching out tight as her body slowly lifted up off of the bed, floating up from the mattress as far as the ropes would allow.

"Oh dear God," Richard whispered, crying again.

Father O'Leary stood by the wall near Richard now, still praying, still clutching his own crucifix and rosary beads.

The twisted smile never left Julia's face as her body levitated up as far as the ropes would allow, her arms and legs straining, joints popping, ropes and tendons creaking.

"Obey," Julia mocked Father James's words again. "Obey. Obey. Obey."

Father James seemed to falter just a bit, to lose just a little focus, like he might be doubting what he was seeing. He pulled the crucifix away from Julia's forehead and backed away a few steps.

Julia collapsed back down onto the bed, writhing and pulling at the cuffs and ropes. She thrashed her head back and forth.

Another flash of lightning lit up the room for a second.

Father James looked to his assistant across the room. "The holy water! Quickly!"

Father O'Leary picked up the glass vessel with trembling hands and brought it over to Father James. He handed the vessel to the old priest, but he was careful not to step inside the circle of salt and iron.

Father James dunked two of his long, large-knuckled fingers into the water and then flicked it at the writhing Julia.

"Leave this woman alone, demon!" Father James shouted. "Leave this woman right now in the name of Jesus Christ!!"

Julia yelled out words in a sing-song voice as she thrashed back and forth on the bare mattress.

"Leave. Stay. Leave. Stay. Leave. Stay. Leavestayleavestayleavestayleavestay ..."

"You will leave this young woman's body in the name of Almighty God!!"

Father James flicked more holy water at Julia and she suddenly stopped thrashing. She looked at the priest through her scraggly dark hair that hung over her face, covering half of it. She spoke with one dark eye on the priest, a cold mist drifting out from her half-smile.

"Where will I go, priest?"

Father James ignored her question. "Name yourself and leave this young woman!"

Julia spoke again with feigned fear. "But where am I going to go? What's going to happen to me? Even Legion was sent by Christ into the swine."

"You'll go back to Hell where you came from!"

"But I need somewhere to go," Julia continued, her voice suddenly deep and threatening. "I need swine to enter."

The bed began to shake, the metal legs tapping at the wood floorboards.

Julia writhed on the bed again, pulling violently against the cuffs attached to her wrists and ankles, the ropes pulling taut, threatening to snap.

Father O'Leary hurried back towards the wall, but he continued praying.

Paul stole a quick glance at Father O'Leary and Julia's father. Richard shook his head back and forth, crying. And the assistant looked ready to run at any moment. Paul wasn't sure how much more these two men could stand.

Father James stepped back inside the circle of salt and iron. He gripped his crucifix in one hand, his bible in the other. He thrust the crucifix at the writhing girl and he began a string of prayers.

"God, Father of our Lord Jesus Christ, I invoke Your Holy Name and suppliantly request You to give me strength against this and every other unclean spirit ..."

Julia's body popped up from the mattress, levitating in the air again, only the cuffs and ropes keeping her from floating up even farther above the bed. Her arms and legs were stretched out as far as they could go, her muscles pulling, her joints popping, her scraggily dark hair hanging down from her head as it lolled from side to side.

"Leavestayleavestayleavestayleavestay!!" she screamed. "Obey. Not obey. Obey. Not obey. Obeynotobeyobeynotobeyobeynotobey ..."

This was how demons liked to talk. They loved the opposites of nature: light and dark, good and evil, yes and no, right and wrong. They loved the confusion of it, the duality of everything.

Paul moved closer to the bed.

Father James showed the first cracks in his faith, a slight stumbling as he witnessed the physical impossibility of the girl floating above the bed right in front of his eyes.

"Swine!" Julia yelled at Father James as she whipped her head back and forth in the air. "I need swine to enter!"

Her head stopped thrashing suddenly and she stared at Father James. "Will you be my swine?" she whispered.

Julia crashed back down onto the bed and there was the sound of rushing wind.

But the wind wasn't from the storm outside—it was coming from inside the bedroom.

Oh God, Paul thought. *This is getting out of control too quickly.*

They all stared in horror at Julia's skin—it seemed like thousands of worms were crawling right underneath her skin.

Father James backed up another step, but he still wasn't outside of the circle yet. He dropped his arms as if the crucifix and bible had suddenly become too heavy for him to bear. He had a confused and horrified look on his face like he couldn't trust what he was seeing anymore.

The worm-like things moved down from Julia's body and into the mattress. They moved under the mattress, their bulk pushing up against the stained fabric.

Shadows moved in the corners of the room, growing darker and more solid, forming into nightmarish shapes. The rushing of wind grew louder, the air became even colder.

Just as Paul was about to rush across the room and push Father James away from the bed and outside the circle of salt and iron, the candles blew out and the bedroom was plunged into darkness.

CHAPTER FIVE

"The lights!" Paul yelled.

"The candles are out!" Richard yelled back in the darkness.

Paul heard the sound of footsteps in the bedroom, but it didn't sound like anyone had run for the door yet.

He couldn't hear Julia thrashing on the bed anymore. She wasn't making a sound now.

"Richard," Paul called out. "The light switch! We need light right now!"

Paul heard the sound of Richard stumbling around the room, feeling his way along the wall for the light switch.

Paul felt around in the darkness for his duffel bag against the wall. He had to work slowly; he didn't want to knock over the still-smoking chaffing dish. His hands touched the wooden black box, and then he moved his hands slowly to the duffel bag, and then to the right. He knew his flashlight was somewhere to the right of his bag where he had left it standing next to the small tape recorder. He needed to get some kind of light on in this room right now; there were things that could appear and move around in the darkness—he had seen them before during other exorcisms; he had fought with them before.

There was the sound of running feet across the wood floor and then the sound of the bedroom door flung open. Then there was the sound of running footsteps out in the hallway, and then the sound of the bedroom door slamming closed.

The assistant had finally run, Paul thought.

Paul turned his flashlight on and shined it at the wall where the small table and candles were. He did not expect to see Father O'Leary still standing there.

But the young priest cringed against the wall, still clutching his crucifix and rosary beads, his lips moving in non-stop prayers. His skin looked so pale in the flashlight's beam, his eyes so wide. He was beyond shock now.

But Paul needed to get through to Father O'Leary.

"Father O'Leary! Re-light the candles! We need the light!"

It took a moment for the priest to even realize someone was talking to him. He looked into the beam of light at Paul, blinking uncontrollably as tears slipped from his eyes.

"The candles!" Paul yelled again.

The young priest nodded and lunged at the table. He found the lighter and dropped his cross and rosary beads on the table next to the candles as Paul shined his flashlight beam at him. He lit the candles and hovered over the flickering flames as if it was his last lifeline in this sudden world of darkness.

If Father O'Leary hadn't run out of the bedroom, then who had?

Paul swept his flashlight beam around the room. Julia was still tied down to the bed and all of the cuffs on her wrists and ankles seemed secure even though she had struggled against them with incredible strength. But she laid very still now, her head turned to one side, her dark hair splashed across her face. She looked like she might be unconscious.

"Julia …" Richard whispered.

Paul whipped the flashlight beam over to the bedroom door where Richard stood next to the light switch. He looked horrified, afraid, and hopeful all at the same time.

"The light switch!" Paul yelled at Richard.

"It's not working!"

Paul swept his flashlight beam around the bedroom. Father James was the only one not in the room. It was Father James who had run.

No, Paul thought. *He hadn't run ... it was worse than that. The demon had jumped from Julia to Father James when the lights went out.*

Richard ran across the room and knelt down by his daughter's bed, brushing her hair out of her face.

"She's alive," Richard whispered and looked at Paul as a lightning bolt from outside lit up the room. In that split second, Paul saw that Richard's face was shiny with tears.

"It's not over yet," Paul told Richard. "Don't untie her until I get Father James."

"Is she still … is that thing still inside of her?" Richard asked.

"I don't know. We can't be sure. There may have been more than one demon." Paul thought of the story from the Bible that the demon had spoken of through Julia's lips before: The story of Christ casting out the demon Legion from a man and forcing them into a group of pigs. Legion. Many demons.

It had been a long time since Paul had dealt with more than one demon possessing a person's body. Usually a person couldn't be possessed unless they allowed themselves to be, unless they opened the door somehow, even just a little bit, and invited them in. Once the door was open, the demon could wriggle its way into that person's life, little by little, inch by inch. Sometimes a person just suddenly felt anxious or depressed for no apparent reason. Or they had strange thoughts, maybe a voice whispering to them to do something terrible either to themselves or to others.

What door had Julia opened? What had she been messing around with? He hadn't noticed any signs of the occult among the possessions of her bedroom that had been laid out in the living room, not even a seemingly harmless Ouija board.

It didn't make sense for her to be possessed this strongly, a possession this total and complete should've taken years. There should've been signs along the way; she should've gotten help long before tonight.

But Paul knew there were rare cases where a demon, or more than one demon, took over someone's body quickly and completely. It was rare, and it must be what he was dealing with tonight.

And now the demon had jumped from body to body—another very rare occurrence. He was dealing with something he'd never seen before, only heard about or read about in case studies.

Paul didn't have time to ponder these things right now. He needed to find Father James.

Thunder rumbled as Paul set his flashlight down on the floor. He grabbed the canister of salt and dumped the last of it onto his hands and rubbed it into his skin to purify them even more. He picked his flashlight back up and looked at Father O'Leary who was still huddled by the table of candles in the corner.

"Help him pray," Paul barked at the young and shaken priest. "Don't untie her and don't leave this room. If Father James comes back in here, don't trust him. He's possessed now."

"That can't be possible," Father O'Leary said as he walked on numb-stiff legs over to the side of Julia's bed.

Julia still hadn't moved a muscle or made a sound. Her eyes were closed and the strange half-smile was gone from her face now.

"We're dealing with a very strong force here," Paul told Father O'Leary. "Your faith must be the strongest it has ever been. Father James's faith may have slipped and allowed the demon a way into him. You don't want to let that happen to you. Stay inside the circle, both of you. It will offer some protection, but it won't replace your faith."

"What are you going to do?" Father O'Leary asked Paul.

"I'm going to find Father James and drive the demon out of him."

Paul grabbed the black box from the floor and turned for the door. He didn't have time to keep this conversation going just so Father O'Leary could be comforted.

He slipped out of the bedroom and closed the door on the flickering candlelight. He was now in near-total darkness with his flashlight beam as his only light.

He shined the light to his left, towards the two doors at the end of the hallway. He crept down the hall, his boots not making a sound as he walked. He shut the flashlight off as he made his way slowly to the first closed door without a sound, like he was a shadow among the shadows. His eyes had already adjusted to the darkness. He opened the door and it didn't squeak or squeal when he pushed it open. He stepped inside a bathroom and glanced around just as another flash of lightning lit up the room from the bathroom window.

There was nowhere for Father James to hide in here. The shower curtain was pulled back revealing the tub, and the door to a tiny linen closet was open.

Paul hurried out of the room and opened the next door which led to a master bedroom. This room took a few more moments to search. He turned his flashlight back on and used the beam to quickly search under the bed and inside the walk-in closet.

As he searched the bedroom, something tugged at his mind. He looked at the artwork on the walls in the bedroom, the décor on top of the dresser. It looked like a woman shared the room with Richard, but then again it didn't. Like he might have been married at some point in the past, and then she left, and he hadn't gotten around to redecorating, maybe like he had wanted to keep everything the same in case she ever came back.

But that didn't feel right, either.

He let his eyes linger on the clothes hanging in the closet a moment longer.

Something was wrong here. He was missing something, but he wasn't sure what it was. He had a sinking feeling that it was something important.

Father James wasn't back here in these two rooms, and Paul hadn't heard anyone in the hallway. He had decided to work his way from the back of the house to the front. But he needed to hurry before Father James either attacked someone or left the house so he could spread the infection of his possession on to someone else.

Paul hurried down the hallway. There was only one more closed door in the hallway besides the door to Julia's room. As he passed the closed door to Julia's bedroom, he stopped for a moment, listening. Everything sounded quiet in there, and he could still see the flickering light of the candles coming from underneath the door.

Everything seemed okay in there, but then again it felt like it wasn't.

Opposites, but similar at the same time. The way demons liked it. Light and dark. Good and bad. Right and wrong. Confusing everything.

Leave. Stay. The words echoed in Paul's mind, the words uttered through Julia's lips. *Leave. Stay. Leavestayleavestay. Obeynotobeyobeynotobey.*

Paul shut the voice away in his mind. He couldn't be distracted right now … he had a job to do here.

He walked down the hall and came to the last closed door on the other side of the hallway. Maybe it was a guest room of some kind, he thought. Or maybe an office or home gym or storage.

He wrapped his hand around the door handle, just about to open it, but then he froze when he heard a sound from the kitchen—a crashing noise. And then he heard the sound of someone giggling; it was a deep voice that was giggling—it was Father James.

CHAPTER SIX

Paul dropped his hand away from the door handle and stared down the hall that opened up to the living room with the archway to the kitchen off to the right. He was certain that the crashing sound and the giggling had come from the kitchen. He had trained his ears through the years to locate sounds in the dark.

Paul clicked his flashlight on and shined it down the hallway as he walked. He could use the heavy flashlight as a weapon if he needed to.

"Father James," Paul said in a low voice. "Come on out and show yourself. You need help. I want to help you."

There was another noise coming from inside the kitchen now, like the sound of someone crawling across the floor.

†

In Julia's bedroom, Father O'Leary knelt beside the young woman's bed. Richard knelt on the other side of the bed. Everything was quiet now, everything very still. The only sound was the occasional rumble of thunder and the dancing of the rain on the roof. But the rain was softer now, the storm beginning to move past them.

Father O'Leary prayed silently, but he also tried to listen for sounds of Paul in the house. But he couldn't hear Paul.

Julia still hadn't stirred. She was very still, but Father O'Leary saw that her chest was rising and falling slightly.

"You like watching her?" Richard asked Father O'Leary from the other side of the bed.

Father O'Leary looked at Richard. The big man's expression had changed and the tears in his eyes had dried up. In the flickering light of the candles from the corner of the room, Richard's face seemed to be changing, morphing into the expression of a madman. He had the same twisted half-smile that Julia had worn earlier, and his eyes seemed to have grown very dark—his entire eyeballs were black.

Father O'Leary didn't answer Richard. His voice was stuck in his throat, his mouth suddenly so dry he was afraid his tongue was going to stick to the roof of his mouth. His body had become both tense and rubbery at the same time, the strength draining out of him now. Even though it was still freezing inside the room, he felt cold sweat trickling down his back and from his armpits. His testicles shriveled and hugged close to his body.

"You like watching her, don't you?" Richard said again, his breath escaping his mouth in a cloud of vapor that hovered over Julia's body for a moment before disappearing into the air.

"What … what are you talking about?" Father O'Leary stammered. "We have to pray. We have to be strong."

"We *are* strong," Richard said and moved his hands to the cuff on Julia's left wrist.

"What are you doing?!"

Julia turned her head towards Father O'Leary, and now she had the same twisted smile on her face, her eyes pure black again. "Come join us," she said to Father O'Leary.

"Oh God, no!" Father O'Leary whimpered and jumped to his feet.

Richard unbuckled the cuff on Julia's wrist and her arm was free.

†

Paul entered the kitchen with the black box tucked underneath his arm. He panned his flashlight beam around the room. He didn't see Father James anywhere. The kitchen was large and open, with a table for four against a wall and an L-shape of cabinets and appliances on the other wall. Another large archway at the other end of the room led out to the dining room, and a door near that archway led out to the garage, Paul supposed.

But Paul didn't worry about those doors and archways. Father James was still somewhere in this kitchen, he was sure of it.

Paul heard a noise from the refrigerator behind him. He whirled around, his flashlight up, the beam pointed at the top of the large refrigerator where Father James was somehow impossibly crammed up on top of the refrigerator in that small space, his body folded in on itself.

"Father James," Paul breathed out. "I know you can still hear me from somewhere inside there. You have to fight this … you have to hold on to your strength."

Father James's eyes were coal-black in his pale face that stuck out from his body over the top of the refrigerator. He opened his mouth wide and his breath misted out into the suddenly cold room. The window over the sink had fogged up.

As lightning flashed, Father James sprung out from the top of the refrigerator like he had been shot from a catapult; a gangly, flying object, large head and open mouth, sharp elbows and knees, large hands open and reaching for Paul.

Paul managed to turn his shoulder into the attack, and he let the black box fall from his hand as he grabbed at the priest's clothing and limbs, and then he twisted and flipped, slamming the old priest down onto the table top in one smooth movement. The table collapsed, the legs flying out. One of the chairs cracked apart in the process.

Father James was back on his feet in a split second, bleeding and damaged, but not feeling it. He smiled at Paul, but it was the same twisted, half-smile Paul had seen on Julia's face, the upturn on one side of the mouth so severe, the eyes so wide and dark.

"In the name of Almighty God!" Paul shouted. The silver crucifix around his neck winked in the light from his flashlight which he'd lost in the quick battle with Father James. The flashlight was on the floor shining a splash of light across the linoleum, shining right on the black wooden box that had landed near the baseboard of the wall.

Paul lifted his hands up and the rings of iron were dark circles on his fingers. Religious tattoos and crosses on his wrists peeked out from underneath the cuffs of his dark sweater.

"I command you to leave this man's body!" Paul shouted, his hands still up and ready to defend himself against this raging animal that had been an old man only moments ago. "You leave this holy vessel! You have no right to be there. You are not welcome in this holy man's body. You are not welcome anywhere!"

For a moment Father James hesitated and his dark eyes cleared a little.

But then Paul heard a scream from Julia's bedroom.

It was a man's scream.

A distraction.

Father James used the distraction and pounced on Paul, knocking him down to the floor.

"You want to know my name?" Father James growled as he hovered over him. "I am the Terror By Night, and I am going to take everything away from you, Paul. Everything that you love."

CHAPTER SEVEN

Father O'Leary jumped to his feet beside Julia's bed. The flickering light of the candles made it seem like there were shadows moving all around the corners of the bedroom.

But the shadows seemed darker, and more solid. Were they coming for him?

The young priest didn't waste any time; panic had overtaken him. He ran around the foot of the bed and bolted for the bedroom door, praying he would be able to get past Richard.

Julia had unbuckled the cuff on her right wrist with her free hand and now she sat up like a piston and began working on the cuffs around her ankles. She would be free in seconds.

And in that moment before he ran, Father O'Leary swore he saw those worm-like creatures squirming underneath the fabric of her sweatpants and underneath the skin of her arms and face.

Those worm things couldn't be real, could they? he kept telling himself. *It was just an illusion from the candlelight.*

Father O'Leary whispered out a string of prayers as he raced for the bedroom door, almost like his mouth was working on its own. His body felt rubbery and weak from pure shock, but at the same time a shot of adrenaline was coursing through his veins causing a fight-or-flight response ... and he chose flight.

For the briefest of moments, Father O'Leary dared to believe that he'd gotten past Richard.

But Richard was somehow in front of him, looming there, blocking the door. The big man grabbed Father O'Leary around his throat with one large hand, clamping down hard, squeezing the air out of him and stopping his movements suddenly.

Father O'Leary's hands went to Richard's wrist and he tried to pull the man's hand away, but Richard was way too strong.

And then Richard pulled something out from underneath his shirt as Father O'Leary struggled in the big man's grip. It was some kind of plastic bottle that looked like a flask, a white bottle with a red plastic cap and some kind of label on it that Father O'Leary couldn't read because black and white spots began to dance in front of his eyes.

But when Richard popped the cap open with a quick flip of his thumb, Father O'Leary could smell the pungent chemical scent.

Oh God, no ... lighter fluid!

The priest heard Julia from behind him; he heard the squeak of the mattress, the squeal of the bedsprings as she got off the bed.

Richard still held Father O'Leary by the threat. Richard spoke in a language Father O'Leary had never heard before.

An inhuman and guttural language.

A demon language.

The half-smile had never left Richard's face.

Richard squirted the lighter fluid onto Father O'Leary's struggling body, all over his black clothing, and then he tossed the plastic container away onto the floor. Then he picked the young priest up by his throat and threw him across the room like he weighed ten pounds.

Father O'Leary flew through the air and then collided with the candles on the table in the corner of the room.

Flames whooshed up.

Father O'Leary screamed.

†

Paul heard the screams from the bedroom. It was a man screaming, and Paul had no doubt that it was Father O'Leary.

He had to help the young priest. He tried to run, but Father James knocked him to the floor with a vicious blow.

Paul hit the linoleum floor and tried to get back up, but a pain exploded in the side of his head. The priest was too strong with the demon inside of him. Paul needed to get through to Father James who was trapped somewhere inside.

Paul crawled backwards away from Father James; he was still on the floor in a crablike position, ready to jump up and defend himself.

Father James walked towards him and loomed over him with an ax.

Where had he found an ax? Who kept an ax in their house?

And now Paul realized what he had overlooked. He had missed the details, the signs, and now Father O'Leary was being injured, maybe even killed, because of Paul's inattention to detail. And now maybe he himself was going to die because of his mistake.

There was no way Julia could be possessed this deeply without other people noticing, without her father or mother seeking help. And now Paul knew why. Richard *knew* Julia was possessed the whole time, because he was possessed, too.

A long time ago the two of them had opened that door, maybe only a crack, but they had let the darkness inside of them. It had grown inside of them, getting stronger and stronger, until it had taken over completely.

Something was inside that other room in the hallway, the one behind the closed door that he hadn't checked. There was something in there that he should've seen, at least guessed at. Maybe it was an altar. Or it was their sacrifice or their symbols and gifts to the Dark Lord and his minions.

Father James swung the ax down, driving the tip of it down into the linoleum floor. Paul moved out of the way just in time and then kicked the old man in the knee, catching him off balance and driving him back away from him. It was a kick that would've normally injured the old man severely, possibly even broken his leg. But the old priest had super strength now and nothing could hurt him.

"Father James!" Paul shouted as he jumped to his feet. "I know you're still in there! You can't let this demon control you! Father O'Leary is in danger. He's hurt. He's dying! We have to help him!"

Paul felt a heat radiating out of the hallway, and Father O'Leary's screams floated out on that wave of heat. He could even smell the smoke. He could hear the crackling of flames.

Somewhere a smoke alarm was sounding off.

Oh God, the house is on fire!

It was Richard and Julia's ultimate sacrifice and their ultimate gift to the Darkness—the killing of a priest.

Father James got back to his feet. His eyes were still black and the half smile was still on his lips.

Paul couldn't keep fighting Father James—it would take too much time. It was just a distraction so he couldn't get to Father O'Leary.

He jumped to his feet and was about to run down the hall into the smoke and heat.

But then something happened in a split second. Something changed on Father James's face. The twisted smile was gone, his mouth dropping down into a frown, his long face jowly once again. His eyes cleared, his black eyeballs turned back to blue again. He was suddenly aware, but confused.

The demon had let the priest go.

But why?

Demons never let anyone go voluntarily—they always held on to the bitter end until they were driven out.

Something was wrong here.

Father James looked at the destruction of the kitchen table and chairs, then down at the ax stuck in the floor, then back up at Paul. It was like he suddenly realized that the house was heating up, smoke drifting into the kitchen, the smoke alarm screeching from somewhere down the hallway.

"What happened?" Father James croaked.

"You were possessed."

Father James shook his head no as if that were impossible, his jowly cheeks quivering.

Paul didn't have time to argue with the old priest, there would be plenty of time to argue about it later if the old man could ever be convinced that a demon had taken possession of his body and controlled him like a puppet.

"You need to call 911!" Paul yelled at the priest. "Use your cell phone if you have one, or there's one in my truck. You need to get out; this whole house is going to be on fire soon!"

"Where are you going?"

"To get Father O'Leary. He's still in the bedroom."

"What about Richard? Julia?"

"It's too late for them now."

Paul saw the confusion on the priest's face, the questions racing through his mind, but he didn't give him a chance to ask them. He grabbed the black box from the floor near the wall and ran down the hallway.

He kicked the bedroom door open and rushed inside. The far wall was engulfed in flames. Father O'Leary had stopped screaming because he was dead. His charred body was slumped down and curled up in the corner over what used to be the end table.

Paul dove down under the low ceiling of black smoke and grabbed his tape recorder and his canvas bag.

Richard rushed at him out of the flames and smoke. The thing that used to be Richard tried to grab at Paul, but his hands touched the black box and he flinched back into the smoke and flames. It was enough of a flinch for Paul to back up towards the door, just enough of a distraction.

Paul backed up to the bedroom door about to leave.

Richard and Julia stood hand-in-hand in the flames that had already caught the bed on fire.

Neither one of them moved. They stood among the flames with the twisted half-smiles on their faces, staring at Paul with their completely black eyes.

Paul hesitated for a moment in the doorway. "There's still time!" he yelled at them over the roaring flames and screeching smoke alarms. "You can repent! He will forgive you!"

Neither one of them answered. Neither one of them moved. They just waited in the flames, smiling.

Paul ducked out of the bedroom and slammed the door shut on the flames and smoke. He thought of stuffing some of Julia's clothes from the living room underneath the door to block the smoke and possibly slow the fire down a little, but he decided not to bother.

This house needed to burn.

Richard and Julia couldn't be saved now, he knew that. They had made their pact with the Darkness a long time ago.

It had been difficult to see before in the darkness inside the house, but now with the roiling smoke it was nearly impossible. Paul felt his way along the hall, past the locked door, then past the archway into the kitchen, and then out into the living room.

The front door was wide open and the night outside was lighter than the inside of the house. The rain was still coming down, but it was a lot lighter than it had been before.

Paul grabbed his coat and hat from the arm of the couch, and then he was out the door.

He heard screams coming from the bedroom as he left the house. Julia's screams. Richard's screams.

Father James waited for Paul in the front yard. He stood in the rain, right in the middle of a large muddy puddle, his shoes caked with mud now, but he didn't seem to notice.

"Where's Tim?" Father James asked.

That must've been Father O'Leary's first name, Paul thought.

"I'm sorry. He didn't make it."

Father James's shoulders slumped, his face hung even lower, like he was fighting back tears. "Richard and Julia?"

"They were possessed all along. I think they drew us here."

"Why?"

"I don't know. To kill us. To sacrifice us. To spread the possession." But Paul thought he might know the real reason why they were brought here and it sickened him. He didn't want to think about it.

He remembered the voice that had emanated from Father James's throat when he'd been possessed.

I am the Terror By Night, and I am going to take everything away from you, Paul. Everything that you love.

"Let's get these vehicles moved back away from the house," Paul told the old priest, gently guiding him by the arm out of the puddle he was standing in.

"But the house," Father James muttered. His voice was slow and thick, like shock was setting in. "The fire …"

"There's nothing we can do about it now. Maybe the rain will slow it down a little before the fire trucks get here."

Paul turned and looked at the house. He saw the flames exploding out of the side window near the back of the house, the flames spiraling up into the night sky, spreading along the roof quickly, like the fire was alive.

No, the rain wasn't going to slow this fire down, Paul thought. Not *this* fire.

I am going to take everything away from you, Paul, the voice echoed in his mind again. *Everything that you love.*

Paul thought of his son. His daughter. His ex-wife.

CHAPTER EIGHT

Paul and Father James were allowed to leave the property after the sheriff had taken their statements. Father McFadden had shown up when the police arrived and he had vouched for what had happened here at the Whittier house.

Paul and Father James had gotten their stories straight before the cops got there. They told the police that they'd been here on the Church's authority to investigate a case of possession, but the father of the daughter had turned violent and started a fire in the house, killing himself, his daughter, and Father O'Leary.

The cops seemed like they believed Paul's story, but they promised to investigate further. But Paul knew they wouldn't find much evidence inside the house—it had been burnt nearly to the ground. But he had a suspicion that they might eventually find the mother/wife's body buried somewhere on the property—sacrificed a short time ago by Richard and Julia.

Before Paul left, he gave Father McFadden a brief account of what had really happened (he'd left out some of the more unbelievable parts of the account to the cops, including Father James's possession), and Paul promised to give Father McFadden a complete written report in a few days, as was protocol. Father McFadden promised that he and the Church would clear things up at the Whittier house and that neither Paul nor Father James would face any further inquiries from the police.

A little while after his conversation with Father McFadden, Paul drove home, driving back down the sloppy trail through the woods.

He dialed Rachael's home number in Cleveland, Ohio as he drove, but got no answer even though it was one o'clock in the morning and she and the kids should be at home. He called Rachael's cell phone after getting no answer on her house phone. No answer on her cell either, so he left a message for her.

"Hi, Rachael," he said into the phone. "It's Paul. Sorry to call so late. I just really need to talk to you about something. Please call me back as soon as you get this. It doesn't matter what time it is, just call me. Please. Thanks."

He hung up the phone.

What else could he say? That she and the kids might be in grave danger right now? The reason she had kept the kids after they had divorced, and the reason she had never allowed Paul much contact with his kids over the last few years, was because Rachael didn't want the disease of his delusions (as she called them) to infect her children.

Damn, if she would just believe him. Trust him this one time.

But she was a firm believer that God was just an abstract idea, if there even *was* a god, which she'd expressed several times that she wasn't sure about yet.

At the time Paul had met Rachael, Paul was wrestling with his own doubts about God. Even though he'd come from a long line of Investigators, he didn't want to believe, he didn't want to follow in their footsteps. He didn't want *that* life.

But after Danny and Lisa were born, and after his own father had died, Paul started changing. And year after year he drifted back towards God. And towards his true calling. He couldn't stay away; he couldn't turn his back on the Voice calling to him.

Rachael didn't understand.

They grew further and further apart. Paul wanted to follow in his father's footsteps after he died. But Rachael didn't want that kind of life for herself, or for her kids.

She always called them *her* kids.

But they were *his* kids, too.

Not anymore. Rachael had filed a restraining order against Paul because of his delusional fantasies that he was some kind of crusading demon hunter for God.

Paul talked to his children on the phone sometimes, but he could hear the resentment in their voices. Now that they were teenagers, Danny seventeen and Lisa fourteen, they were growing away from him. Rachael thought it would be easier if she just told the kids that Paul wanted to stay away from them rather than saddle their children with the idea that their father was mentally ill. What if the kids feared becoming mentally ill themselves? Rachael had argued. What if they believed Paul's sickness could be passed down genetically?

And Paul had reluctantly agreed to stay away from his own children.

Paul knew Rachael's worst fear was that one or maybe both of their children would end up like him, living in this fantasy world of God and demons and possessions.

Rachael felt (irrationally anyway, because Rachael was a big believer in science) that keeping their children away from Paul would keep them from being exposed to his sickness, like he had some kind of virus that could be caught by close proximity.

Paul sent birthday and Christmas cards every year. He shipped Christmas presents in the mail. He called his kids every few weeks and tried to talk to them—as long as they would let him, anyway. As long as Rachael would let them.

It crushed him that he wasn't allowed to see his children anymore; it crushed him that he wasn't allowed to be in their lives, to know them. Why would God allow that? Why did God call him to this duty that drove him away from his family?

Yet, on the other hand, a small part of him was glad that he wasn't around his family, that they weren't close to the evils that he faced, that they were safe from the darkness he was drawn to and duty-bound to fight.

Yes, maybe God was working in His mysterious ways even though Paul wasn't happy about it.

Feeling his children were far away and safe had always comforted Paul a little.

Until tonight.

Until the warning.

He had to be sure his family was safe.

†

Paul drove down his neighborhood street in Boston and pulled up to his row house that was squeezed in between two other homes that lined the narrow street. His Ford Bronco rumbled with power as he eased it into his driveway. He was sure his neighbors weren't too happy about hearing the throaty growl of his truck pulling into the driveway at two thirty in the morning.

Paul shut off his truck and grabbed his coat, hat, and canvas duffel bag. He got out of the truck and shut the door as quietly as he could. A quick glance around told him that a few lights were on here and there in the other houses, but he didn't see anyone peeking out the window at him.

His body was sore from the fight he'd had with Father James. He knew it would probably be worse in the morning. But he would take a few aspirins and keep going—he had felt worse than this before. Much worse.

He unlocked his front door and entered his dark home. He flipped on the light switch which lit up the lamp next to the armchair in the living room. He closed his front door and locked it. And then he engaged the deadbolt, listening to the loud thunk of metal thumping into the wood frame of the door.

After he hung his coat and hat on an antique coat rack near the front closet door, he dropped his canvas bag down beside the recliner next to the couch. He went to the kitchen for a drink.

The kitchen was as Spartan and minimal as the rest of Paul's home. Not much in the way of décor, and nothing that didn't serve a purpose. The sink was empty and gleaming, the dishes put away. The countertops were bare except for the toaster, the coffee machine, and four ceramic canisters that held coffee, tea, sugar, and salt.

He flipped on the light over the stove instead of the harsh fluorescent lights overhead and the yellowish light provided a cozy glow in the small kitchen. A small four-seat table was shoved against the wall and it served as the dining room table. A large iron crucifix hung on the wall above the table.

Paul opened the cabinet next to the refrigerator that housed a few recipe books, a holiday dinner set passed down from his mother that he never used, little jars of spices, cold medicines, and some other odds and ends. And there was a bottle of vodka.

He poured himself half a glass of vodka. He popped two aspirins into his mouth and chased them down with the fiery liquid. He set his cell phone on the kitchen counter and sat down at the table with the glass of vodka in his hand. He sat in the kitchen, listening to the hum of the refrigerator and watched the cell phone like Rachael might call at any minute.

But he knew better than that.

He knew he would have to call her again tomorrow.

CHAPTER NINE

Cleveland, Ohio

Danny walked home from school down the wide streets of Parma, a suburb of Cleveland. The Victorian-style houses were set close to the street with only small squares of green lawns in front of them. He walked underneath ancient trees that ran in a line down both sides of the street between the sidewalk and the road. Cars and trucks were squeezed into the driveways that ran down along the sides of the houses, many of the driveways leading to free-standing garages in the backyards.

It was almost Halloween and many of the front porches were already decorated with fake skeletons, jack-o-lanterns, and other spooky decorations. The weather was cold, the air chilly, but at least it hadn't snowed yet.

Danny was almost five foot ten inches tall and he thought he might grow a few more inches in the next couple of years. His dad was six foot two, so maybe there was hope for a few more inches for him.

The thought of his father entered his mind, and he tried to push it away. Why think about him? Paul didn't want anything to do with him or his sister. He never came to Cleveland anymore, and he had made it perfectly clear that he didn't want them coming to visit him in Boston.

Danny mentally shrugged. He didn't care.

But that was really a lie—he did wonder why his father didn't want much to do with him or his sister. But what could he do about it?

His father left them when Danny was seven years old. Danny remembered crying and begging him not to go. He begged him on the phone to let him come see him in Boston. But Dad always said no. Not right now. Not a good time. Busy working.

Whatever kind of work *that* was.

Danny didn't even know what his father did for a living. Something to do with a big Catholic church in Boston, but he was always so vague about the details whenever Danny asked about it.

Maybe he was a janitor there or something and he was too embarrassed to admit that to his kids. Or maybe he was a drunk. Or a bum living off of the Church.

Danny didn't know if his dad had a girlfriend or had remarried. He didn't know much about him at all.

Whenever he talked to his father on the phone, he tried to ask him questions, but his father always found a way to turn the conversation back around to Danny's life.

He saw a picture of his dad in his mind as he thought about him. Maybe it was a distorted picture, distorted by time, a picture he had seen when he was fourteen years old, which was the last time Paul had come to Cleveland to visit him and his sister. But he remembered Paul as being tall and strong. He had dark hair and tanned skin even though he hardly ever seemed to go outside. He was quiet, brooding, and he didn't waste a lot of time with words. In fact, nothing seemed to be wasted with his father: no extra words, no unnecessary movements, no possessions that weren't useful; he was a master of efficiency in every way.

Oh well. He pushed the thoughts of his father away, not sure why he was even thinking about him.

Danny was thin, but he was lean and beginning to show some muscle. He had taken a weightlifting class this year even though he had been a little nervous about it. And, of course, Danny got the class with many of the football and basketball players in it. On the first day of class, the coach let the students split up into groups of three or four guys each, and Danny joined up with the two weakest and skinniest and most nervous-looking kids in the class. But, after a week of working out, the coach switched some of the groups around. He took Danny aside and asked him why he was working out with those two. The coach had seen Danny pushing himself, far out-lifting them already, and he knew those guys he was with weren't even trying. So the coach put Danny with another group.

Danny managed to get along with the other two guys in his new group—both of them were on the football team, one of them a starting receiver—but he wouldn't exactly call them friends.

But, little by little, Danny felt that he was beginning to come out of his shell, and he knew that the weightlifting had been a big help, a confidence booster. Maybe after—

Danny stopped walking, his thoughts jarring to a stop.

He stared down the sidewalk at a man who stood half a block away.

Danny glanced around. There weren't too many people out on the street right now. There was an old man working in his garden. There was a woman sitting on her porch, talking on her phone, braying out a shrill cackle.

He wasn't sure what bothered him about the man standing half a block away. He was long past being afraid of strangers—he was too big now for someone to abduct him and throw him into a van.

Wasn't he?

Danny started walking forward again.

The man wasn't moving.

He just stood there on the sidewalk. Motionless. He was dressed only in a short-sleeve white Polo shirt, tan khaki pants, and brown shoes; the cold weather didn't seem to bother him. He was about as tall as Danny but a little bigger and broader in the shoulders. He was just an average blond-haired, pale-skinned guy standing alone on the sidewalk. That's all. Nothing to be worried about.

But Danny was worried.

He stepped off the sidewalk and out onto the road, giving the stranger a wide berth as he passed him.

Danny didn't want to stare at the man, but he couldn't take his eyes off of him as he walked by, like he wanted to see where the man was at all times.

It was the strange expression on the man's face that gave Danny the creeps. The man was smiling, but it didn't look like a regular smile—it looked like a twisted, half-smile that didn't touch his lifeless, dark eyes.

The man didn't make a move as Danny walked by, except to turn his head slowly so he could follow Danny with his dark eyes.

Danny even waved at the man, a weak, half-wave. But the man didn't wave back. He didn't say anything. He just watched him with that strange smile on his face.

Once Danny was past the man, he started running. The panic that had been slowly building up inside of him as he walked past the man had erupted and he just started running. He was afraid of the man, even though there didn't seem to be a reason to fear the stranger. The man had done nothing wrong; he hadn't made any kind of threatening gesture towards Danny. But Danny couldn't help feeling afraid.

He ran for two blocks and then stopped and turned around, breathing hard as he stared down the sidewalk.

The stranger was gone.

It was nothing, Danny told himself. *Just some weirdo out for a stroll.*

Danny hurried home, constantly peeking over his shoulder. He looked around one last time to make sure the stranger hadn't followed him all the way home before he stomped up the porch steps to their front door.

When Danny stepped inside the house, he saw his mother with the cordless phone cradled between her ear and her shoulder. She paced as she talked, sighing and wearing an exasperated look that told Danny she was talking to his dad.

He found it strange that the thought of his father had just popped into his mind on the way home from school, and here he was calling the house. But that didn't mean that he had any desire to talk to him.

Danny rushed upstairs to his room and stretched out on his bed.

The stranger he'd seen on the way home had really gotten to him more than he would've expected. The guy was definitely creepy. But there was more to it than that. The fear he'd experienced ran deeper, like to a subconscious level. And he couldn't shake the feeling that he'd seen that man before, or at least someone like him. He'd seen that strange smile and dead-eyed stare, those black eyes.

But where?

In his dreams, maybe?

Danny popped up from bed. He needed to get up and move and get the thought of the creepy guy out of his mind. It was just some man; that was all. Danny was older now, he couldn't be afraid of the bogeyman anymore.

He was hungry. Maybe he would grab a quick snack before dinner.

CHAPTER TEN

Rachael nodded at Danny when he came down the stairs and headed for the kitchen for his afterschool snack. She held the phone away from her face, her hand clamped over the mouthpiece.

"It's your dad," she whispered.

He nodded like he already knew that.

"You want to talk to him?"

"Maybe later," he grumbled and went into the kitchen.

Rachael put the phone back up to her ear.

"I don't know how to explain it," Paul said into her ear, continuing his conversation without missing a beat," but I think you and the kids might be in some kind of danger."

"Paul, please," Rachael said, her eyes darting to the archway that led into the kitchen from the dining room. She moved into the living room, closer to the front door so Danny wouldn't overhear her. "Don't start with this stuff," she hissed into the phone.

"I need you to believe me," Paul said. "I just want you to be on the lookout for anything strange."

I'm already talking to someone strange, Rachael thought, but she didn't say it.

"Is there anywhere you can go for a few days?" he asked.

"I'm not going to put my life on hold, and my children's lives, just because you're getting another one of your premonitions."

She heard her ex-husband sigh on the phone, and then he was quiet, already conceding to her.

"Just promise me that you'll be careful," Paul finally said.

Rachael softened just a bit. For a split second she heard a voice from the past—the *old* Paul—the Paul who was happier, more relaxed, a Paul who loved life and wasn't such a fundamentalist crazie like he was now. She had never been sure what had changed Paul so much. It seemed to have started after Danny and Lisa were born, and then it was like he became more and more religious, and more and more paranoid to go along with it. And when Paul's father died, Paul had changed completely by then.

Paul had told Rachael about how his own father had begun Paul's training as an exorcist and Investigator for the Church. He never went into too much detail about the training, but he told her that there were a lot of physical preparations and studying and praying involved in the training. He had been trained to become strong in body, mind, and spirit—a true warrior in every sense of the word.

By the time Paul was eighteen years old, he had rebelled during that training. He wanted a different life for himself than his father had in mind for him. He got out of the house, out into the world and fell in with a street gang for a short time. He was even arrested, but never charged with the crime of attempted murder. That was something else from his past that he never went into too much detail about with Rachael.

Eventually, Paul worked two jobs so he could afford to attend a community college where he studied science. The college was where she and Paul had met. Paul seemed so quiet when she met him, but not a nervous kind of quiet; he seemed like a strong and stoic man. But it was his curiosity about the world that had attracted her to him. He had seemed so passionate about learning, about discovering new things, like so much of this was brand new to him. And it *was* new to him, she came to find out. He'd been home-schooled by his father, forbidden to learn much about science and medicine. When he hadn't been home-schooled, he had gone to religious schools, some Catholic, and some not Catholic.

Paul had always promised that when he had children he would never raise them up like that, filling their minds with a doctrine and giving them no other choices or the freedom to make up their minds or draw their own conclusions about life. Rachael loved that about him.

They grew closer together and eventually they got married. It was a small ceremony, and Paul's mother and father refused to attend. And when Danny and Lisa were born, Rachael meant to hold Paul to his promise he had made so long ago about not raising his kids in a strict religious environment.

But then Paul started to change.

"I will be careful," Rachael finally told Paul on the phone. "I'm always careful with my kids."

She thought about asking him what was going on in his life, but she knew he would dodge the question with vague answers. She also thought about asking him why he was suddenly so concerned about her and the kids, but she knew she wouldn't really get an answer. And she didn't want to open that particular can of worms even if he did confide in her. She didn't want to entertain his fantasies and go along with them, to in any way justify his worries.

They made a few more generic exchanges with each other, and then she hung up the phone after promising him again that she would keep an eye out for anything strange and be extra cautious these next few days.

She felt bad. She knew Paul really loved his children (and she was sure he might still love her), she just wished his mind wasn't so screwed up. But she had to think of her children first, and she couldn't allow them to be around him while he was living this delusional life of his.

Rachael looked out the front window with the cordless phone still in her hand. She could hear Danny in the kitchen making a sandwich or something. She could go into the kitchen and remind him that she was going to make dinner soon. But it didn't matter, Danny would still eat dinner, too. Now that he was lifting weights in school, he was always hungry, and all he ever seemed to gain was muscle.

She stared out at the street and realized that a blond-haired man had been walking slowly past their house on the sidewalk. She hadn't gotten a good look at him, and now he was almost past their house and out of view of the window. He was dressed in tan pants and a white, short-sleeved shirt even though it was pretty cold outside.

A chill ran over her skin as she stood there in front of the living room window. And then she hurried over to the front door and locked the deadbolt.

Had the man been smiling at her as he walked past their house?

She shook her head as she walked away from the front door and headed to the kitchen, not willing to let Paul's paranoia get to her.

CHAPTER ELEVEN

Boston, Massachusetts

It was Saturday, and Paul worked on his report for Father McFadden.

He was upstairs in one of the spare bedrooms in his house that he had converted into an office. This was the smallest of the three bedrooms, but it had the most furniture in it. The other bedroom was a guest bedroom even though he didn't hold out much hope that his children would ever use it anytime soon.

Where the rest of his home was minimal and Spartan, his office was crowded and cluttered. A large desk was crammed against a wall with two large wooden filing cabinets stacked on top of each other on each side of the desk. Two tall bookcases took up another wall, all of the shelves crammed with books on Christian history, demonology, witchcraft, the dark arts, histories and cases of exorcisms.

Much of the walls around the room were covered with cork boards which Paul had tacked newspaper articles, internet printouts, and notes to. Many of the articles and internet printouts overlapped each other. He subscribed to eight newspapers and he scoured them for articles about anything paranormal. He had stacks of old newspapers in the corner, ready for recycling. He constantly searched the internet for any signs of the Darkness. He believed something was happening, perhaps signs of the End Times, and there were clues scattered around, they just needed to be found and pieced together.

Paul sat at his desk typing on his ancient desktop computer. The computer was old, but the motherboard and memory had been updated, along with a lot of new software added to it. On the desk beside the keyboard were his notes he'd written down after the failed exorcism the other night, and the small tape recorder he always kept with him.

He had listened to the recording a dozen times now and then he took more notes. He could hear his voice on the recording and the voices of Father James, Father O'Leary, Richard, and Julia. He re-lived the exorcism time and time again through that recording. He heard the rushing of wind when the electricity went out. He heard himself screaming at Richard to get the lights back on. He heard himself screaming at Father O'Leary to re-light the candles. And he also heard the running feet in the darkness and the slamming of the bedroom door that he now knew had been Father James bolting from the bedroom. The possession of Father James had happened so quickly, it seemed to have been almost instantaneous.

But he heard other sounds on the tape now as he listened to it over and over again, subtle sounds in the background when he turned the volume up all the way. He heard a whispering in the background, but it was more than one voice whispering—it was many voices. The voices were faint, but they were there among the background static. The voices in the background seemed to be whispering words in another language. Maybe Latin, but if it was Latin then it was a bastardized version of the language. Paul could only pick out a few words that he recognized.

And as the tape went on, he heard himself leave the bedroom and leave Father O'Leary alone with Richard and Julia. Then he heard Richard attack Father O'Leary. He heard the fear in the young priest's voice. He heard him crash against the wall, the flames whooshing up. He heard the young priest's dying screams.

Paul leaned back in his office chair, the old chair squealing in protest. He took a break from his report. He was a slow and methodical writer. And he was even slower at typing.

Legion

The name and the story from the Bible stuck in his mind. My name is Legion: for we are many, is what the demons had said to Jesus in the Gospel of Mark before He cast them out and into a heard of swine.

And the demons inside of Julia, and then Father James, they had referenced that story and the name Legion from the Bible.

But they weren't Legion. No, they were someone else. The Terror By Night, the demon inside Father James had told him that. Paul didn't know the demon's real name, but he was certain he had been dealing with one (or many) powerful demon.

Paul got up and left his office. He went downstairs and walked through the living room to the kitchen for another cup of coffee. He'd gotten up early even though he hadn't fallen asleep until three o'clock in the morning. After tossing and turning from eight o'clock until eight thirty, he decided that he couldn't sleep anymore and he got out of bed.

He was worried about Rachael and the kids. He was also worried cops were going to be banging down his front door because of the three burnt bodies in the Whittier house. But Father McFadden had promised to take care of all that, and he had promised Paul that he wouldn't be charged with any crimes.

Still, Paul felt terrible. The exorcism had gone badly, worse than he could've imagined.

How had he not known Richard was possessed along with Julia? How come he hadn't figured it out more quickly?

It had all been a ruse.

But why?

To get them to the house? To get *him* there?

Just to give him a warning?

Paul felt a shiver run through his body as he sipped his coffee.

He glanced at the door in the kitchen that led out to the garage. He never parked his Bronco in the garage because he couldn't fit it inside. The garage was divided unequally into a woodshop on one side, and a home gym on the other side. The gym consisted of a multi-station exercise machine with stacked weights, a bench and squat rack with a complete set of Olympic weights, a rack with dumbbells that went up to fifty pounds, a treadmill, a speed bag, and a canvas punching bag wrapped in duct tape that hung in one corner. The woodshop was a long counter with a large table saw next to it, and other various tools scattered along the counter. Two of the black boxes that he constructed were in pieces on the counter, waiting to be put together and painted. A pegboard took up much of the wall above the counters where he hung his other hand tools.

Paul thought that he should go out to the garage and work out right now. Take a break from the report, from these thoughts that tormented his mind.

He thought about calling Rachael again, trying to convince her again that this was very real.

But he didn't.

He was supposed to meet Father McFadden this evening at the hospital to visit Father James.

Maybe a quick workout and then a shower would make him feel better. He had wanted to have the report ready so he could give it to Father McFadden at the hospital. But it would have to wait. He still needed to do more work on it.

Paul drank the rest of his coffee and headed back upstairs to change into his workout clothes.

CHAPTER TWELVE

Cleveland, Ohio

Danny saw the man again.

It was Saturday and he had ridden his bicycle over to his friend Pete's house. They were supposed to shoot some baskets in his driveway. Pete had a basketball hoop attached over the garage door at regulation height and they used to shoot the ball a few times a week in the summer.

But Pete wasn't home.

"He went to his father's house," Pete's mother had told him. "He didn't tell you?" she asked with feigned shock. "That little stinker. And you rode all the way over here."

Danny could feel the mock sincerity oozing from her and he just wanted to leave, but she stood in the doorway with that stupid, fake smile plastered on her face.

"That's okay," Danny said and offered a fake smile to counter hers. "Could you have him call me when he gets back?"

"I *sure* will," Pete's mother over-jubilantly exclaimed.

He wondered if she was on some kind of prescription medication that she might be overindulging in, something that set the chemicals in her brain on a constant excited little dance.

Danny hurried off the front porch, back to his bicycle where he had dropped it in their front lawn. No doubt Pete's mother was probably frowning at the placement of his transportation as she stood at one of the front windows staring at him with that smile still plastered on her face.

He was thinking about that smile on Pete's mother's face when he rode home. He was thinking of how eerie her smile had been, and how it had reminded him of the stranger's smile he'd seen on his way home from school yesterday.

When he was almost in front of his house, right in front of the driveway, he brought his bicycle to a screeching halt on the sidewalk.

There was someone at the back of his house, by the corner, near the driveway that led to the free-standing garage.

It was a man.

The same man he'd seen yesterday.

But the man was gone now.

Had he even really been there?

Maybe he had imagined the man because he'd just been thinking about him and that odd, twisted half-smile of his.

No, he was sure he had seen him at the back corner of their house. And now the man had ducked back behind the house. He was somewhere in their backyard right now, hiding from Danny.

For a moment Danny was paralyzed with fear and indecision. He stood on the sidewalk, straddling his bike, clutching the grips of the handlebars harder than he realized. He stared down the empty driveway. His mom's car was gone.

He sprang into action.

He jumped off his bike and ran with it up across the front yard. He dumped his bike on the front lawn near his mother's meticulously arranged shrubs and flowerbeds that ran the length of the front porch in front of it. He knew he'd get an earful from his mom later about leaving his bike in the front yard.

"You want someone to steal your bicycle?" she would say. "Why don't you just leave a sign on it that says: Free?"

But he didn't care about getting yelled at right now. Right now he needed to get inside and lock the front door. He needed to see if Lisa was home, make sure she was okay.

Danny got to the door and found that it was locked. Of course it was locked, his mom was gone. He shoved his hand into his front pocket and dug out the key to the door. He could imagine the man walking briskly down the side of their house from the back corner where he had been hiding. He could imagine the man's plain brown shoes crunching along the gravel driveway, his gait quickening.

After he pulled the metal storm door open, Danny stuck the key into the lock of the front door with trembling fingers. He constantly glanced back at the front corner of the house, expecting the man to spring out at him and jump at the railing of the front porch, clamoring over it like a spider. Or maybe he was sneaking up from the other side of the house. Danny's eyes darted to that corner.

He finally got the door unlocked and pushed his way inside. He turned around to slam the door shut. The door had a large piece of glass in it that took up most of the top half of the door and it rattled in the loose frame when he closed the door. He realized that this barrier of glass was a poor defense against an intruder if that intruder wanted to barge his way in. There was the storm door on the outside of the front door; it was just a thin metal and glass door, not much extra protection. But he had forgotten to lock the storm door, and he wasn't going to unlock the front door again to do it.

He backed away from the door, the floorboards of the one hundred year old house creaking underneath the carpet as he took each step.

"Lisa!" he called out.

No answer.

He took a few quick steps over to the stairs and yelled up the steps. "Lisa, you up there?!"

Still no answer. She was either ignoring him, which was possible, or she was out with Mom. It was Saturday and they might have gone grocery shopping.

Danny felt frightened suddenly, like a small child that had been forgotten and left behind at home.

Stop it! Danny told himself. *Calm down. Think!*

Danny slowed his breathing down and made his panicked mind think logically. The man probably wasn't even out there. He might have imagined the whole thing. He had only seen him for a split second. Or maybe the man had been their neighbor, Arthur. Or maybe it had been someone cutting through their backyard.

The back door!

Danny raced through the living room and then through the dining room, the glass plates and bowls tinkled inside the hutch as he thundered past it. He ran through the kitchen to the mudroom where there was a guest bathroom and a door that led outside. He got to the door and was relieved to find that it was still locked. This door also had a large plate of glass in it. What was the deal with these doors and the large glass panels?

He pulled the curtain away from the door's window and looked out through the glass. He pushed his face against the glass so he could see as much of the driveway, garage, and backyard as he could.

Nobody was out there that he could see.

He backed away from the door, making sure the deadbolt was locked. He thought maybe he should check each window on the first floor and make sure all of them were locked. But he knew his mother always kept them locked if they were closed.

The basement. Maybe he should check the windows in the basement. They were small, maybe too small for a man that size to squeeze through, but maybe it wouldn't hurt to check. And then he remembered that there was another door that led outside on the first landing of the basement. They hardly ever used it, but he knew he wouldn't be able to relax until he checked to make sure it was locked.

He walked into the kitchen and stood there for a moment, looking at the sliding pocket door that opened up to the stairway which led down to the dark basement. There was no lock on the sliding door.

For a moment, he imagined he heard noises coming from behind the sliding door, from somewhere down in the basement. It sounded like a sneaky noise, maybe a jiggling noise, like someone trying to open the door that led outside.

Come on, Danny! he told himself. *Don't act like a scared little kid. Go down there and check the door. Once you know it's locked, you will be able to breathe easier.*

Part of Danny wasn't ashamed of being frightened a little bit. There was a strange man outside his house, a strange man he'd seen yesterday on the way home from school, and now that man could possibly be trying to break in to their home. But he wouldn't be breaking in to steal anything out of the house. No, his plans were going to be much worse than that.

Danny wasn't sure where those thoughts had come from.

He forced himself into action and made himself march across the kitchen. He thought for a split second about grabbing a knife from the block of knives on the counter, but decided against it.

He pushed the sliding wood door aside and stared at the wooden stairs that led down into the darkness.

He flipped on the light switch and it made a clicking sound. The door that led outside was only six steps down on the landing. This door also had a glass pane in it, but it wasn't as big as the ones in the front door and the back door. And the glass was covered right now with a solid curtain.

Danny looked at the door handle. It was still. No one was rattling it. All he needed to do was go down there and check it.

He hurried down the steps before he could change his mind. He grabbed the metal door handle, expecting it to jiggle in his hand when he did.

But it didn't.

And the door was locked.

Danny breathed out a sigh of relief and stood there for a moment. He let his hand drop down away from the door handle like the strength had drained out of him. He hadn't realized how tense he'd been. But he was safe now. The man out there (*if* there was a man out there) wasn't going to get inside unless he broke one of the windows. And then Danny would be on the phone dialing 911 before the man had a chance to—

The door handle jiggled.

Danny stared down at it like he couldn't comprehend what he was seeing.

He lifted his hand up towards the curtain to push it aside. But it didn't feel like it was his own hand anymore, it was like he was watching someone else's hand and arm pushing the curtain aside.

Once he ripped the curtain to the side, he saw the man's face right on the other side of the glass.

CHAPTER THIRTEEN

The man stared at Danny through the glass. It was the same blond-haired man he had seen yesterday. He had the same half-smile frozen on his face, a smile that wasn't really a smile. And his dark eyes watched Danny. The man's eyeballs were pure black; Danny could see that now that he was so close to him.

Danny let the curtain drop back in place and he backed away from the door. He stumbled back up the basement steps, scraping his shoulder against the plaster wall on the other side of the stairwell in the process, knocking down an old framed picture from the wall.

Only one thought pounded in his mind: he needed to get to the cordless phone; he needed to call the police.

He froze when he heard a voice calling out to him from the living room.

"Danny!" his mom sang out. "We're home! Come help us with the groceries. And how many times have I told you about leaving your bicycle in the front yard?"

Danny sprinted out to the living room and slid to a stop. He stared at his mother and his sister as they sauntered in from outside. The front door behind them was wide open—the stranger could come inside the house anytime he wanted to.

"The guy out there …" Danny tried to yell but his sentence came out as a wheeze of words. He ran past his mother and sister to the front door and slammed it shut. He twisted the deadbolt locked.

"What's wrong?" Mom asked, annoyed but beginning to become concerned. She stood in the living room with four plastic grocery bags gripped in her hands, two in each fist.

"You didn't see the man outside?" Danny asked as he peeked out through the curtain over the door.

"What man?" Rachael asked.

"You *had* to have seen him when you pulled up in the driveway! He was right outside the door to the basement!"

†

Rachael's stomach dropped and she felt the tingling of fear dancing across her skin. She knew her son, and she'd seen him overreact before, heard his share of embellishments and pranks over the years, but this was different.

Her son was really scared right now.

"Okay, just calm down, Danny," she said more out of habit than anything. But she didn't feel calm anymore. "When did you see this man?"

"I saw him yesterday when I was walking home from school. I know I should've told you about it but—"

"*Today*, Danny. When did you see him today?"

"I came back from Pete's house, he wasn't home," Danny said, spilling his words out in a rush. "And when I got back home I saw the man in the driveway by the back corner of our house. He was just staring at me, and then he went behind the house. I ran inside. Locked the door."

"Mom?" Lisa said. Her eyes were dinner plates of fear as she still held two plastic grocery bags bulging with food.

"It's okay, baby," Rachael assured her daughter, but then she looked back at Danny, waiting for him to continue.

"I checked the doors and windows," Danny continued quickly. "And then I checked the door in the basement steps and he was jiggling the handle."

Rachael marched into the dining room and set her bags of groceries down on the "good" table reserved for company. The bags flopped over and vegetables and a few cans of food spilled out of them. She hurried over to the cordless phone that sat on an antique desk and dialed 911.

"The door in the basement was locked, but he was still trying to get in," Danny said as Rachael waited on the phone, listening to it ring.

She nodded, indicating that she had heard her son's words, but her eyes kept darting to the archway that led to the kitchen—and to the basement.

The operator finally answered the 911 call. "911," a woman's voice said in a calm voice. "Is this a medical emergency or a police emergency?"

"Police," Rachael answered. "I just got home and my son told me there was someone outside …"

"… he was outside the basement door," Danny told her again. "Jiggling the door handle. Trying to get inside …"

"… he was outside our house, at the door that leads to the basement steps," Rachael said into the phone as Danny talked to her. "He was jiggling the door handle. Trying to get inside."

Danny now looked less afraid and full of energy. He bolted out of the dining room and into the kitchen.

"Where are you going?" Lisa asked him and followed him into the kitchen. She set her bags of groceries on the small breakfast table in the corner of the kitchen.

Rachael, the cordless phone still up to her ear, followed both of them into the kitchen. She saw Danny at the back door, pushing the curtain aside and peeking out through the glass.

"Is the man still outside?" the 911 operator asked Rachael about the same time her daughter asked Danny the same question.

"I don't see him," Danny said, and then he hurried back into the kitchen to look out the window over the sink.

"We don't see him," Rachael said into the phone.

"I've got an officer on the way," the operator told Rachel in a practiced calm voice. "Just stay inside and keep your doors and windows locked."

"Yes, we will. Thank you."

"The officer should be there in about five minutes. Would you like me to stay on the line with you?"

Rachael watched Danny as he ran over to the sliding door that opened up to the basement steps. The door was still open all the way. Her son clamored down the six steps to the landing below where the door was that led outside. He threw the curtain back boldly and looked out the window. He tested the door handle to make sure it was still locked as he peered outside.

"I still don't see him anywhere," Danny said.

"Ma'am?" the 911 operator said into Rachael's ear.

"I'm sorry," Rachael said, clearing her throat a little. "No. I'll hang up and wait for the police. Thanks."

"If you need to call back for any reason," the operator said, "please don't hesitate."

"I won't. Thanks."

Rachael pushed the END button on the cordless phone and held onto it.

"This is where he was, Mom!" Danny said from the basement landing. "Right outside this window."

More waves of fear tingled across Rachael's skin. She remembered Paul's words, his warning that she and the kids might be in danger.

†

Danny told his mom everything as they waited for the police. He recounted every detail that he could remember.

And then when the police showed up—which was only one officer, a giant African American man named Officer Booker—Danny retold everything to him.

"He didn't say anything to you?" Officer Booker asked Danny.

Danny sat on the couch next to his sister, and the officer and his mother sat in the two arm chairs.

When the cop had first arrived, he'd walked around their house and then walked around the free-standing garage. Rachael was outside with him (she had told Danny and Lisa to stay inside), and she opened up the garage so he could look around inside. But he didn't find anyone hiding anywhere.

Now the officer sat in the recliner in the living room, barely seeming to fit his bulk inside the arms of the chair.

"No," Danny finally answered the officer. "He didn't say anything to me either time I saw him. He just stared at me and he had this weird smile on his face, like only half of his mouth was smiling." Danny tried to mimic the smile. "Like this."

Lisa broke out into a giggle, trying to stifle it with her hands. Rachael gave her a warning look.

Officer Booker smiled at Lisa and then looked at Rachael, turning serious again as he looked at her. "We'll do a few more drive-bys past your house tonight and tomorrow. And I'll turn this description in to see if anything pops up. If you see this man again, call us right away. And if you do see him again, and if you are able to, try to get a photo of him with your cell phone or a camera."

Rachael nodded.

"Until then, just keep your doors and windows locked. Peek out several windows before you go outside. Sounds like this guy might've been casing your house, maybe he thought you were all out of the house and tried to see if he could get inside. Trying to find an unlocked door."

Danny didn't think the stranger was just some normal, run-of-the-mill burglar, but he didn't say anything. He had seen the man's dead eyes and his twisted smile. He could feel it in his soul that this man was evil. And even though he felt safe now inside their locked home in the daylight with the gigantic Officer Booker in their living room, he was sure that later tonight he wouldn't be able to sleep; he would probably be peeking out of his upstairs bedroom window every few minutes, waiting for a shadowy figure to slowly wander up their gravel driveway, the soles of his brown shoes crunching down the pea rock of their driveway with each step.

Officer Booker stood up and apologized that he couldn't do more. And then he left.

CHAPTER FOURTEEN

Boston, Massachusetts

Paul met Father McFadden at the hospital.

Father McFadden was in his mid-fifties and if he hadn't been wearing the black clothing and white collar of a priest, he might have looked more like a lawyer or even a corporate executive. He was a little over six foot, almost as tall as Paul, but slighter in build; not skinny, more like the athletic build of a long-distance runner or bicyclist. He had dark hair that was beginning to show streaks of gray at his temples which made him look more distinguished than old. He exuded a sense of confidence and quiet authority—like he'd been in a position of power for some time and he'd been born for just that purpose.

Paul shook hands with the father. They gave each other a grim smile, and Paul stared at Father McFadden with haunted, dark eyes.

"How is he?" Paul asked about Father James.

"He's a little better. He's still a little uncertain about what happened that night at the Whittier house. He still doesn't want to believe all of the … the details."

Paul nodded.

They got a quick cup of coffee in the hospital cafeteria and sat down at a corner table far away from the other people.

"I should've seen the signs as soon as I got to the Whittier house," Paul said after sipping his black coffee. "I should've reacted faster."

"It's not your fault. Luckily you were there or it could've been much worse."

Paul nodded, thinking of how Father James hadn't wanted him there in the first place.

"I didn't save Father James," Paul said. "I didn't drive the demons out of his body and into the box."

Father McFadden watched Paul, not moving a muscle.

"The demon … those demons inside of him … they left on their own."

"They don't do that," Father McFadden said.

"I know. But this time they did, like they suddenly had somewhere else to go."

"Maybe they went back into Julia."

Paul shrugged. "Maybe."

Father McFadden finally moved, taking a sip of his coffee.

"When I got to the house, Richard Whittier, Julia's father, he seemed normal at first."

"But now you believe he was possessed the whole time."

Paul nodded. "Yes."

"Do you think he was perfectly possessed?" Father McFadden asked.

Paul didn't answer right away. Father McFadden was referring to a phenomenon where a person was so deeply possessed by a demon or an evil spirit that they didn't even know they were possessed. It was a rare condition—Paul had never seen it in person before—but there had been many reports of it throughout history.

"I don't believe he was perfectly possessed," Paul finally answered. "But I do believe he was possessed before I got there. I believe he and his daughter were voluntarily possessed for quite some time, and Richard was just hiding his possession and waiting for the right time to attack."

"But why go through all that? Was it just to get a priest there to perform an exorcism? Just a random attack on the Church? On humans?"

"I don't know," Paul said, shaking his head. "Maybe. But one thing that bothers me is what the demons said to me when they were still inside of Father James, right before they let him go."

Father McFadden waited patiently.

"They told me that they would take everything away from me. Everything that I loved. And then the demon taunted me, asking me if I wanted to know its name. It told me that it was the Terror By Night."

"But the demon never told you its *real* name."

"No."

"I will pray for you. And you should pray, too. Your faith must be strong right now."

"I'm still worried about my ex-wife and my children," Paul told the priest. "I can't help but think that the demon was threatening my family. My children. I called Rachael, tried to warn her, but she doesn't believe me." He hesitated for a moment. "I may have to go there soon."

"Of course," Father McFadden answered. "I understand."

†

Paul and Father McFadden rode in the elevator together up to Father James's room on the fifth floor. The old priest was the only patient in the room. He looked even older now than when Paul had seen him at Richard and Julia's house. He looked thinner, his body somehow longer underneath the sheets. His face seemed longer, too. His jowls hung down more. The bags under his eyes were larger and darker. The deep creases of his wrinkles were more pronounced underneath the bright and harsh lighting of the hospital room.

A TV was turned on in the corner of the room high up on the wall, but the sound was turned down low.

"Father James," Father McFadden said as he entered the room. He walked over to his bedside and took the man's large hand in his own. Father James's other arm was hooked up to an IV.

Paul felt a little uncomfortable. He knew the old priest didn't like him to begin with, and he probably liked him much less after what had happened in the Whittier house. Paul moved over to the window in the room and looked out at the streets of Boston five stories below them.

"How are you feeling?" Father McFadden asked as he pulled up a chair next to the bed. Normally the question might have sounded disingenuous, but from Father McFadden it sounded heart-felt. If he had the inclination, he could be a hell of a convincing politician. He even looked the part.

"Better," Father James answered and even managed a weak smile. "They're going to release me tomorrow morning. They say I don't have any serious injuries, just some bumps and bruises. And some minor smoke inhalation."

"I'll make sure there's a car here for you in the morning," Father McFadden said and patted the man's liver-spotted hand lightly.

Father James smiled and closed his eyes. "I have so much to do …"

"You don't worry about any of that. Take as much time as you need to rest and recover."

Father James smiled and nodded, his eyes still closed, his breathing deeper and even.

Father McFadden glanced at Paul who still stared out the window, and then he got to his feet as silently as a cat burglar. He motioned with his head that they should leave.

Paul was ready to go.

As they started to walk out, Father James's voice stopped them.

"Paul," he croaked. His blazing blue eyes were open again and staring right at Paul. "Might I have a word with you?"

Paul glanced at Father McFadden who nodded.

"I'll just step out into the hall for a moment," Father McFadden said.

After Father McFadden left the room, Paul came back around the foot of Father James's bed and sat down in the same wooden, lavender-cushioned hospital chair that Father McFadden had been sitting in. The chair looked like hotel furniture to Paul, sturdy but too ugly to steal.

Father James stared at Paul.

"How much do you remember?" Paul asked.

"Some. Not everything. Father McFadden told me that I was possessed by a demon."

Paul nodded. "The demon jumped from Julia into you when the lights went out in her bedroom."

Father James nodded and his eyes looked distant for a moment like he was suddenly back there in the Whittier house again. "I should have stayed outside the circle of salt like you told me to."

Paul nodded, but didn't comment. He agreed that maybe the priest should've heeded his advice that night, but he also wondered if it would have done any good. It turned out that they had been dealing with more demons than they had anticipated. They had been dealing with stronger demons than they had been ready for. They had been dealing with two people who were more deeply possessed, and *willingly* possessed, than any of them had imagined.

"I'd always been taught that a demon couldn't possess a person unless they allowed it somehow, unless they opened that door, like inviting a vampire inside," Father James said. "I'd always believed that as long as one's faith was strong, they were safe from possession."

Paul nodded, but he'd seen possession of the innocents before. He'd read about it many times; there were many accounts of it throughout history. He'd seen such terrible things before, but this moment wasn't the time to talk about those things. This was the time to listen to Father James and try to comfort him.

The old priest shook his head and closed his eyes. Then he opened them again like he didn't want to be in the dark, even if it was behind his own eyelids. His blue eyes, normally fierce, were now watery and vulnerable.

"I'm ashamed I was so weak," the priest whispered. "So egotistical. Perhaps those sins, those weaknesses, they allowed the door to be opened to the evil spirits."

"Maybe," was all Paul said.

Father James was quiet for a long moment, just staring up at the ceiling through half-closed eyes. Paul thought the priest might be falling asleep and he wondered if he was sedated.

Paul got up to leave, and Father James's hand shot out and grabbed his forearm, his large hand gripped Paul's arm with surprising strength.

Father James stared up at Paul from the bed. "I'm frightened, Paul. So … so scared. I saw things while I was …" he let his words trail off like he couldn't even say the word "possessed" now.

Paul didn't say a word.

The priest licked his lips like his mouth had suddenly gone dry from fear. "If that thing got inside of me that night, then it can do it again.

It can find me wherever I go and get back inside. I don't have anywhere to hide. I'm afraid my faith is not strong enough anymore."

"It will have to be, Father."

"No … you don't understand. Something terrible is coming. I saw flashes of … of terrible things. They've been waiting and waiting, patient, and now they're ready to attack."

Paul gently pulled his arm out of Father James's grasp.

"We'll be okay," Paul told him, but he didn't feel that way. He could still hear the demon's words uttered through Father James's throat: *I am the Terror By Night, and I am going to take everything away from you, Paul. Everything that you love.*

"No, we won't," Father James snapped at Paul, his eyes watering now. "We won't be okay. You have to prepare. You have to be ready."

Paul nodded. "Do you want me to send Father McFadden back in here?"

"No," Father James said and plopped his head back down on the pillow. He looked miserable, like a hunted man with nowhere to hide.

Paul left the hospital room and met up with Father McFadden in the hall. He told Father McFadden everything that Father James had told him. He didn't feel like he was betraying the old priest's confidence, because Father James hadn't asked Paul not to tell Father McFadden anything. Maybe he was too ashamed to look Father McFadden in the eyes right now and admit that his faith hadn't been strong enough that night.

†

Paul drove home as night fell on Boston. He stopped at a take-out deli and ordered a roasted turkey sandwich to go. He took the meal home and sat down at his small table in his immaculate and silent kitchen.

He chewed his food slowly and then stopped suddenly. His body was frozen for a moment. His mouth fell open and the half-chewed food spilled out of his mouth. His hands trembled on the table as he stared across the kitchen.

But he didn't see his kitchen anymore.

He was somewhere else now.

He saw a vision.

Water. Screams. Darkness. Death.

Oh Dear God!!

Paul was on his feet without remembering that he stood up. He looked down at the table now that the vision was gone. He saw the chunk of food he'd been chewing down on the table, just a piece of mushy pulp now. He didn't even remember spitting it out.

It felt like he couldn't breathe for a moment.

And now he felt an incredible and sudden loss. His body ached, his heart ached, his soul ached.

No Oh God no Please God no ...

Paul rushed to the kitchen counter and grabbed his cell phone. He flipped quickly to Rachael's name and tapped the screen with his trembling finger. He held the phone up to his ear and listened to the ringing.

At least it was ringing.

Then he heard a recorded message.

"The number you are trying to reach is not in service at this moment …"

Paul tried Rachael's home phone. He dialed the number and listened to the ringing. It rang five times and then went to a recorded message.

"Hi, Rachael," Paul said after the beep. "It's … uh, it's me, Paul. I was just calling to make sure everything's okay." How could he tell her that he was having visions that some kind of harm was going to come to her and the kids? But he couldn't say that. If he did, she would never call him back.

"Just please call me when you get this."

Paul hung up the phone and paced around the kitchen. He looked back at his plate of food on the table, but the thought of eating turned his stomach right now.

Oh God, what should I do?

He wondered if he should call the airlines and reserve a seat for tomorrow or the next night.

Yeah, maybe he should do that.

A surprise visit to see his kids.

Of course Rachael would be furious with him. But he would have to deal with that when the time came. At least he would be there in the same city with them in case they needed him.

He grabbed his small address book out of the drawer in the kitchen and flipped it open to the letter "A" for airlines. He had flown so much on the same airline for the last ten years that he should have this phone number memorized. But he looked the number up and dialed it into his phone.

Moments later he had a reservation for tomorrow night. It was the soonest reservation he could make on such short notice.

Until then, he would keep trying to call Rachael, keep trying to get through to her. Maybe once he got a hold of her, he could let her know he was coming out to see the kids. If she blew up, he could always cancel the flight. But at least he would hear from her and know that she was okay.

CHAPTER FIFTEEN

Cleveland, Ohio

Danny sat in the back of the police vehicle with the back door open; his legs were sticking out, his feet on the running board, his legs bunched up in front of him, his torso bent over. A wool blanket was wrapped around his shoulders over his drenched clothes. He was wet. He was freezing. He was in shock.

Danny stared at the dark lake underneath the evening sky. The last traces of sunlight were a gory red line on the western horizon. A line of cop cars and an ambulance were parked along the side of the road up and down the guardrail, except for the area where his mom's car had crashed through.

A tow truck was backed down onto the embankment that led down to the water's edge, ready to pull his mom's car out of the water.

The ambulance had just gotten there five minutes ago. Two paramedics rushed towards Danny who sat very still in the back of the police car. One of the paramedics shined a light into Danny's eyes and took some vital signs. They wanted to take Danny to the hospital, but a cop instructed them to wait until he asked Danny some questions.

Two divers were down in the water looking for Danny's mother and sister who were still inside the car.

His mom and his sister were dead. Danny already knew that. They'd been down there underneath the murky water way too long now. It wasn't a rescue mission anymore. Now it was just a retrieval mission.

Danny watched all of this with a strange detachment, like he was watching some action movie, a film where the hero might rescue the victims in the nick of time. It didn't even feel like his life right now. He was still in shock and he shivered uncontrollably.

Officer Booker approached Danny as the divers dipped back down below the surface of the water. He could see their lights rippling underneath the water. But he couldn't see his mom's car underneath the dark water. The cops had set up spotlights on the bank, shining light down to the marshy water's edge of the large lake. All of the cop cars had their red and blue flashing lights on and the lights gave the whole scene an odd strobe-light like effect.

Danny looked at the gigantic police officer as he walked towards the car. He recognized the officer as he walked towards him—he was the same officer who had come to their house when the smiling man had been trying to break into their basement door.

Officer Booker stood right in front of Danny now, looking down at him with large dark eyes filled with compassion. He seemed to be fighting back tears.

"Danny," Officer Booker said.

Danny stared at the large man, but he didn't say anything.

"Who else was in the car?"

"My mom and my sister," Danny said in a low voice.

A red sedan was parked way down at the end of the line of police cars and emergency vehicles up on the side of the road where traffic crept by as rubberneckers gawked at the accident scene even though a cop in uniform waved at them frantically to move along. The red sedan was owned by a man in his late fifties who gave a statement about what he had seen. He'd been following Danny's mom's car, and he said it looked like the car just kept on going straight instead of slowing down and following the sharp curve in the road when it reached the lake. He said he hadn't even seen the brake lights—like the car never even slowed down. The car crashed through the guardrail, sped down the embankment and plowed right into the water. And then it sank. The headlights and taillights were visible for a moment underneath the water, the man said, and then they disappeared underneath the dark surface of the water.

The man said he tried to get to the passengers in the car, he tried to help them. After he called 911 on his cell phone, he ran down to the shore and saw Danny walking out of the water. He looked dazed, he seemed to be in shock, and he was shivering uncontrollably. The man said he dove into the water and tried to get to the mother and daughter, but he couldn't do it. It was too dark and he wasn't that great of a swimmer.

But at least he had helped Danny up to the bank and watched him until the police arrived five minutes later. He felt good about that at least. He told the cops over and over again that he had done what he could, but he wished he could've done more. But he was so out-of-shape, and he wasn't an expert swimmer. He couldn't get to the other two in the car.

Danny watched as the tow truck backed down a little more on the muddy embankment until it was as close as it could get to the water without sinking down into it.

A diver lifted his head up out of the water.

"Find 'em yet?" a cop shouted at the diver, lifting his hands up in a universal questioning gesture.

The diver gave the thumbs down signal and shook his head—the equally universal sign for bad news.

Danny's heart sank as he watched from the back of the police car. He knew they were gone, but he had dared to let himself hope just a little bit.

"Son, what happened here?" Officer Booker asked Danny in his deep and gentle voice.

Danny shook his head slowly as tears filled his eyes. Seeing the diver shake his head no had pounded the reality home—his mother and his sister were dead. His entire family was gone in the blink of an eye.

"Who was driving?" Officer Booker asked patiently.

"My mother," Danny answered and his voice sounded so far away to his own ears and it felt like he wasn't himself, like this situation wasn't real, like it was happening to someone else.

"Did she lose control of the car?" the officer asked.

Two paramedics waited near Officer Booker, watching Danny like two mother birds. If they felt like they needed to swoop in and take Danny to the hospital, then they would. And they had already told Officer Booker that. They had checked Danny for signs of concussion and water in his lungs, but he seemed okay. He didn't have any obvious head wounds or any other wounds except for a few minor scratches on his arms and hands. But they reminded Officer Booker that Danny could still have a brain injury and they wouldn't be able to tell without a CAT scan.

"I don't know," Danny said as tears slid out of his eyes. "I guess so. I can't remember."

Danny tried to remember back to when they had been driving in the car. Where had they been driving to? Where had they been driving from? It was all a blank to Danny right now. Had Mom been speeding? Had she been upset about something?

"I can't remember anything about the accident," Danny said again.

"Officer," one of the paramedics stepped forward. "Memory loss can be a sign of a brain injury. We need to get him to the hospital. We can't wait much longer."

Officer Booker nodded and moved out of the way so the paramedics could do their job. They walked Danny to the waiting ambulance and helped him up into the back.

Danny did remember something about the accident, something that had happened right before the crash. But he didn't want to tell Officer Booker or any of the other cops about it because it didn't make any sense.

He had seen the blond-haired man with the twisted half-smile right before the accident. He was the same man he had seen on the sidewalk while walking home from school, the same man he'd seen at his house outside the basement door, the same man he'd seen right on the other side of the glass.

Had the man been standing in the middle of the road?

Had his mother swerved to avoid hitting the man?

Had the man been standing on the side of the road and then Danny screamed at his mom?

Had Danny distracted his mother at the worst possible moment?

Had all of this been his fault?

CHAPTER SIXTEEN

Paul got the phone call as he was working on his report to Father McFadden.

He sat at his desk in his office, the door slightly ajar. Sometimes he listened to classical music as he worked on his reports or did research, but not now. It had been difficult enough to concentrate on this report and he didn't need any distractions. He was having some trouble putting into words the evil he had witnessed at the Whittier house, the power the demons had possessed. They had been waiting for him and the two priests. And Paul should have sensed it.

And now three people were dead and who knew how badly Father James's psyche had been damaged. Maybe Paul couldn't have saved Richard and his daughter—maybe they were too far gone after willingly giving themselves as servants to the dark side—but he should've been able to help Father O'Leary and Father James; he should've been able to protect them.

And when the demon vacated Father James's body so quickly after its warning, Paul couldn't help but think that the demon had sought out his family who he was no longer able to protect.

He had called Rachael several times throughout the night and the morning. He still wasn't getting through on her cell phone, still getting the message that her service was out of order. He had left five messages on her home phone.

No returned calls yet.

Which didn't necessarily mean anything. Rachael usually took her time calling him back.

The report for Father McFadden was almost finished—he wanted to have it done and delivered to him before he left for Cleveland. He'd read it over and over again, changing a word here and there, but he was sure that it was ready now. All he had to do was print it out.

His flight was supposed to leave at seven thirty this evening, and he already had his two bags packed and waiting by the front door.

He sat there for a long moment, staring at the computer screen, the arrow from the mouse hovering over the print button on the screen.

And then the phone call came.

He ran downstairs to the kitchen and picked up the cordless phone on the counter. He looked at the number—he recognized the Cleveland area code, but he couldn't place the phone number immediately.

He answered the phone.

It was Rachael's mother.

"Paul, it's Gail." Her voice was steady and he recognized her deep, throaty voice. She had been a lifelong smoker until recently when she had been diagnosed with emphysema.

He and Gail had had their differences over the years, but they remained at least on speaking terms. Paul had gotten along a lot better with Rachael's father when he was still around.

"I'm afraid I've got some bad news," Gail said and then her voice cracked. "Some really bad news."

Paul felt his world tilting, trying to slip away from him. He gripped the phone tighter like it was his only lifeline to this world right now.

He knew what was coming.

From a million miles away he heard a tear-jerked voice tell him that Rachael and the kids had been in a car accident. Rachael and Lisa hadn't made it.

"Danny?" Paul managed to say.

"He's okay," Gail said, recovering quickly from crying. She sniffled. "He's still in shock about the whole thing, but he's physically okay. He stayed the night in the hospital, but he's coming back here with me today."

Paul tried to talk but he couldn't find his voice for a moment. All he could hear was that growling voice coming from Father James's mouth.

I am going to take everything away from you, Paul. Everything that you love.

Paul stumbled over to his kitchen table. He pulled a chair out, the legs scraping along the floor, and he plopped down. He felt like he couldn't talk, like he couldn't breathe. His whole body ached so badly, worse than he ever would've thought possible.

"The funeral's this Saturday," Gail said and left the words hanging in the air, a silent question wondering if he was going to make it.

"Okay," Paul said and exhaled a held breath. He breathed in as tears slipped out of his eyes. He saw flashes of his daughter, so many memories of when she was a baby, a child, recent photos sent to him through e-mail.

And now she was gone.

"I'll be there," Paul said, fighting to control his voice. He thought of telling Gail that he already had a flight booked for this evening, but he couldn't say the words. He had known something was going to happen, but he had been too late. Perhaps only hours too late. If he had driven … he thought for a moment. But no, he still wouldn't have made it to them in time. He should've left two days ago; he should've left for Cleveland right when he got home from the Whittier house. Oh God, he had failed again. But this time he had failed his family.

Gail didn't answer him. She didn't say anything.

"How did this happen?" Paul asked.

Gail was silent for another moment; there was just a wheezy breathing on the other end of the phone. "The police are still investigating," Gail told him. "But it looks like Rachael, like she just … just lost control of her car going around a turn by a lake. The car … it crashed through the guardrail and drove into the lake. Danny was able to get out of the car … but Rachael and Lisa … they …"

The lake.

The sudden visions of being trapped in a car underneath dark water came rushing back to Paul. He had seen a premonition of what was going to happen to them, but he hadn't acted on it soon enough.

The knife blade of guilt ripped through him and he had to push back a sob.

"No one else was involved with the accident?" Paul finally asked. He would've thought they might have been run off the road by someone.

"No. There was a witness. An older man who tried to help but … but he couldn't help. He saw the whole thing. He said Rachael seemed to just drive right down into the water."

"Oh God," Paul said and shuddered.

Gail sniffled and then got control of herself. "Paul, we need to talk about Danny. I can't take care of him by myself. And my son, he's too busy with his family in Seattle. Besides, I think it's time Danny was around his father now."

"Yes," Paul croaked out. "Yes, I agree. I'll be there tonight."

CHAPTER SEVENTEEN

Cleveland, Ohio

Danny stood next to his father at the funeral. It had been almost three years since Danny had seen him in person. It had been that long since his father had come to Ohio to visit him and his sister. Danny wasn't angry at seeing his dad now, he wasn't bitter, or sad … he wasn't anything, he didn't feel anything. He felt hollow inside. Empty.

The funeral took a little while. Uncle Martin from Seattle said a few things, but then he broke down crying. Grandma Gail tried to say a few words but she cried and then she had trouble catching her breath. She had to inhale some oxygen from the tank she wheeled around with her and Uncle Martin and his new wife helped her back to her seat.

Some of Danny's mother's friends and co-workers said a few things. They tried to emphasize the good things, tried to remember the good times, but they all said that this was a terrible and unexpected tragedy, and that both his mother and sister were in a better place now. A brave schoolmate of Lisa's stood up at the podium and said a few things, reading from a paper she held with shaking hands, trying not to cry.

There were tons of flowers and cards, one gigantic card from the Junior High School that Lisa attended with hundreds of signatures all over it.

After the funeral, Paul drove Danny and Gail to her house in the vehicle he had rented—a Lincoln Navigator. A few friends stopped by Gail's house and she had some refreshments laid out. But her visitors only stayed a few hours and then they were gone.

Danny excused himself and went to lie down in the guest bedroom where he had been staying since he got out of the hospital. He had packed an overnight bag and grabbed a few books from his house after leaving the hospital, and that was the last time he had been in his own house. The overnight bag of clothes and the stack of books were in the closet with its door halfway open.

He lay in bed on top of the covers, still fully dressed from the funeral except that he had kicked off his shoes at the bottom of the bed. He felt exhausted even though he hadn't done anything physical for the last few days.

He held a necklace in his hand. It had been his mother's necklace and he had added a charm from the bracelet that Lisa always wore. It was his last connection to them, a keepsake he could carry around with him in his pocket and hold whenever he wanted to, a talisman that would hopefully help keep the tears and crushing grief at bay for now.

He had almost drifted off to sleep when he heard a voice whispering to him. It was coming from inside the bedroom … from inside the closet.

It was his mother's voice.

"Danny …"

He sat up like a piston and stared at the half-open closet door with the long, skinny mirror attached to it. The door creaked open a little, inch by inch.

"Danny … I'm not dead. Come in here with me … come in here and see me …"

Suddenly, Danny was underneath the dark water again, struggling to hold his breath. He could see the dim lights underneath the water … dashboard lights from his mother's car.

Danny sat bolt-upright in the bed, breathing hard, his blood rushing in his ears, his heart pounding against his ribcage. There was a sheen of perspiration on his face and for an irrational split second he thought the perspiration was the cold water from the lake.

He still held the necklace bunched up in one fist.

He looked at the closet door across the room. It was almost shut now, only open a crack. For a moment he expected it to creak back open.

That door had been open before, hadn't it? Why was it closed now?

He finally got his breathing under control and his heartbeat slowed down from a sprint to a jog. The blood rushing in his ears had lessened and now he heard another sound.

Voices.

But not from the closet. These voices were coming from the living room. It was his grandmother and his father. They were talking in low tones, but not whispering. Yet he couldn't make out what they were saying.

He got up and crept to the bedroom door that was ajar. He pulled the door open a little and slipped out into the hallway. He walked down to the end of it, close enough to hear, but not close enough to be seen from the kitchen.

"The arrangements were already made a while ago," Grandma Gail said. "If any event such as this were to happen, you were always going to be the one to take care of the children."

"Thank you," his father answered.

"There are a few more things that need to be taken care of," Grandma said and there was a pause and a tinkling of china like they might be sipping tea. "I set up a meeting with the lawyers on Monday morning. Just some papers to go over and sign. Assets to be switched over, the house to be put up for sale or rented out. And we still need to pack her stuff up. Keep what you and Danny want and put the rest in storage or donate it. She had a will and certain pieces of furniture and heirlooms have already been promised to some family members."

"I understand," Paul said. "Whatever Rachael's wishes were, I want to respect them. I don't want anything else … just my son."

My son?

He was going to live with his father? In Boston?

But what if he didn't want to go? Didn't he have a say in any of this? He was seventeen years old, still a minor, but he would be eighteen in nine months. Old enough, he thought, to have a say in his own life.

Danny felt like rushing out into the living room and disrupting their little tea party. He felt like expressing the feelings that were raging inside of him now.

But he didn't.

Instead, he crept back to the guest bedroom and lay back down on the bed. He kept one eye on the closet door, the nightmare still fresh in his mind as he lay there.

†

Forty-five minutes later Danny heard his father leave the house. He heard his rental tank outside start up and then drive away.

Danny got up and went out to the living room. His grandmother wasn't there, but the TV was on with the sound turned down low. He heard the clinking sound of dishes in the kitchen. He went to the kitchen and found his grandmother cleaning up even though everything was immaculate.

She looked at Danny as he entered, and she smiled at him with such a sweet smile that he couldn't help smiling back.

"Danny, you're up. Did you get some sleep?"

"A little," he mumbled.

"Come on, sit down." She gestured at the small table in the kitchen. "Are you hungry?"

"Not really."

"How about a few cookies? I made some last night." She didn't wait for him to answer. She brought a plate of cookies over from the counter and set them down in front of Danny.

Danny sat down at the table and picked up a cookie while Grandma Gail poured him a big glass of ice-cold milk and brought it to the table. He felt like he was on autopilot as he bit off small pieces of cookie and chewed them up without really tasting them.

He looked at his grandmother as she stood next to the table. "I'm going to Boston to live with my dad?"

Gail smiled, but this time it was a sympathetic smile. She pulled a chair out and sat down. Danny could hear her ragged breathing; she was winded from just the little bit of activity that she'd been doing.

"You heard me and your father talking," she said.

"He's not my father," Danny blurted out before even thinking about it. "He's hardly been around for the last few years."

"I know …"

"I shouldn't have to live with him if I don't want to. I'm almost eighteen years old," he added in case she might have forgotten.

"Danny," she said and her throaty voice was suddenly stern, her light eyes focused on him. "I need to tell you something and you need to listen to me."

He didn't say anything.

"You may not like what I'm going to say. You may not even believe it."

Danny still didn't say anything—he just waited.

"The reason your father hasn't been around is because your mother asked him *not* to be around. She even got a restraining order against him. He wasn't allowed around you or Lisa unless he had your mother's permission."

Danny was shocked. "But why? What's wrong with him? I mean, obviously there's something wrong with him if Mom had a restraining order against him. And now you want me to go to Boston with him?"

"Danny," she warned. "I'm not finished."

He was quiet, waiting for her to finish what she had to say. The cookies and milk were forgotten in front of him.

"You have no idea what your father does for a living, do you?"

"No. He doesn't really talk too much about himself."

Gail nodded. "That figures. Your mother wanted it that way; she didn't want you to know too much about what your father does."

"Why would she want it that way? What's going on?"

"I'm trying to explain that."

"What does he do for a living?"

"He works for the Church. For many churches. He's an Investigator."

"Investigator? Like what, a detective?"

"Sort of. He investigates claims of supernatural phenomenon."

Danny was silent for a moment. Then he shook his head no like he didn't understand. "Why wouldn't my mom want us to know about that? Why would it be such a big deal?"

"It's complicated," his grandmother answered. "Your father is a very … and your mother was …" Grandma Gail paused like what she had to say next was difficult and Danny was afraid she was going to start crying. But she took a deep and wheezy breath and got her bearings. "Your mother, I'm afraid, was not a very religious person."

Danny could attest to that. He and Lisa had never been forced to go to church or read the Bible even though his grandmother, and obviously his father, were believers.

"I'm not saying she didn't believe in God," Grandma Gail continued quickly like she was defending her daughter, "but she didn't like organized religion, and she wanted you and your sister to make up your own minds about your beliefs."

"That's what I want to do," Danny told her. "Make up my own mind. And I don't want to go live with Paul. I have school here. My friends." Danny thought of the school he hated, of the kids he couldn't get along with. He thought of his only friend Pete who seemed to be avoiding him lately.

"Danny, listen to me. These are the facts. I would love to take you in, but I'm too old and I don't have the physical energy for it anymore. Your Uncle Martin and Aunt Sue are too busy with their family. But that's not even the real reason. You *belong* with your father whether you want to believe that or not. You and he deserve at least a chance to get to know each other. Just try it out for a while. When you turn eighteen and graduate from high school, then it will be up to you. You can go wherever you want then."

Danny didn't say anything—he just had a sinking feeling that his whole life was spiraling out of control, like he was trapped in a raging river and he had no way to stop himself. He felt like the last of his family, his grandmother, was kicking him out.

"And I think you *need* to get away for a while," Grandma Gail said. "Get away from your house, from this city, this state. There are going to be too many reminders here of what happened."

Danny's mind flashed back to the night of the accident. He still couldn't remember anything about it, but he still remembered the man at the side of the road, staring at him with his dead eyes and smiling at him with his twisted half-smile. He regretted not telling the police about that detail—his only real memory—but there were a few reasons for that. One was that he couldn't be completely sure that he had seen the man on the side of the road, or if he had been a figment of his imagination. And two, if the man had really been there, then Danny couldn't help feeling like the accident was somehow his fault.

"Just think about what I've said," Grandma Gail told Danny. "Your father is a good man. At least try to get to know him. I never totally agreed with what your mother did, keeping your father's life a secret from you, and I wish I would have interjected. I didn't want to interfere with her life. But I wish I had now."

Danny's grandmother looked so sad. He had to keep reminding himself that not only had he lost a mother and a sister, but she had lost a daughter and a grandchild.

"Don't you want me around?" Danny finally asked. He felt childish and bratty even saying such a thing, and he immediately regretted it. He knew it was a low blow, a punch to his grandmother's gut. It was a pathetic last resort and plea for her to let him stay.

But she gave him a warm smile and reached out and caressed his cheek. "Of course I do. And I've treasured having you around so close to me all these years. But now it's your father's turn to be in your life. And *your* turn to be in his."

PART TWO

CHAPTER EIGHTEEN

Danny sat in the airplane seat next to his father. They had stayed in Cleveland for nearly a week after the funeral. Danny packed some of his stuff in a storage unit that his grandmother had rented for him. Anything that wasn't kept in storage or given away to other family members was donated to charity. Danny collected his most treasured memories in a shoebox which included his mom's cell phone, an assortment of photos, a few greeting cards, a folded-up picture his sister had drawn, some jewelry. But he kept his mother's necklace with his sister's charm on it in his pocket.

He had packed several boxes of his stuff that Paul (he still couldn't quite call him Dad yet, and Paul seemed fine with that) had shipped off to Boston. Danny only brought along two large suitcases of clothes and a carry-on bag on the flight.

Danny and Paul had made mostly small talk while they packed up his mother's house. Uncle Martin and Aunt Sue had stayed an extra two days to help with the chore, but they kept complaining about how badly they needed to get back home and get back to work.

Danny had tried to say goodbye to Pete, but again he wasn't home. He left a message on Pete's cell phone, letting him know about his mother and sister and that he was going to live with his father for a while. He hung up the phone, knowing his only friend was no longer his friend. Besides his grandmother, he had nothing left in Cleveland anymore.

His grandmother's words kept echoing in his mind: *You need to get out of town for a while. Get out of this state. You need to start over.*

And as much as he didn't want to, Danny decided to look at this as an adventure, a strange journey that he was about to embark on.

He had never flown on a plane before and it was exciting. The flight from Cleveland to Boston wasn't that long and his father had booked first-class seats for them. Maybe his dad was rich.

It was a nighttime flight and they were supposed to be in Boston at about ten p.m. Danny figured he should be tired as he sat on the plane, but he wasn't. He didn't say much to his father—Paul wasn't much of a talker—so Danny just stared out the window at the darkness.

"I'm going to use the bathroom," Paul told him.

Danny looked at him and nodded.

No smile from his father, no pat on the head. Just a dark and stoic look. He got up without a sound and went down the aisle.

Danny looked back out the window, but there wasn't much to see except the darkness. He couldn't even see the nighttime lights below because of the cloud cover.

But then he saw a pale face materializing behind his own face in the reflection on the window's glass. The pale face had that twisted half-smile, the same dead and dark eyes.

Oh God ... it's him! He's found me! He's on the plane!

Danny jumped and turned around in his seat. He saw a stewardess leaning over his father's empty seat towards him. She was smiling, but she didn't have the twisted half-smile he'd seen in the reflection in the window. And her eyes weren't dark and dead, they were greenish-blue and cheerful.

"Do you need anything, sweetie?" she asked.

Danny just shook his head no. For a moment he couldn't speak.

"Something to drink?" she asked. "A Coke or Pepsi?"

Danny just nodded, agreeing to whatever she said.

"Okay, sweetie. Be right back."

Danny let out a breath that he felt like he'd been holding the whole time.

†

They landed in Boston on schedule. They got off the plane and had to wait thirty minutes to find their suitcases—Danny's two suitcases and Paul's one.

Paul carried his own suitcase and Danny's extra suitcase, the heavier one.

They stepped out into the chilly night air and walked to the parking area where Paul had left his Ford Bronco.

These last few days had been strange for Paul. He was dealing with the ache of loss for his daughter and ex-wife, yet he was treasuring this time he spent with his son.

His son seemed okay about everything so far. Paul had expected a big fight with him about coming to Boston, but Danny had been fine with it. Paul talked to Gail before they left, and she told him that she had already talked to Danny about going to live with him. She also hadn't told Danny everything about Paul's life—that part was up to Paul.

And Paul loved Gail for that.

How much should he tell Danny? Paul wondered.

Everything.

But when?

It would take time. He and his son had made a lot of small talk, more than they ever had on the phone or through e-mails.

Paul had found out some of his son's interests, including his passion for basketball. But Danny told him that he was too nervous to try out for the high school team. He learned that Danny didn't have a girlfriend at the moment, and he only had one person he called a friend, a boy named Pete, even though apparently Pete was turning into a snob lately.

They'd lost themselves in the work of packing the house up and Paul let Danny take his time with his own room.

Even though things had gone relatively smoothly, Paul knew that it was going to take some time for Danny to work through his grief. Paul had been with many grieving families over the years. And he was grieving himself for his own daughter, and his ex-wife who he had never hated, who he had never stopped loving. And when she didn't want him to be a part of his children's lives, he didn't hate her for it, he respected her decision after he followed his true calling to God. She accused Paul of making a choice between religion and his family. But it was more than that, deeper than that. He wanted both, but he couldn't turn his back on God and his calling and the talents and skills he had been blessed with to help people.

You mean helping people like Richard and Julia? his mind whispered. *Like Father O'Leary? Father James?*

He pushed the voice away.

But these demonic attacks had been stronger than he had ever experienced before. And then the demons went after his family, they killed his daughter and tried to kill his son. And Paul knew they weren't done yet. No, this was far from over.

And his only responsibility now was protecting his son, because he knew they would come for him again.

"Cool ride," Danny said, breaking Paul's train of thought as they walked towards his truck.

"Thanks," Paul muttered. "It's a 1978 Ford Bronco. It's old, but still in great shape."

They got inside the truck and Paul started it up. The engine roared to life, rumbling with power as it idled in the parking lot.

"It's got a 302 under the hood," Paul said just to say something. He felt a little nervous and a little foolish—he wasn't good at small talk. "That's an eight cylinder engine," Paul explained.

"Not good on gas?" Danny guessed.

"Not the greatest," Paul answered and gave him a smile.

Paul put the truck in gear and they headed home.

†

They didn't talk much on the drive to his father's house which was in a crowded neighborhood of Boston. The neighborhood reminded Danny a little of Cleveland, but with more hills and trees. The streets seemed a little narrower and winding, the houses huddled a little closer together.

They parked in the driveway. It was late and his father's truck sounded loud in the dark. He wondered off-handedly if neighbors ever complained. But then again Paul looked like a guy you wouldn't mess around with. He had seen his dad's bulging muscles and intricate tattoo work when they were packing up the house and Paul had stripped down to a long-sleeved shirt with the sleeves rolled up to the elbows. He remembered that his dad was muscular and strong, but for some reason Danny hadn't remembered all the tattoos his dad had. He thought about asking his dad about his tats, but decided to wait for another time.

They got their bags and suitcases out of the truck and brought them to the front porch. The house looked small and squeezed in close to the other houses on each side of it. There was only a small strip of grass on each side of Paul's house.

The house was two stories, but the second story was only built over the house and not the garage. It was a neat and clean house and looked like it had been repainted recently. The small square of front lawn was mowed and trimmed. A line of small shrubs stood in a line in front of the porch railing. There were no garden gnomes, no signs proclaiming this as home-sweet-home, and no real décor of any kind on the front porch, not even plants in pots. Nothing but a generic doormat that had WELCOME printed on it.

Inside, the house was just as neat and minimal as the outside. Paul hung his coat on the old-fashioned coat rack next to the closet door. And Danny hung his coat next to his father's after setting his suitcases down.

Danny looked around the small, cozy living room. He saw a couch, a recliner, a coffee table, an end table. All of the furniture was hard and tan and neutral. Both tables were clear of any knickknacks and only a few religious paintings and icons hung on the walls. The floor was wood planking and shiny with polyurethane.

As he looked around, Danny did not notice a TV anywhere.

"No TV?"

"No. Sorry. I've got a radio."

"How do you have no TV?"

"I don't watch much TV," Paul said and shrugged. "But I can get one if you like," he added quickly. "And cable service. Whatever we need."

Danny didn't answer, but he would like a TV in his bedroom. "Yeah," he muttered.

"We'll work on it tomorrow," Paul promised.

There was an awkward silence for a moment, and then Paul exploded into nervous action. "Over here's the kitchen."

Danny followed his dad into the neat and spacious kitchen. The countertops were clean and nearly bare—there were only four canisters, a toaster, and a coffee maker on them.

"That door over there leads out to the garage," Paul told Danny. "Some storage out there. A small woodshop. And I've got gym equipment and some weights. You're welcome to use the weights and machines if you want to."

Danny nodded. He didn't think he'd really be interested in a woodshop, but he had gotten into weightlifting in school recently and he wouldn't mind sticking with it.

"I don't have a lot of food in the house right now," Paul continued. But we can go to the grocery store tomorrow."

"Okay."

"I got an extra room for you upstairs."

Danny followed Paul back out to the living room to grab his suitcases. He followed his father up the creaking steps to the second floor where there was one bathroom and three small bedrooms.

Paul showed Danny his own bedroom with its neatly-made bed and a dresser that was covered with framed photographs. He showed Danny his cramped office.

"What's all that?" Danny asked, pointing at the corkboards on the walls with the newspaper articles and internet printouts covering them, along with handwritten notes stuck everywhere in between.

"My work," Paul said and left it at that.

Danny left it alone, too. "I see you at least have a computer. An old one."

Paul nodded.

"Wi-Fi?"

Paul shook his head no.

"We could get Wi-Fi with the cable so I can use my I-Pad and laptop," Danny suggested.

"Yeah. Of course."

Paul showed Danny the guest bedroom which was even more plain and neutral than the rest of the house. Danny set his suitcases down next to the bed.

My new bedroom, Danny thought.

My new life.

He felt depressed. He always felt depressed these days.

Danny told Paul that he was tired and that he wanted to go to sleep. He brushed his teeth in the hall bathroom and changed into a pair of sweat pants and a thermal shirt. It was chilly in Paul's house. Did he even have the heat turned on? But Danny didn't complain.

He lay there in the dark with the bedroom door halfway open. Paul had left the light in the guest bathroom on for him in case he needed to get up in the middle of the night.

Danny was glad Paul had left the bathroom light on; he didn't want to be by himself in the dark right now.

He lay there for a while, staring at the shaft of light shining into his bedroom from the hallway. He listened to the creaks and groans of the old house—new noises he would have to get used to. Other than those noises, the house was silent. Danny didn't hear Paul anywhere in the house. He figured Paul had gone to bed, but he wasn't sure.

Danny couldn't sleep. He rolled over and turned on the lamp next to the bed and reached underneath his bed for his shoebox. He rolled over on his side, almost like he was curling his body around the shoebox as he went through the photos, staring at them for a long time.

He couldn't believe his mother and sister were really gone.

God, he missed them so much.

A noise at his door startled Danny. He turned around and sat up in bed. He looked at the doorway and saw Paul standing there. He was dressed in a pair of gray sweatpants and a long-sleeved shirt that didn't conceal his muscular body too well.

"You okay?" Paul asked.

Danny wiped the tears out of his eyes quickly.

"It's okay to grieve," Paul said.

Danny nodded. He thought Paul might enter the room and come over to his bed, maybe sit down next to him, perhaps try to console him or maybe even give him a hug. Danny didn't want any of that right now, and it was almost like Paul *knew* that.

Paul stood motionless in the doorway.

"It's just not fair," Danny said even before he realized he was going to say anything. "I can't remember anything about the accident."

"Don't be so hard on yourself," Paul told him. "Give it a few more days. Or a few weeks. I'm sure the memories will come back."

Danny only nodded.

"You may not be remembering because you don't *want* to remember right now. It may be your own mind's way of protecting you."

Danny didn't say anything.

"I'm not a doctor," Paul said. "But I know some people at the church you can talk to."

Danny sat very still, just watching Paul in the doorway.

"But only if you want to," Paul added quickly. "No pressure."

"Yeah. Thanks. I think I just want to be alone for a while."

Paul nodded and stepped out of the doorway without a sound. He closed the door, but left it open just a crack. A slim shaft of light poured in from the hallway.

Danny lay back down, curling his body around the shoebox again. He picked up a photo of his sister, stared at it a moment, then buried his face in his pillow and sobbed.

CHAPTER NINETEEN

Danny woke up in the darkness of the bedroom.

For a panicked moment Danny didn't know where he was. He thought for a few seconds that he was back home in his house in Cleveland, Ohio; he thought he was waking up from a nightmare that his mother and sister had drowned in a lake after they had crashed their car into it.

But then it all came rushing back to him.

He wasn't at home anymore. He was at his father's house. At Paul's house. And his mother and sister were dead.

He sat up in bed in the darkness and realized that he must've turned off the lamp beside his bed in the middle of the night, but he didn't remember doing it. The bedroom door was all the way closed now and no shaft of light from the guest bathroom shined in. He couldn't even see the strip of light underneath the door so the hall bathroom light must be off.

The streetlight from outside the only window in the bedroom shined in and allowed him just enough light to see half of the bedroom which was washed in a yellowish-orange light, but the other half of the room, the part of the room with the closet, was still in darkness.

Something had awakened him from a sound sleep—some kind of noise.

He didn't like being in the dark, and he mentally cursed Paul for turning off the hall bathroom light when he had promised to keep it on all night.

Then another thought occurred to Danny, a thought that sent an icepick of panic through him—maybe the electricity had gone out. Maybe he was trapped in this darkness for a moment.

Danny heard a voice whispering from the darker side of the room.

A familiar whisper.

His mother's voice.

"Danny ..."

Danny stared into the dark side of the room, towards the closet. He couldn't see anything over there.

Why was it so dark in here? It shouldn't be this dark.

He heard the closet door creaking open. He heard the sound of wet footsteps on the wood floor. He heard the squish of water from each saturated footstep. He caught the scent of murky water and rot in the air. He heard wet breathing, the gurgling of lungs full of liquid trying to work.

And then he saw the shadow of a woman shuffling towards the foot of his bed in the darkness, emerging from the blackness. She was getting closer and closer to the lighter side of the room.

"Danny … come down here with me … I'm so lonely …"

Danny spun around in his bed and pawed at the lamp, fumbling with it, almost knocking it over. He didn't hear the wet footprints or gurgling breathing anymore; he only heard the rushing of blood in his ears from his hammering heartbeat.

The rushing in his ears sounded like …

…water …

… rushing water … dark … only the flickering lights from the dashboard of his mother's car …

Paul burst into Danny's bedroom just as he managed to get his lamp turned on.

"You okay?" Paul asked as he stood a few steps inside Danny's bedroom with the door wide open behind him. The light from the hall bathroom shined into the room from behind Paul, silhouetting him.

"Uh … yeah," Danny breathed out.

"You were screaming."

That shocked Danny a little—he didn't remember screaming.

"It was just a nightmare," Danny finally said.

Paul didn't respond. He just stood there.

Danny looked past his father at the light coming from the hallway. He was sure that the light hadn't been on a moment ago, but now it was. He wanted to ask Paul if he had just turned the light on, but he didn't.

"Wake me up if you need anything," Paul said, and then he walked out of the bedroom, leaving the door halfway open.

Danny let out a long breath, his heartrate slowing back down to a normal speed and his trembling beginning to subside. He was afraid to look across the bedroom at the closet door, afraid he would see wet footprints on the wood floor leading from the doorway to the bed, maybe the slimy remnants of a plant from the bottom of the lake spread across the floor like a black banana peel.

But he made himself look, and there were no footprints on the floor.

It had seemed so real.

And then he remembered seeing brief flashes in his nightmares of the crash that had killed his mother and sister. He remembered feeling suspended in the cold, dark water. He remembered the lights flickering on the dashboard of the car. The headlights were also flickering as the electrical system in the car shorted out.

Maybe his memories were beginning to come back.

But did he want them to?

Danny rolled over and noticed that the shoebox wasn't on the bed anymore. Had he knocked it off the bed in the middle of the night? The last thing he remembered was crying into his pillow.

He leaned over the side of the bed and looked down at the floor. He didn't see the shoebox on the floor with its contents spilled out.

He got off the bed and got down on the floor on his hands and knees. He checked underneath the bed, steeling himself, praying that he wouldn't see his mother stuffed under there, grinning at him, reaching for him with bloated fingers.

The shoebox was safely tucked underneath the bed. He hadn't remembered putting it back there. But he also hadn't remembered turning off the lamp next to the bed.

Maybe he had just been overly-exhausted.

He needed sleep, he knew that, but he was afraid it would be a while before he fell back to sleep so he got back in bed and just laid there with the lamp on.

CHAPTER TWENTY

Before Paul and Danny had gotten back to Boston from Cleveland, Paul had called Father McFadden and expressed his apologies for the lateness of his report about the exorcism at the Whittier house. But with what had happened with Paul's ex-wife and children, Father McFadden completely understood.

Paul had stayed up late into the night and read through the report of the Whittier exorcism a few more times. He had included everything in the report, including his own failings. It had been a difficult report to write, a difficult experience to re-live in words. Paul had been to nearly a hundred investigations over his ten year career. Most of them had been in the United States, but he had been to a few outside the country: one in Ireland, two in Mexico, three in Canada, and one in Italy. Many of the investigations had been ordered by Father McFadden, but Paul worked for other churches. But of all of the investigations he had been sent to, and of all the things he had experienced, the Whittier exorcism (and the death of his daughter and ex-wife after it) had been the worst by far.

He printed out the report this morning and slipped the papers and a copy of the tape recording into a large manila envelope. He folded the tab down and sealed it with a blob of hot wax. He pushed a stamp with the Lambert family crest down into the wax—the seal was from a family line that went back centuries, longer than he had ever imagined until he began training under his own father to become an Investigator and he had learned about their family line.

Paul left the large yellow envelope on his desk for the wax to cool. He got up and left his office. He crept down the short hallway and looked at Danny's half open bedroom door. He peeked inside and saw that Danny was still asleep with his lamp still on.

It had been a rough night for Danny. When Paul had rushed into his son's bedroom in the middle of the night after hearing his screams, Danny had told him he'd just had a nightmare.

But Paul suspected worse. He suspected the demons that had warned Paul, the demons that were after his family, the Terror By Night, were after his son now, trying to take the last member of his family away.

Paul couldn't let that happen.

He decided to let Danny sleep a little longer. He knew he needed his rest; he needed to build his strength up.

Paul went downstairs, carefully avoiding the creaky parts of the steps. In the kitchen, he set out a box of Special K cereal and almond milk for Danny's breakfast. He was pretty sure Danny wouldn't find this meal appetizing, but it was all he had for breakfast. Maybe they would go to the grocery store if Danny was up to it, and then he could pick out some food he liked. Maybe they could pick up a few slices of pizza at Al's for lunch.

He grabbed a big bottle of water out of the refrigerator and headed out to the garage. He needed a workout. He was afraid the pounding on the punching bag might wake Danny up, and if that happened then so be it.

Danny needed to get up soon. They had some things to discuss.

†

Danny jumped awake to a dull pounding noise. At first he thought the pounding might have been a headache throbbing inside his skull, but then he realized that the pounding was reverberating throughout the house. It was a low thump, barely audible, but definitely there.

He got out of bed and turned the lamp off. He slipped out into the hallway. His dad's bedroom door was wide open, the bed neatly made.

Danny hurried downstairs and the pounding was louder down here. Paul wasn't in the living room. Danny peeked out through the blinds that covered the front windows, but he didn't see Paul outside anywhere. He hurried to the kitchen and the pounding was even louder in here. It wasn't a rhythmic pounding, it was more random than that.

It was coming from the garage.

What was Paul doing in there?

Danny rushed across the kitchen to the garage door and opened it slightly, peeking out through the crack. He saw Paul brutalizing a punching bag with blows. The interior of the garage was gloomy, but

Danny saw Paul clearly. He wore only his pair of sweatpants—he had stripped off his shirt.

Paul had the body of a warrior. His large, angular muscles were spider-webbed with thick veins. A scar ran down along his left side, and he had a few other smaller scars on his arms. But perhaps the most striking and surprising thing about Paul's body were the tattoos that covered much of his skin. A large crucifix took up much of his back. The top of the cross started at the back of his neck and went all the way down to the waistband of his jogging pants; both points of the arms of the cross reached out to each of his rear delts. There were a series of words written in places near the cross, sentences in fancy script. Danny couldn't read them from where he was standing, but he guessed they were quotes of Scripture. Paul had smaller tattoos on his chest, abs, and arms; many of them were smaller crosses and more writing.

Paul's punches to the bag were pulverizing solid thumps. He was powerful, but also lightning-fast. A sheen of perspiration covered his body and his dark hair was slicked back with sweat.

Paul stopped punching when he noticed Danny standing in the doorway.

"You're up," Paul said.

"Yeah," Danny answered, and he opened the door all the way and stepped down into the garage.

"There's some cereal on the table. Milk in the fridge. We'll go to the store in a little while so you can pick out some stuff to eat."

Danny nodded. "Okay."

Danny spotted the woodshop on the other side of the garage, but he didn't walk over to it. He saw the scattered pieces of wood on the countertop underneath the pegboard of tools, but he didn't ask about them.

"Go ahead and eat something," Paul said.

Danny nodded and left the garage.

He walked over to the kitchen table and stared at the cereal box. Special K? Not really his kind of cereal. He looked for more cereal boxes in the pantry and cabinets, but Special K was his only choice. Maybe he could sprinkle some sugar on it. He grabbed the milk out of the refrigerator, but then he noticed that it wasn't even really milk—it was something called almond milk.

Cereal was now out of the question. He looked for alternatives to his breakfast in the fridge and cabinets. No sodas. No sweet tea. No junk food in the freezer or snack cakes in the pantry. Paul was obviously a health nut.

Deciding to skip breakfast, Danny went back upstairs. He was on his way back to his bedroom, but he stopped by the office door like he was suddenly drawn to it.

He could still hear the slight pounding from downstairs, so he ventured inside to snoop around a little. He walked to the wall of bookshelves and studied the titles of some of the books—but some of the titles were written in a language he didn't understand.

Clauicula Salomonis

Lemegeton.

The Grimoire of Solomon.

There were dozens and dozens of books on demonology, classifications of demons, histories of demons. There were cases after cases of demonic possessions and exorcisms. There were books on the occult, witchcraft, and the dark arts. There were books on outdoor survival, self-defense, and weapons training. There were a dozen different bibles in different languages—and some of them looked ancient. Speaking of ancient, on the shelves next to the books were a few odd sculptures and small statues carved from stone. Crosses and crucifixes hung on the walls all around the room.

Danny's eyes were drawn to Paul's large desk. The top was cluttered with papers and a few open books, like Paul had been working there recently. The messy desk and office were a contrast to the rest of his neat and orderly house. This room was cluttered where the rest of the house was sparse. This room looked lived-in, it looked used, it had technology (a computer, a printer, a phone, the internet). It was like this room was the focus of Paul's life and the rest of the house served only basic functions like shelter, sleep, and food.

He spotted a manila envelope in the middle of the desk with an old-fashioned wax seal on it—just like out of some medieval film. Danny picked up the envelope and turned it over carefully. He read the two words written across the front in neat handwriting: *Father McFadden*

He laid the envelope back down on the desk and went over to the corkboards. He studied the cutout newspaper articles and internet printouts.

Girl in Arkansas: possible demonic possession case.

Satanic objects found at a murder scene in Los Angeles.

Mysterious circumstances surround a death in Rome, Italy.

Ritualistic killings near the Texas/Mexico border.

Some of the articles had words or phrases underlined or highlighted in a yellow marker. Some of the articles had handwritten notes on them, the same neat handwriting that was on the yellow envelope on the desk.

Danny walked over to a small closet and opened the door. He saw dark clothing hanging in a line right in front of him—they looked like trench coats, sweaters, jackets, a few pairs of pants. On the floor there were a few pairs of black boots that laced up in the front. And next to the boots was a dark canvas bag bulging with something inside. There were weapons leaning against the corner in the back of the closet behind the hanging clothes. They looked like swords and staffs, but not replicas—the real thing.

But what really caught Danny's eye were the stacks of black boxes on top of the closet. They were all small and rectangular, and they were all painted black. But Danny could see hundreds of symbols carved into the wood boxes. Maybe it was Hebrew writing, he thought. Or Greek. Or some other language. Some of it looked like symbols or hieroglyphics. But the strangest thing was that each box was wrapped tightly in some kind of metal wire.

He reached up to the boxes and brushed his fingers across the wood surface in between the strands of wire. The surface of the box was glossy like some kind of polyurethane had been applied over the black paint; but he could still feel the symbols etched into the wood.

He wondered what was inside all of these boxes. He was about to pull one down when Paul's voice froze him.

"Help you with something?" Paul asked.

Danny whirled around to the door, his heart stopping for a moment at the sound of Paul's voice.

"Don't touch those," Paul said, staring at him. He stood in the doorway and he had his sweatshirt back on now. Both his shirt and pants were stained with sweat from his workout, and he had a small towel draped over one shoulder. Obviously he was done working out and Danny hadn't even realized the pounding from down in the garage had stopped.

"I was just … looking around …"

Paul nodded like he could see that.

"I saw your workshop in the garage, and I saw the pieces of wood on that countertop. Did you make these boxes?"

Paul nodded again. "Yes."

Danny stared at Paul, and he realized now that he could be an intimidating man. But in that moment he made the choice that he wasn't going to be intimidated anymore, not by his father, not by kids at school, not by anyone.

"What are the boxes for? What's in them?"

"It's a little difficult to explain. It might be a little hard to believe."

"Try me."

Paul didn't answer.

Danny glanced back into the closet for a moment, and then looked back at Paul. He had expected Paul to be angry for catching him snooping around in his office, but he didn't seem to be mad, so Danny pressed on with his questions.

"What about these clothes? And that duffel bag? And those weapons in the back of the closet? What's all of that stuff for?"

"It's for my work, but there's a lot to explain—a lot that we need to talk about."

"What exactly is it that you do for a living?" Danny asked his father, looking him right in the eye.

"I'll tell you. I want to tell you everything very soon. I promise. But first I need a shower and we need to go to the store and get some food for you."

Danny just nodded in agreement.

"I see you didn't like the choice for breakfast," Paul said like he was trying to change the subject.

"I wasn't hungry," Danny lied.

"How does a slice of pizza for lunch sound? I know a good place down the street that we could stop at before we go to the store."

That sounded good to Danny. But what he wanted even more than food right now were the answers that Paul promised he would give.

CHAPTER TWENTY-ONE

After Paul was done with his shower and dressed in his usual long-sleeved and dark attire, he took Danny to Al's Pizza and Subs. It was lunch time, but it wasn't too crowded inside yet.

They split a pepperoni pizza and a small salad. Paul ate most of the salad and Danny ate most of the pizza. Cassie, Al and Sue's daughter, waited on them and Paul caught Danny staring at her. He tried to keep his smile to himself.

After they were finished eating, Paul drove to the supermarket in his rumbling Bronco. They loaded up on frozen dinners and junk food. This wasn't Paul's idea of a healthy diet, but after what Danny had been through, he wasn't going to harp on his nutritional choices just yet. Danny was young; his body could still recover from the poisons in these processed foods.

After the supermarket, they stopped at a department store and bought a flat-screen TV for Danny's bedroom. And Paul had already scheduled the cable installation for the next morning as promised.

They drove back home and put the groceries away and set the TV up in Danny's room. They made some dinner: frozen fish sticks and tater tots for Danny and some leftovers for Paul.

After dinner was over and the dishes were washed and put away, they sat down at the small kitchen table. Danny had a cold can of Coke in front of him, and Paul poured himself a small shot of vodka.

This wasn't going to be easy for Paul and the alcohol would help him relax a little. Paul was about to talk about things he hadn't talked about in years, things he hadn't even thought about in years. He was going to have the same conversation that his father had had with him almost twenty years ago.

Paul remembered that conversation. They hadn't had it at a kitchen table—it had been at St. Mathews Church, in the courtyard. His father had brought him to the place where he worked. Of course Paul had already known somewhat of what his father did for the church; it was no secret in his family that he had come from a long line of Investigators, some of whom were endowed with certain Gifts of the Spirit.

At first Paul had resisted the calling. He didn't want that kind of life for himself—his father's life. He had rebelled and ran away. It broke his mother's heart and she died a few years later. But Paul's father, Saul Lambert, had carried on with his calling.

Paul had met Rachael and they had fallen in love. They had planned to have a family. But when Paul saw the signs of evil in the world, when he saw glimpses of what hid in the darkness, moving like shadows, he began to feel the calling pulling at him. And then when he got his own Gifts of the Spirit—visions and the ability to sense demons—he knew he couldn't turn his back on God's gifts.

He tried to convince Rachael to come with him on his journey, but she was convinced that Paul was losing his mind. After their children were born, she was even more resistant.

Paul had to walk away from his family. He had no choice. But he'd never stopped loving them and he wanted Danny to know that. Sometimes God forced choices on people, hard choices, but people were always free to choose. Paul wanted both worlds, but he couldn't have them both. He had made his choice.

Paul downed his shot of vodka. He was ready to tell Danny everything.

†

Danny watched Paul, this stranger who was his father, this stranger who he didn't know much about who sat on the other side of the table. Danny's mind slipped back to when he was a young kid, to his memories of his father. They were pleasant memories. He remembered a strong and happy father. He didn't remember too many arguments between his mother and father, but even when there were arguments, it was his mother who had done the yelling—not his father. Even though his father was a strong man, he had always been a gentle man. Of course, Danny's memories were from over ten years ago—the memories of a seven, eight, and nine year old boy.

"I investigate instances for the Church," Paul finally said.

"Yeah, Grandma Gail told me. Paranormal stuff."

"Yes, sort of. Hauntings and possessions."

"Possessions? You mean like exorcisms?"

Paul nodded.

"You're an exorcist?"

"In a way."

"So, you're a priest."

"No."

"I thought only priests could perform exorcisms."

"An exorcism is a Catholic ritual, but anyone can perform an exorcism. But you have to remember that no person casts a demon from a person's body—only God can do that. The exorcist, whether he's a priest, pastor, or an average person, is only a tool. But whoever performs the exorcism, their faith in God must be extraordinarily strong."

Danny pictured Paul standing over someone strapped down to a chair, commanding the demon to leave their body.

"You also said hauntings," Danny reminded him.

"A haunting, whether it is a place or an object, is just an item that a demon has attached itself to."

Danny thought about that for a moment.

"What do you think of when you think of a ghost?" Paul asked.

"I don't know." Danny shrugged. "A dead person whose spirit hasn't travelled to the other side yet."

"Possible," Paul said. "But doubtful. Not in my experience at least. Demons can take many forms. They can take the form of ghosts. They can take the forms of loved ones and try to pass themselves off as these loved ones."

Danny felt a chill run through his body as a flash of last night's terrible dream played in his mind. He pushed the thought away.

"I've never really believed in ghosts and demons," Danny said.

"What about God?"

"I'm not sure. I guess He could be real."

"Many people your age have doubts, Danny. It's natural. We're all given free will by God, and we're allowed to choose what we believe."

Danny was silent for a moment. He took a sip of his Coke. He was suddenly very thirsty.

"How did you get this job, investigating haunted houses and possessed people?" Danny asked.

"My father was an Investigator. And his father before him. And his father before him. Going back centuries."

A sudden connection clicked in Danny's mind. "Wait a minute. You want me to follow in your footsteps? Become an Investigator like you? Is that why you're telling me all this?"

"I didn't say that," Paul said in a gentle voice. "I would like to see you do this, but only if it's your true calling. Remember, you always have a choice. God always gives you a choice."

Danny was quiet for a moment, afraid he had offended Paul somehow. "I don't know anything about this kind of stuff," he finally said.

"There's a lot of training involved."

"So, what's in those boxes upstairs that you make? The ones wrapped in metal wire."

Paul sighed. "It's actually iron wire. It has to be iron."

"Why?"

"I know this may be a little difficult to believe. But one of my Gifts of the Spirit is summoning demons out of people who are possessed and forcing them into these small wooden boxes."

Danny just stared at Paul for a moment. He opened his mouth like he was going to say something, but then he stopped, thinking it over for a few seconds. "Are you … you're trying to tell me that there are demons in those boxes?"

"There's a piece of ancient parchment inside each box. Once I learn the demon's true name, the one given to it by God, then I can write it down and force the demon inside the box."

Danny felt a peculiar tilting of his world, like everything he'd thought that was real just became questionable, and everything he thought was a myth had become real. Here was his father, a person he hadn't seen in almost three years, telling him that he was an Investigator for the Church and that he ran around casting out demons from people and from places and then stored them in little black boxes in the top of his office closet.

He expected him to believe this?

Danny stood up and paced around the kitchen. He needed to move around. He felt like he might be sitting in the house of someone who might not be totally sane.

He thought about the restraining order that his mother had had on Paul. And now he wondered if Paul might be crazy, if his mom had known that Paul could be crazy and possibly even dangerous.

"I know it's a lot to handle all at once, Danny. But there are Gifts of the Spirit that have been running through our family for centuries, passed down from father to son. I told you about my Gift of summoning demons. And I've had the Gift of visions for years. You probably already have Gifts that you don't even recognize. You have to be ready for them if you experience them."

Danny didn't respond. He walked over to the sink, suddenly feeling nauseous. He felt like he needed to get out of this house, get away and try to think about all of this.

"You may see visions," Paul told him. "You have to be ready for them."

CHAPTER TWENTY-TWO

Danny left the kitchen.

Paul got up and followed Danny into the living room.

Danny went to the front closet and got his jacket from the coat rack.

"Where are you going?" Paul asked. "I didn't think we were done talking."

"I'm just going out for a walk."

"Danny, you have to be careful."

Paul knew that Danny thought he was crazy right now. He knew all of this was going to be difficult to wrap his mind around. He wanted to tell him that the demons that had killed his mother and sister would still be after him. But he didn't, because he was afraid of pushing Danny too far away right now. He would need some time to realize these things on his own.

Danny turned to the front door, about to leave, but then he looked back at Paul. "Is it okay if I go for a walk down the street? Think some things over."

Paul didn't answer.

"I just need some fresh air. Some time alone. All of this … it's just a lot to think about."

Finally, Paul nodded. He didn't feel good about letting Danny go outside, but he had to let him go. He had warned him to be careful, but maybe he hadn't warned him enough yet.

†

Danny walked down the sidewalk in the late afternoon light. The sky was overcast, the air humid and chilly, and it felt like it might start drizzling at any moment.

He followed the line of homes squeezed in tight next to each other, some underneath the shade of one hundred year old trees.

After he crossed an intersection, the houses got a little bigger, the lawns a little more spacious, the driveways longer. At the next intersection he saw a large park across the street that was full of ball fields. Some of the ball fields were fenced in. Near one of the baseball fields was a basketball court—just a concrete slab with four basketball nets, two on each side which made two full courts beside each other. Both of them were empty. There were hardly any people at the park, a couple of kids played on a playground set in the distance at the other side of the fields, and their parents were huddled up on benches watching them.

Danny stopped walking and sat down on a park bench that was close to the basketball courts. The basketball courts made him think of Pete and how they used to shoot baskets in his driveway. And that made him think of home. And thinking of home made him think of …

He squeezed his eyes shut, fighting back tears.

God, he just wished he was back home again with his mother and his sister, not stuck in this city with a father who might be more than just a little delusional.

What was he supposed to do?

He jumped when something touched his foot. He opened his eyes and looked down at the faded, orange basketball touching one of his sneakers like it had just rolled through the grass towards him. The ball looked old, the orange-peel texture nearly worn down smooth.

"Hey! A little help?"

Danny looked up at the basketball courts twenty yards away and saw a lanky kid his own age standing at the edge of the concrete slab. He wore baggy shorts and an oversized T-shirt that was a little too big for him even though the weather was cold. He had blond hair, large eyes, and a wide and friendly smile. He held his hands up, ready to catch the basketball whenever Danny decided to throw it back to him.

Danny grabbed the ball, stood up and threw it at the kid.

"You wanna shoot some hoops?" the kid asked.

Danny shrugged. "Sure."

He trotted over to the court, glancing around. He still didn't see any other kids playing on any of the other fields. Probably inside their warm houses playing video games or watching TV, he thought.

The kid caught the ball and shot a basket from the edge of the court. The ball bounced off the rim.

Danny ran past the kid and caught the bouncing ball.

"I haven't seen you around here before," the kid said as Danny shot the ball … and missed.

"Just moved here from Cleveland."

"Oh Wow. Cleveland. Lebron James."

"Yeah," Danny said and smiled.

Danny caught the ball and tossed it to the kid. The kid shot and made it. The ball bounced right back to him, and he passed it back to Danny.

"Name's Ricky. What's yours?"

"Danny Lambert."

"Cool. What brought you to Boston?"

Danny shrugged and shot the ball. He noticed that the sky was darkening quickly, the night rushing in much faster than he had realized.

"Moved in with my dad," Danny finally answered. His shot missed and he ran to grab the ball before it bounced over to the next court. It felt good to run around, his body already warming up in the chilly air. He could see his breath as he huffed and puffed. He grabbed the ball and turned around and fired a pass back at Ricky who waited in the same spot.

Ricky caught the ball and stared at him, smiling. But his expression seemed strange, his eyes a little darker, a little colder. His smile seemed suddenly fake, a malevolent grin hidden just underneath the surface.

Danny felt a chill run up his spine, his balls crawling.

Something was wrong here.

At first Danny thought this kid was with a pack of friends and they were going to come running at him from the other fields, playing a game of kick-the-shit-out-of-the-new-kid, and then give him some kind of warning to stay off their turf.

But the danger seemed different than that—it felt darker, more dangerous.

And Danny noticed that he couldn't see the kid's breath like he could see his own. In fact, it didn't even look like Ricky was breathing at all.

But he was smiling at him as he held the ball.

"Where's your mom, Danny?"

Danny felt a pang of fear knife through him. His muscles felt suddenly rubbery and they tingled with energy at the same time, like his body couldn't decide whether it wanted to run away or collapse in a fetal position on the concrete.

"I need to go," Danny said. "It's getting dark," he added as if he needed some kind of excuse.

"It's dark where your mother is, Danny," Ricky told him.

Danny swallowed hard as the kid stood motionless, ball under one arm now. He just stood there, staring at him and smiling.

"I came here to give you a warning," Ricky said.

Danny didn't say anything.

"Don't go with your father. You don't want to see what he's going to show you. You don't want to be there when that happens."

Ricky turned to shoot the ball. When he turned, Danny noticed that the back of his head was caved in and matted with blood; a few dark chunks of glistening brain were mixed in with the blood that clung to the back of his head.

How did he not see that before?

No way he could have missed it.

Drops of blood dripped down from Ricky's matted hair and plopped down on the concrete. Little drops of blood were everywhere. There was even a small clump underneath the basket that looked like a piece of meat or brain covered with blood.

Ricky made his shot—a swoosh, nothing but net. He turned and looked at Danny with the severe half-smile on his face, the same smile Danny had seen on the blond-haired man back at his house in Cleveland as the man struggled to get inside the basement door.

Danny didn't bother saying anything else.

He ran.

And he heard the pounding of sneakers on the concrete as the kid chased him.

Would the kid catch up to him? How fast could the dead run?

Danny didn't waste any energy turning around to find out. He ran, listening for Ricky's footsteps or shouts from behind him, but he could only hear his own sneakers slapping the sidewalk and his heavy breathing. He expected to feel the dead kid's fingertips touch his shoulder or the back of his neck at any moment. He knew the feel of the kid's flesh would be ice-cold and slimy. It would feel wet, like from under a cold lake. And that touch might stop him in his tracks. That touch might make him pass out right there on the sidewalk.

When he crossed the intersection to his dad's street (without even stopping to look for cars), he slowed down and glanced behind him.

He didn't see Ricky running after him. He didn't see anyone on the sidewalks. It was darker than he had noticed and he saw lights on in most of the houses—cozy, yellowish lights, people tucked safely away inside their homes, protected from the creatures that prowled the night out here.

A hand fell on Danny's shoulder and he let out a scream, whirling around, his hands up to ward off the dead kid who must've used a shortcut through some backyards to cut him off before he got home.

Paul defended Danny's strikes easily, and then he backed up a step.

"Danny, what is it?"

Danny stared at Paul, and he wanted to burst into tears. He was happy his father had come looking for him, but at the same time he hated him, hated that all of this was from his dad and his cursed family line.

And it was true. Danny had just seen that. Either he had the Gift of visions as Paul had suggested, or he was going crazy, perhaps breaking down from the stress of his mother and sister's deaths. Neither option really seemed that great to him right now.

"It's late," Paul said.

"Yeah," Danny breathed out. "Sorry. I was trying to hurry back."

Paul stared at Danny like he didn't believe him.

CHAPTER TWENTY-THREE

Danny went straight up to his bedroom when he got home. The cable guy had come and set up the cable and internet before he and Paul had had their little chat about exorcisms, possessions, visions, and demons trapped inside little wood boxes. He tested out his TV and was satisfied. He left it on the Cartoon Network for now, and he knew he was going to leave it on all night while he tried to sleep. Maybe he would feel better under the comforting, flickering light of the TV.

After a quick shower, a snack, and another can of Coke—which Paul seemed to frown on but thankfully said nothing about—Danny went to his room again and shut the door. His door handle had a lock that a skeleton key would fit, and he thought about asking his father for the key. But he didn't.

He turned the volume down on the TV and checked the closet which had a few cardboard boxes of storage on the top shelves (no little black wooden boxes, thank God), but was mostly empty except for Danny's clothes on hangers and his two empty suitcases on the floor. His boxes with his posters, knickknacks, sports equipment, and other possessions that he and Paul had shipped from Cleveland hadn't showed up yet. Maybe it would be here in the next day or two. Danny couldn't wait to get his basketball posters up on the walls, his boxes of trading cards that he collected, books and comics stacked on a bookshelf, the things that would make this room his own room.

He closed the closet door, making sure it was shut securely. He checked underneath the bed—nothing under there except a few dust bunnies and his shoebox. He checked the only window in the bedroom; it looked out onto the strip of dormant grass that served as the side yard between Paul's house and the neighbor's. He looked as far as he could out the window and he could see part of the front yard, the sidewalk, and the street beyond that. He had almost expected to see Ricky standing on the sidewalk under the glow of the streetlight, his basketball tucked underneath one of his thin and pale arms, his caved-in head glistening in the yellowish-orangish light, the light casting sharp shadows on the kid's face, making his half-smile even more menacing.

But Ricky wasn't standing down there on the sidewalk.

Danny left the curtains open so some of the streetlight would beam into the bedroom, and then he went to his bed.

Maybe Ricky hadn't been there at all today.

The thought of hallucinating seemed as scary as seeing dead people walking around, talking to him and giving him warnings.

Almost as scary.

Was he losing his mind? Was he cracking up from all the stress?

He didn't know. He just wanted to fall into an eight hour dreamless sleep. His body needed the rest. His mind needed the rest.

†

Danny woke up in darkness. His TV was off. The bedroom door was still closed. The light from the streetlamp shined in through the window and Danny saw the person standing at the foot of his bed, just beyond the line between the dark and the light.

It was his mom.

She stood there in the darkness, her arms reaching out for Danny, bits of muck and lake bottom plant-life hanging from her arms. Water dripped from her hands, her arms, her stringy hair, and her wet dress that clung tightly to her body. Her eyes were pure black, lost in shadow. Her mouth hung open like her jaw might be broken. A gurgling sound came from somewhere down deep inside her throat like she was trying to breathe through water.

"Danny …" she whispered. "Danny … come down here with me. I'm so lonely …"

Danny jumped up in bed onto his feet in a crouch like he was ready to spring off the bed and escape. The headboard crashed into the wall behind him as he backed up into it. The mattress squeaked from his sudden movements. The bed shook.

He heard a ticking at the bedroom window. He tore his eyes away from his mother and saw the blond-haired man at his window, standing outside like he was floating on the night air two stories up. The streetlight lit half of him up and kept the other half in shadow, but Danny couldn't mistake that smile and those dark and dead eyes.

The man clicked on the glass of the window with his long, yellowed fingernails.

Danny screamed.

He fumbled with the lamp next to his bed, trying to turn it on. He heard the wet footsteps in the room with him, the squelch of water on the floorboards, the tapping at the window. But he didn't look at either one of them; he concentrated on the lamp, he concentrated on trying to twist that little knob.

"... isn't real, this isn't real, this isn't real ..." Danny kept whispering like a mantra.

The bedroom door flew open and the overhead light came on.

Paul stood in the doorway, looking alarmed and angry at the same time.

"Danny! You okay?!"

Danny stared back at Paul. He shook his head no and tears spilled down his cheeks even though he didn't want to cry in front of his father. "I don't think so," he finally said.

†

Paul and Danny sat at the kitchen table. It was almost five o'clock in the morning.

Paul made a pot of strong coffee for himself and gave Danny a can of soda which he cradled in front of him.

At seventeen years old, Danny was already almost as tall as Paul, and he already had wide shoulders and naturally long limbs. He looked like he was beginning to fill out his frame with muscle. But right now, to Paul, he looked so small and vulnerable, curled up in the kitchen chair in front of the table.

"What did you see?" Paul asked him after they were quiet for a long time.

Danny didn't answer for a long moment. He just trembled and sipped his can of Coke, staring down at the table.

"What did you see, Danny?" Paul asked again in a gentle voice.

"It was just a nightmare," he whispered.

"And earlier tonight, when you went out for a walk? You were running from something, weren't you?"

Danny looked up at his father with a lost look in his eyes. "I saw a kid my own age at the basketball courts. He said his name was Ricky. But he was dead. Or he should've been. He had a big … like a wound at the back of his head. Like his head had been smashed in or something."

Paul only nodded. "Could be Ricky Doleman. He used to live a few streets over from me. He was playing basketball in his driveway a few years ago and chased the ball out into the street. He was hit by a car."

Danny let out a long breath and shook his head no. "You're saying I saw a dead kid? That I shot baskets with a dead kid?"

"I'm saying a demon came to you disguised as that form. They don't reveal their true forms very often. Sometimes they mask themselves as someone else and try to weasel their way into someone else's life."

Danny shook his head no again. "No. This can't be real."

"It is," Paul said with more force. He didn't want to scare Danny away, but he needed him to see the truth. "It's real and it's dangerous. They're after you, and they're after me."

"But why?"

"I think they're afraid of me because I can trap them. I know they hate me. They hate the family line I come from. They want to hurt me by hurting you and my family. And I think they might be afraid of you, too."

"Of me? Why? I can't do anything like what you can do."

"Not yet. And you don't even know what your Gifts are yet; what powers you might have inside of you."

"It's not fair," Danny said. "I never asked for this. I never did anything to them."

"They don't care about fairness and they don't care about your concerns," Paul said and then sipped his coffee. His throat was suddenly very dry.

"I don't remember anything from the accident," Danny said after a long moment.

Paul nodded.

"But I do remember something right before we crashed." Danny hesitated like he didn't want to say more.

"Come on, Danny, we can't have any secrets between us right now," Paul said even though he was still holding on to some very big secrets of his own. He couldn't tell Danny everything all at once.

"I saw someone at the side of the road," Danny finally said. "He might have been standing in the road. I'm not sure. I might have yelled at Mom when I saw the man. I might have distracted her just long enough to ..."

Danny wiped away at his sudden tears.

Paul waited patiently.

Danny described the blond-haired man to Paul. And then he told Paul about the two times that he had seen the man before: once on the way home from school and once outside the basement door when he had been jiggling the door handle and trying to get inside.

"Why didn't you tell me about this man before?"

"I don't know. I thought it was just some crazy guy. And then when I remembered him from the accident, I started wondering if I'd seen him at all. No one else had seen him but me. I started wondering if I was going crazy. And now the nightmares of Mom and the kid at the basketball courts ..."

"You're not going crazy. As much as you may not want to believe it, this is real. And the sooner you come to terms with that, the sooner you can learn to defend yourself, and the stronger your faith will become."

"If God is so good, then why is He doing this to us? Why is He allowing this to happen?"

"He gives all of us a choice. You can't help the family line you were born into. But you still have a choice—you can choose to ignore the family line and the calling, or you can choose to embrace it. You can pretend that what you've been seeing were hallucinations. And you can choose to try to run away and hope that the dark spirits don't get to you. Or you can choose to fight back."

Paul got up and poured another cup of coffee. He noticed the time on the microwave oven. It was getting close to six o'clock in the morning now. The first light of morning was lightening up the kitchen window. There was no sense in going back to bed now.

"I want to fight," Paul heard Danny say from behind him. Danny's voice was strong. And it was angry.

Paul turned around and saw that Danny was looking straight at him, his dark eyes seemed darker, his jaw was set, his jaw muscles clenched. He looked bigger now, stronger.

"I want to make them pay for what they did to Mom and Lisa."

Paul nodded and kept his expression neutral. But on the inside he was happy. This was the first major step for Danny—belief. Sometimes it was the most difficult step.

"Okay," Paul said. "We can begin training soon."

Danny didn't say anything; he just nodded.

"In a few hours we're going to Mass at St. Mathews. I want you to wear your nicest clothes. The darker the better."

CHAPTER TWENTY-FOUR

Danny wore the black pants and shoes that he had worn to his mother's funeral. But he picked out a different shirt and put that on. Then he pulled a dark sweater on over that.

He was ready.

They drove to the church in Paul's rumbling Bronco. Even though the truck was old, the engine had been rebuilt and it was like brand new. Paul explained the importance of having a reliable vehicle, and having one with both power and speed, one that could be used in both the city and off-road if need be.

"But gas for this thing must be outrageous," Danny said.

"The Church pays for that. And they pay for my house. And they pay me a nice salary."

"Wow," Danny said.

"I provide an important service for them. I go to places and do things many others can't or won't. And one day, so will you."

†

St. Mathews church looked like a small city to Danny. The buildings took up over one city block. Paul parked his truck in a massive parking area that was as big as a Wal-Mart parking lot, but much cleaner and with perfectly mowed and trimmed grass islands that broke up the rows and rows of cars and trucks.

They walked to the main sanctuary. It was a massive building with wide sidewalks that ran through meticulously landscaped lawns and shrubbery that led up to the massive doors that were opened wide, welcoming in the congregation. Statues of angels rimmed a cathedral with a steeple that rose up into the gray sky with a cross on top.

Danny and Paul sat in the last row of pews with most of the congregation bunched up in the first half of the rows of pews, closer to the dais. Paul had his large manila folder on his lap, the one Danny had seen on his desk in the office, the one with the neatly printed name: Father McFadden.

Danny's eyes wandered up to the high ceilings, the gigantic wooden beams that stretched across them. He gazed at the windows of stained glass art, rows and rows of them.

He looked back at the congregation in front of him as they settled in. Many of them glanced back at him and Paul, stealing peeks. They seemed both offended and nervous that Paul was attending the service.

Danny was secretly amused and prideful. He always thought Paul was a badass, and now he could see the fear and the respect in other people's eyes. He could see them wondering about his father, the mystery of the man in the black clothing who sat in the last row. And now he had this boy with him. *His son, perhaps?* their eyes questioned.

†

After the service was over, Paul introduced Danny to Father McFadden. They had walked down a labyrinth of wide halls to meet with him at his office door which was wide open.

Father McFadden was an inch or two taller than Paul, but he was thin and had the rigid posture of a lamppost, yet he somehow managed to seem at ease at the same time. He had a warm smile and a twinkle in his gray eyes, but Danny sensed power and authority coming from this man.

"Danny, I'm so glad to finally meet you," the priest said as he shook Danny's hand in a warm and firm grip.

"Yes, sir. Thanks." Danny didn't know what else to say.

Father McFadden's face fell into a frown. He dropped his head a little. "I was so sorry to hear about your loss."

Danny felt an instant ache in his chest and a tightening of his throat. The compassion in the priest's expression and voice almost brought him to tears.

"Thank you," Danny croaked out.

Danny pushed his thoughts away from his mother and sister, and he pondered his father who stood beside him. It was still a little difficult for Danny to wrap his mind around the idea that his father came from a long line of Investigators that stretched back before the Middle Ages. And it was even more difficult for him to believe that he might be an Investigator himself eventually.

"I have a few things to discuss with Father McFadden," Paul said as he looked at Danny.

Danny could tell he was being brushed off and it hurt his feelings a little. He had already told Paul that he wanted to learn the ways of the family line. He thought today would be his first day of training.

But he didn't dare question it—not with both Father McFadden and Paul staring at him.

"There's a beautiful courtyard just down that hall outside," Father McFadden said to Danny. "Just take a left out the door and walk to the end and then take another left. And don't worry, we'll have plenty of time to get to know each other soon."

It was like the priest had read his mind, and Danny could read between the lines: *You're not ready yet for the secrets that we will be discussing behind these closed doors.*

Danny managed a smile. "It was nice meeting you ..." Danny hesitated, searching for the right word.

"Father," Paul helped.

"Father," Danny repeated with a smile of embarrassment.

†

Danny walked down the hall and his hard shoes echoed slightly off the high stone walls. He turned a corner at the end of the hall and walked down another short hallway that seemed to come to an end, but then he saw a doorway tucked into the wall on the left just at the end. A set of concrete steps led from the open doorway down to an ornately designed metal gate. He could see the gray daylight beyond the gate lightening up the bottom of the steps.

He descended the steps and pushed through the metal gate. He expected the hinges to squeal, but the gate worked like it was brand new even though it looked centuries old. It seemed that there must be dozens and dozens of maintenance people to keep up with this church, which seemed more like a compound to Danny.

The courtyard was beautiful.

The walkway beyond the iron gate opened up to a rectangular courtyard that was a little smaller than a football field. The grounds were a series of small grass fields broken up by lines of hedges and walkways that meandered their way through. There were also stands of shrubs and flowers, some arranged around concrete and marble statues. The whole courtyard was closed in on all sides by the high walls of the church buildings and the gray sky formed the ceiling above.

Danny found a bench and sat down. It was chilly out here, but not too cold. He had his jacket with him and he pulled it tighter around him.

He was startled when a young priest sat down right beside him. He hadn't even heard the man walk up to him.

"Hi," Danny said, letting out a slow breath of air.

"Hello," the priest said. "I'm Father Norman." He extended a hand in greeting.

Father Norman was maybe in his late twenties, Danny guessed. He was a good-looking man with features that seemed chiseled from marble like some of the statues in the courtyard. He had jet black hair and eyes, and a quick and disarming smile.

Yet something set Danny on edge about the man. He took the priest's offered hand and gave it a shake, a little surprised by the man's strength.

He also noticed the ends of intricate tattoos peeking out from underneath the cuff of the priest's sleeve when he extended his hand.

†

Paul laid the manila envelope on Father McFadden's desk and sat down in one of the two chairs in front of the desk. Father McFadden's office was spacious with bookshelves lining some of the walls and antique furniture scattered about tastefully. A large Persian rug covered the wood floor underneath the chair Paul sat in. A fire crackled in a stone fireplace ten feet behind Father McFadden's chair. Two tall narrow windows stood on each side of the stone fireplace that rose all the way up to the twelve foot ceiling.

The room was comfortable and cozy.

Paul got right to the point about the report, and then he again told Father McFadden his concern about the warning the demon had given him through Father James when he was possessed. He reminded Father

McFadden about Father James's fears he had voiced when he saw him at the hospital, his sense of hopelessness and fear.

"He has been through a lot," Father McFadden said. "But he's back home resting comfortably now."

"It was my fault," Paul said, and he'd had the same thought hundreds of times now but it never lessened the guilt he felt. "I should've seen the signs sooner."

Father McFadden nodded, seemingly neither agreeing nor disagreeing. Like a politician.

"An evil legion is after me," Paul finally said. "They are after everything I hold dear. They've already struck my family. I tried to warn Rachael, but …"

Again Father McFadden nodded.

"I should've gone to Cleveland sooner whether she wanted me there or not. I had a plane ticket booked the evening of the accident, but I … I should've left sooner. I should've been there to protect them."

"If you had gone there, your ex-wife would've called the police," Father McFadden said. "You would have broken the restraining order and went to jail."

Paul didn't say anything. He didn't need to; the father was right. He would've been arrested and Rachael's car would've crashed into the lake either way. Just hearing the sensible way the priest said it eased Paul's conscience slightly, but only slightly.

"We all make choices, Paul. That is God's gift to us—our free will. Rachael made her choice. I'm sorry your children were caught in her decision."

Paul sighed and looked away.

"But you still have your son."

Paul nodded and looked back at Father McFadden. "I can't help but think that Danny is who the demons were really after the whole time. They want to cut the line I come from before Danny can become an Investigator."

"How much have you told your son about that?"

"A little. Not everything."

Father McFadden sat very still. The fire popped and a glowing ember struck the metal fire screen.

"He's already showing signs of the Gifts," Paul said. "He's been having nightmares, but I believe they might be visions. I think he can see the demons when they come to him in the disguise of his mother. And other people."

"Dear God," Father McFadden whispered. "The poor boy."

"He's agreed to begin the apprenticeship. To begin the training."

"And he's certain about that."

"Yes. He wants to fight back. He wants revenge."

"Not the best reasons …"

"But it's a start," Paul interrupted quickly.

Father McFadden nodded again, his body very still in his chair behind the desk.

"When the next assignment comes, I need to take Danny with me. I need to be by his side at all times. I need to be there to protect him."

"Yes, of course. And you think he will be ready for an assignment?"

"He will have to be. I'll have to give him a crash course."

Father McFadden jumped to his feet from behind the desk and strode quickly across the room to a two hundred year old table against the wall. He poured himself a glass of scotch. He turned to Paul, lifting an empty glass, offering a drink to him with the gesture.

Paul nodded and stood up as Father McFadden poured another glass. He walked over to the father and took the glass from him. He gulped down the scotch in a few swallows.

"There is something else?" Father McFadden asked. "Something else you want to talk to me about?"

"I believe that Julia's father, Richard Whittier, was perfectly possessed. He may not have known he was possessed until the demons took over at the very end, until we were there to exorcise the demon from Julia."

Father McFadden stared at Paul and then poured another drink for himself.

"Do you believe in perfect possession?" Paul asked the priest.

The priest was silent for a moment as he sipped his second drink. He looked at Paul and shook his head. "I've heard of cases of perfect possession, but I've never witnessed it before."

Paul nodded. "I have one favor to ask of you. It's a big favor."

Father McFadden braced himself for Paul's request.

†

"You must be Paul Lambert's son," Father Norman said to Danny. A smile still played at the young priest's lips, but his eyes were intense.

Danny smiled back. "How did you know?"

"I can see the resemblance."

"Really?" Danny didn't think he really looked like Paul all that much.

"Yes. The structure of your face. The build of your body. Especially the eyes. Same dark color. Same intensity."

"You know my father?"

"Everyone knows your father here."

"So you know what he does."

"It's supposed to be a secret, but ... you know how talk spreads." The priest still had that small smile on his lips as he stared at Danny.

Danny felt a creepy feeling swirling in his stomach. He felt the chill in the air around his face and neck, the coldness sneaking down underneath the collar of his jacket, traveling down his spine. He couldn't help shivering a little.

"What about you?" Danny asked. "Are you an Investigator for the Church?"

The young priest seemed astonished. "You think I am?"

"Maybe," Danny said. "You have tattoos on your wrists." *Just like Paul does,* Danny wanted to say, but didn't because he noticed in these few moments that this man's tattoos were different than Paul's.

Father Norman looked down at the tattoos on his wrists that barely poked out of his shirt cuffs like he'd never noticed they were there before. He pulled down on the cuffs of both sleeves, covering them up. Then he jumped to his feet and gave Danny a strange smile that reminded him a little of the blond man's smile.

"I really need to get going now. It was nice to meet you, Danny. It was really good talking to you. I hope to see you sometime soon in the future."

As the priest stood in front of him, Danny's entire body tensed like he was either ready to run or fight. Yet he wasn't sure why he felt this way.

"Yes," Father Norman said, still smiling. "I think we'll all get to know each other real well in the very near future."

"Danny!"

Danny turned at the sound of Paul's voice.

"Danny, you out here?"

Danny jumped to his feet, his spirits lifted a little now that Paul was somewhere out here in the courtyard with him and this young priest who had suddenly given him the creeps. He couldn't see Paul yet with all of the shrubs, plants, and trees in the way, but at least he was here.

He looked back at Father Norman.

But the young priest was gone.

"Danny," Paul breathed out when he walked up to him. "It's time to go."

Danny looked around the courtyard, searching for Father Norman, but he didn't see him anywhere.

"What's wrong?" Paul asked him.

He couldn't have walked away that fast, Danny thought, and then he looked at Paul and shook his head a little. "I was just talking to someone out here."

"Who?"

Danny felt a sinking feeling in his stomach as he stared at Paul, but he wasn't sure why. "He was a young priest. Maybe in his late twenties. He said his name was Father Norman."

"I've never heard of a Father Norman around here. I'll ask Father McFadden about it next time I talk to him."

Danny just nodded.

"Come on," Paul said. "Let's get going."

Danny didn't say anything else; he just walked with Paul out of the courtyard.

CHAPTER TWENTY-FIVE

The next day Paul dropped a stack of books down on the kitchen table next to Danny who was slurping the milk out of the bowl of sugary cereal he had just eaten.

Danny looked at the title of the book on top of the stack: *History of Demon Possessions in the United States*. The book looked old. And it looked like it had a lot of pages.

"You want me to read all of these books?"

"In time. Let's start with the first one. It's a good introduction."

And that was how Danny's training began. He studied for a few hours in the morning after breakfast and then he would exercise in Paul's homemade gym in the garage for an hour. Then an hour for lunch. And then more studying and more studying.

†

Only a week had gone by before Paul and Danny were summoned to St. Mathews by Father McFadden.

The nightmares hadn't come back during the whole week of Danny's training and he was happy about that.

The weather in the Northeast had turned very cold in the last few days and snow flurries danced in the gray daylight in front of the windshield as they drove to St. Mathews.

The church buildings still seemed busy with activity even though it wasn't a Sunday. There were a lot of vehicles in the parking lot where Paul parked his Bronco.

They got out and walked briskly across the sea of pavement to one of the many buildings set off from the main sanctuary.

Inside the building, Danny followed Paul through a maze of hallways until they found the wide hall that they had walked down a week and a half ago.

The door to Father McFadden's office was open as it had been before, an invitation to come in, an expectation that someone was arriving at any moment.

"Come on in, Paul, Danny," Father McFadden called out from inside his office a split second after Paul knocked on the doorjamb.

They entered the office, and the room seemed bigger than Danny had remembered. The shelves of rare books and displays of antique furniture were imposing, but the crackling fire in the stone fireplace gave the room a warm and cozy feel, especially with the flurries of snowflakes swirling around outside the two tall windows on each side of the fireplace's stone wall.

"Please sit down," Father McFadden gestured at the two chairs in front of his desk.

Danny sank down into the chair on the left and he noticed a manila envelope in the middle of Father McFadden's desk. It looked similar to the envelope that Paul had brought to the priest when they were here before. But the envelope on top of Father McFadden's desk was thinner and the handwriting was a scrawl of letters, not the careful and neat handwriting from Paul's hand.

"I'm sorry to ask for your services so soon after your last investigation, Paul. And with the family matters you've been attending to …"

"I want to help," Paul answered quickly.

Father McFadden slid the manila envelope towards Paul.

He took the envelope, but he didn't open it.

"There's a haunting in a house in upstate New York. The house sits on a very large piece of property which is situated well outside the limits of the nearest town. There are two priests who have been trying to help the owners with this … uh, this problem, but they need more help."

Paul nodded.

"Robert and Helen Tully own the house. They just bought it six months ago. They're in the middle of renovating it."

Again, Paul nodded. He betrayed no emotion as he sat like a statue in his chair.

"The two priests are from the local Parish; they've been there for two weeks now—in essence staying with the couple night and day. But no progress has been made yet. In fact, the hauntings seem to have gotten worse."

Paul sat and waited.

"All the arrangements have been made," Father McFadden continued. "Mr. and Mrs. Tully have agreed to let you stay in the house as long as you need to. Any other details you need to know are inside the envelope."

"Thank you, Father," Paul said and stood up suddenly.

Danny jumped to his feet because Paul had done so, mimicking his actions.

"Thank you for your services," Father McFadden said, and then he looked at Danny. "And thank you, Danny, for agreeing to help."

Danny just nodded at Father McFadden, and he felt his heart stop for a moment in his chest. Of course he was sure he would be traveling with Paul, he was sure Paul wasn't going to leave him behind in his house while he was gone. But just hearing the words from Father McFadden made it seem somehow more real.

This is real. This is really happening.

"I'll be in touch when we get to the house," Paul told Father McFadden.

Father McFadden looked back at Paul. "I'm afraid there's no phone reception out there. You will be replacing the two priests—Father Severino and Father Hopkins—and they will send word to me that you made it there safely."

"When should we leave?" Paul asked.

"As soon as possible. Today, if you can."

"We'll go home and pack. We should be there by late evening."

"Thank you. And again, I apologize for the haste with this assignment."

Paul shook his head no and gave the priest a grim smile.

Father McFadden was up on his feet and around the desk in a flash. He moved with surprising speed for a man of his age, Danny thought. The priest offered a hand in farewell to Danny.

"Good luck. You're sure you can handle this, Danny?"

Danny nodded, but he didn't feel so sure.

Father McFadden shook Paul's hand and Danny moved back a few steps to give the two men some space.

"Be careful," Father McFadden said, and it was like he had some kind of ominous feeling about this assignment.

"I will," Paul answered. "I always am."

†

Paul and Danny drove back home and each of them packed a suitcase.

Danny grabbed his duffel bag and his suitcase out of his closet and laid them on his bed. He took out four sets of pants and shirts and threw them into the suitcase, not being too neat about it. He added a few pairs of thermal underwear, pairs of thick socks, two extra wool hats, and an extra pair of cloth gloves.

He saved room in his suitcase for the shoebox hidden under his bed. He opened the shoebox before setting it inside, inspecting the contents. He rifled through the photographs, looked at the pictures on the cell phone, and caressed the pieces of jewelry, especially his mother's necklace with his sister's charms dangling from them—a combination of their favorite pieces of jewelry. He used to carry it with him in his pocket, but now he was paranoid about losing it, so he kept the necklace tucked away in the shoebox.

He set the shoebox inside the suitcase and stuffed the clothes around the box like they were padding. He shut the suitcase and zipped it up. Then he stuffed his duffel bag with an extra coat, hat, and gloves. He added a few books to the bag—the next books in a line of books Paul wanted him to read. He threw a few notebooks and a pack of pens on top of the books.

He grabbed his wallet, his IPod, and his earbuds.

He was as ready as he would ever be.

†

On the drive out of Boston, Danny didn't know how to feel. He was both scared of what might be lurking in this house that they were going to, yet he was also excited in a strange way, like this was an adventure.

Paul lectured Danny about his duties as an apprentice as they drove I-90 towards western Massachusetts.

"Apprentices are supposed to obey the exorcist's commands at all times, no matter how unreasonable they might seem."

Danny nodded.

"You, as an apprentice, are never to engage with a dark spirit. You never speak to a possessed person or to a demonic spirit. You never engage in conversation with them."

Danny nodded.

Paul looked at him.

"I got it," Danny said and smiled.

"This is serious stuff, Danny. There's no way I can prepare you for what you might see in this house we're going to."

Danny had read many case studies of exorcisms and he had an idea of what could happen there.

Paul drove in silence for a moment, driving five miles faster than the speed limit, passing slower-moving trucks and mini-vans. The roar of the Bronco's motor was loud inside the cab.

"What was in the envelope that Father McFadden gave to you?" Danny asked.

Paul hesitated for a moment before answering. "Just some background information on the assignment."

"Can I read it?"

Paul didn't react to Danny's question, but Danny couldn't help feeling that his request had bristled Paul somewhat. "Not right now," he finally said.

"But don't you think I should? I mean, wouldn't that be a part of the training?"

"Not right now," Paul said a little more forcefully.

Danny wondered why Paul wouldn't let him see the contents of the envelope if he was training him. It bothered him, but he pushed it away in his mind to ponder later.

"What are the signs of demonic possession in a person?" Paul asked like he was changing the subject. He stared straight ahead as he asked the question, his hands gripping the steering wheel, the iron rings wrapped around each middle and third finger. He wore his usual dark clothing: black boots, black pants, and a black shirt with his silver crucifix hanging down from his neck.

The tattoos on Paul's wrists poked out from underneath his shirt's cuffs just a little, and it reminded Danny of sitting on the bench with Father Norman in the courtyard at St. Mathews.

Paul's floppy hat hung over the side window in the back where their suitcases, duffel bags, and Paul's black canvas duffel bag were stowed.

"Increased strength is one of them," Danny finally answered Paul's question. "Like superhuman strength." He thought for a moment. "Speaking in languages that the possessed person would not have known before. Vomiting up objects, especially metal objects. Levitation. And …" Danny sighed. He couldn't remember the next one.

"Gnosis," Paul told him.

"Yeah," Danny said. "Gnosis."

"And gnosis is …?" Paul asked.

"The ability of the possessed person to know things about other people that they couldn't possibly know. Like secrets."

"Demons may know secrets that people keep. They may reveal these secrets in the middle of an exorcism to embarrass the exorcist and humble him or disable him."

"So an exorcist should have no secrets," Danny said.

Paul glanced at Danny, pinning him there for a moment with his dark eyes. "We all have our secrets."

Danny nodded and then found himself looking away, not wanting to stare into Paul's eyes any longer.

"Demons may reveal secrets, but they also tell lies," Paul added as he passed another car. "You must be ready for both of them."

†

Paul pulled off the highway in upstate New York. He exited down a ramp and then drove a quarter of a mile to a small gas station.

"Time to fill up this thirsty beast," Paul said with a forced smile. He seemed like he was trying to be relaxed about this trip to a haunting, but Danny could tell that he was nervous and jittery underneath his façade. He wondered if Paul was always this nervous going to an assignment or if it was this one in particular.

Paul got out of the Bronco after parking it next to an aging fuel pump. He looked back in at Danny. "You need to use the bathroom?"

Danny shook his head no.

"You want anything from the store? Something to drink?"

"Yeah. A soda, please."

Paul nodded like he already knew the answer. "Coke or Pepsi?"

"Either one."

"Hungry?"

Danny shook his head no.

"We'll stop somewhere to eat when we get closer to the house. Maybe a diner or something. Or even McDonald's if you want."

"Okay."

Paul slammed the door shut.

Danny got out of the truck to stretch his legs as Paul pumped the gas into the Bronco after paying with a debit card.

A debit card from a church bank account, Danny figured. He remembered Paul telling him that the Church paid for his house, the utilities, and gave him a nice monthly income for his services.

Services I may perform one day, Danny thought as he watched Paul pump the gas.

Danny found it difficult to imagine doing something like this for a living. But then again, he hadn't really begun his training yet. Maybe after their time in this house, Danny would feel a little more confident. Right now all of his training, which was really just a lot of reading, was all blurring together. For some reason, he found it difficult to concentrate on what he was reading, and remembering it all. But he guessed maybe that was because all of this was new to him.

Paul hung the nozzle up after he finished pumping the gas. He screwed the cap back on his tank and shut the little flap.

"You want to come inside with me?" Paul asked.

"Nah, I'll wait here."

Paul nodded and then turned to walk away. He hurried across the snowy parking lot to the gas station store.

Danny walked a few steps away from the Bronco and looked around at the desolate landscape—a land of gently rolling hills with a thick blanket of snow covering everything. There was a small stand of woods across the street, but everything else in the distance was snowy fields. There were a few buildings farther down the wide and lonely road to his left. To his right Danny could see the highway ramps half a mile away. The vehicles that traveled along the river of highway reminded Danny of ants traveling back and forth on their little missions.

He looked back to his left and exhaled a long breath, watching the mist cloud up in front of his face.

And then he heard a noise from his right—a soft crunching and dragging sound.

He looked back to his right, towards the highway in the distance again, and he saw an old man stumbling up to him from the road. He hadn't seen the man before when he had just looked that way towards the highway exit, but the man was there now. He was dressed in layers of old clothes wrapped around his frail body. He held a threadbare coat closed over everything with gnarled hands that were protected from the elements only by a pair of fingerless cloth gloves.

Danny glanced back at the gas station to see if Paul was on his way back to the truck yet.

He wasn't.

The old man was closer now, within forty feet. He was shuffling through the snow, but he was moving fast.

He's probably going to ask me for money.

Danny felt a twinge of guilt as he hurried back to the side of the truck. He would've given the man some money, but he didn't have any.

"Boy ..." Danny heard the old man call out over the chilly wind.

Danny ignored the old man's call and opened the passenger door which screeched out a squeal.

"Boy ... hey, boy ..."

Danny hopped inside the truck and slammed the door shut. He pretended he hadn't heard the old man. He even slapped the door lock down, but then he felt silly being afraid of this old man. What was this old man going to do except give him a guilt trip?

He glanced back at the gas station store, but he still didn't see Paul coming back to the truck. He didn't even see Paul anywhere inside the store through the windows.

What was taking him so long?

A pounding at the passenger window startled Danny. He jumped and whirled around, staring face-to-face with the old man on the other side of the glass.

"I'm sorry," Danny yelled before the old man had a chance to speak. "I don't have any money!"

The old man's face was a roadmap of wrinkles. White stubble dotted his thin jaw and pointy chin. His gray eyes were set deep in his face. The man seemed to be in some kind of pain, squinting like he had a headache.

"Don't go to that house," the old man told Danny.

For a second Danny couldn't respond to the old man's words. He couldn't even breathe.

Had he heard the old man correctly?

"There's danger in that house for you," the old man said.

"What … what are you talking about?" Danny finally stammered out.

"Terrible danger for you in that house," the old man said again, his eyes locked on to Danny's eyes.

The sound of the driver's door opening tore Danny's eyes away from the old man. He turned and saw Paul opening the door.

Paul sat down inside the truck with a plastic bottle of Coke for Danny and a paper cup of steaming coffee for himself. He set the coffee cup in a cup holder in the center console and then handed the bottle to Danny.

"Thanks," Danny whispered. He took the bottle and looked back out the passenger window, afraid of what he might see … or *not* see.

The old man was gone.

Danny turned around in the passenger seat and looked out the rear window of the truck, but he didn't see the old man anywhere.

He could feel Paul's eyes staring at him.

"What's wrong, Danny?"

"Nothing," Danny muttered and turned back around in his seat. He buckled his seatbelt around him.

"You saw something," Paul said. It wasn't a question.

Danny didn't answer.

"You can't fight these Gifts you've been blessed with," Paul said after he closed his door on the cold air. He stuck his key into the ignition of the Bronco, but he didn't start it yet.

"Your visions are trying to tell you something."

Danny sighed. He knew he needed to be honest with Paul and tell him what he saw. "I saw an old man. He looked like he was homeless, I guess."

Paul nodded. "Did he say anything?"

Danny wanted to tell Paul the truth, but at the last moment he decided not to, but he wasn't sure why.

"Not really," Danny finally answered. "He was just banging on the window. Scared me a little."

Paul just stared at Danny for a long moment like he was searching his eyes for a lie, like he was looking for a tell on his face that would give him away. Danny held Paul's gaze for as long as he could and then he looked out the window at the rolling hills of snow.

Paul didn't press any further. He twisted the key and started the truck.

Danny couldn't get the old man's words out of his mind.

There was danger waiting in that house for him.

Now there were new feelings trying to creep into Danny's mind. Thoughts that he'd never considered before. What if these visions weren't sent by God? What if there was something wrong with his mind? What if there was something wrong with Paul's mind, too?

He couldn't help feeling that Paul was keeping secrets from him.

Dangerous secrets, maybe.

PART THREE

CHAPTER TWENTY-SIX

Danny and Paul got to the house just as the daylight faded in the western sky in soft blues and grays, the sky dying a winter day's death. The eastern horizon was already dark with stars twinkling in the blackness. It was cold out here in the middle of nowhere, colder than it had been in town only twenty miles away.

The large house sat in the middle of a vast snowy field, like maybe there were acres and acres of farmland all around the house—or land that *used* to be farmland some time ago. At the far edges of the flat land was a line of dark trees.

They had driven down a long road to get to the house. The road was really more like a trail through the woods which consisted of wintery, skeletal trees.

The house was huge—three stories high with a long front porch and a big attached garage that jutted off from the left side. The house's exterior was covered with white siding that looked gray now and black shutters hanging on each side of each window. There wasn't much in the way of landscaping; many of the plants were now dormant for the winter. There were no trees anywhere around the house.

Two vehicles were parked in front of the garage—a gray sedan and a white Dodge Durango, and both of them were covered with a blanket of snow.

Danny could tell that the house looked old and in need of some repair even from this distance as they pulled up to it. The house gave Danny a creepy vibe; it was the only building sitting out here in the middle of this vast field with no trees or other vegetation around it. It looked unnatural to him. It looked like an aberration in the middle of nature. The structure looked lonely and out-of-place.

Paul parked his rumbling Bronco next to the gray sedan and shut the engine off. And then it was very quiet. The only sound was the whistling wind that flowed freely above the square miles of flat fields.

"You sure you're ready for this?" Paul asked.

A little late now, Danny thought, but he didn't say that. "Yeah. I really don't know what to do, though."

"Just watch me and do everything I tell you to. Okay?"

Danny nodded.

"It will be okay, Danny. The most important thing is that you keep your faith strong. Dig deep down and hold on to your faith."

Again Danny nodded. He wasn't sure about his faith anymore, but he would try. He could at least do that.

"Father Hopkins and Father Severino have been told that you were coming with me. They know that you're my apprentice and they will treat you as such. As far as the owners of the home know, you're just an assistant. No need to go into a lot of details with them when we don't have to."

Danny nodded, not sure why the story needed to be different for the owners of the house. But he didn't question it.

"But what exactly are we going to do here?" Danny asked and glanced at the house that loomed in front of them. "I mean, what's the first thing you do when you begin a …" Danny searched for the right word … "an assignment?"

"I know this is tough on you. I know you probably feel like your world has been turned upside down."

"That about describes it."

"I know all of this is a lot to take in at one time. I didn't expect to have an assignment so soon. I had expected to have more time to train you, to explain procedures and protocols, to prepare you. And I wanted more time for your faith to become stronger. That's important. The most important thing."

Danny nodded, but then a random thought entered his mind: he had never really seen Paul pray. And they certainly hadn't ever prayed together yet.

But Danny didn't say anything.

"I know this is a crash course in apprenticeship," Paul said, tearing Danny away from his thoughts. "But I believe you're going to learn so much here. More than you could've ever imagined."

Danny's throat was suddenly dry and he forced himself to swallow.

"I'll do everything you tell me," Danny finally said. "I will try to learn."

"Just follow me once we get inside. Do everything I tell you. No hesitations. No questions. Okay?"

"Okay."

Paul reached over and patted Danny on the shoulder. It was the first real show of affection from Paul since they had come to Boston.

They got out of the truck and left their bags inside. They would come back for them later, Paul told Danny as they walked towards the house.

A middle-aged priest opened a door next to the garage. He was a short man, slightly overweight, and he had thinning dark hair and large brown eyes. And Danny saw fear and desperation in the man's eyes. He saw defeat. It was like the priest's eyes had seen things that they couldn't un-see.

But the priest managed a smile. "I'm Father Al Severino."

"Paul Lambert," Paul answered and gestured towards Danny. "This is my son and my apprentice, Danny."

Danny climbed the few steps up to the door and shook the priest's offered hand. The man's handshake was soft and clammy, like he was too exhausted to grip Danny's hand properly. Dark bags under the priest's eyes showed that he hadn't slept much recently.

"Father Andrew Hopkins is inside with the owners, Robert and Helen Tully," Father Severino said as he backed out of the doorway to let

Paul and Danny inside. He closed the door behind them after they were inside.

They stood in a mudroom where they shed their coats and hats and hung them on an old-fashioned coat rack carved from wood. They stamped the snow off of their boots.

"No need to take your shoes off," Father Severino said. "The owners are in the middle of remodeling the house." He paused a moment. "Of course, they haven't been able to get much done lately."

Danny looked past the priest at the doorway of the mudroom that opened up to a kitchen.

"This way," Father Severino said, gesturing towards the archway.

Danny watched Paul as they walked through the kitchen. Paul's eyes were constantly moving, they seemed to be taking in every detail and storing them in his memory. Their shoes clomped on the wood floors as they walked through the kitchen. It was a large kitchen with a table in the far corner with four chairs around it. Tall upper cabinets that ran all the way up to the nine foot ceiling were mounted on one long wall with the window in it and a shorter wall next to the archway that ran to a corner. The counters were cluttered with collected knickknacks, cardboard boxes of remodeling supplies, and a few tools here and there. A plastic dish strainer next to the double sink underneath the one window in the room was full of drying plates, cups, and silverware.

Danny set his bottle of Coke down on the countertop to his right, and he followed Paul and Father Severino from the kitchen out to a wide hallway that ran from the front of the house towards the back of the house. Down the hall to their right, the front door stood at the end of the hall.

Down the hall to their left was a set of stairs that led up to the second floor. There were other archways in the wide hall that led to other rooms and Father Severino veered right, heading towards an archway closer to the front door.

Voices drifted out of the room … a quiet conversation.

They followed Father Severino into the sitting room. Another priest, dressed in black clothes and a white collar, stood up from a recliner. This priest was older than Father Severino and stick-thin. He had close-cropped gray hair and a sunken face shadowed with gray stubble. He reminded Danny of the homeless man who had pounded on the passenger window of Paul's Bronco only hours earlier at the gas station.

The resemblance was so striking that Danny nearly stopped in his tracks and nearly stopped breathing.

But it couldn't be possible. This couldn't be the same man. It was just a coincidence.

The homeless man hadn't been real, Danny reminded himself.

There's danger in that house for you, the homeless man's voice whispered in his mind.

"This is Father Andrew Hopkins," Father Severino said as Paul shuffled forward to shake the old man's hand.

"And Robert and Helen Tully," Father Hopkins said, turning to introduce the middle-aged couple sitting on the couch. They stood up simultaneously, both fit and trim, but at the same time disheveled and ragged.

Haunted, was the word that came to Danny's mind.

Danny could tell from the eyes of these four people that they had gone through hell already in this house.

The room they were in seemed to be some kind of formal sitting room to Danny. Or at least that was what it would become once the remodeling was finished. The floors were bare panels of subflooring waiting to have wood planking nailed down over them. The trim around one of the windows was peeling with cracked paint and the other window's casing had already been sanded and the paint scraped away. A rumpled canvas tarp was spread out across the floor underneath the windows where it had collected paint chips and dust. A few hand tools lay on the tarp and the window sill.

It looked to Danny like all of the work had ceased in this house at one moment. One day they were busy working, and then they just stopped. And they never went back to work again.

There were two other antique-looking chairs in the room on the other side of the large coffee table that sat in front of the couch.

After introductions, Robert and Helen sat back down on the couch, close to each other, nearly huddling together like they were cold. Or scared.

"Robert, Helen, this is the expert I told you about—Paul Lambert. This is who we call when things … get out of hand."

"I hope you can do something here," Helen said and searched Paul's eyes for an answer.

"We will," Paul told her. "With all of us together, and with God's help, we will drive every unclean spirt out of this house."

Danny felt a chill run down his spine just from hearing Paul's words. Not only the words, but the conviction in his voice.

The air inside the house was warm and Danny's throat was suddenly dry. He hated to interrupt, but he really needed a drink from his Coke which he'd left on the kitchen counter. And he needed to use the bathroom.

"Mr. and Mrs. Tully?" Danny said.

They looked at Danny.

"This is my son," Paul said. "He'll be assisting me while I'm here."

They both smiled, but the smiles looked fake to Danny and he wasn't sure why.

"Could I use the bathroom?" Danny asked them.

"Oh, of course," Helen said and rocketed back up to her feet from the couch. "Where are my manners?" She seemed like she wanted to move, but her feet stayed rooted to the spot on the floor. "How rude of me. Do you two want something to drink? Or eat?"

"No thanks," Paul answered for Danny with a forced smile. "We ate at a small diner in town."

"Judy's?" Father Hopkins asked.

"Yes," Paul answered.

"Good food there."

Paul nodded in agreement.

Robert was up on his feet with a nervous smile smearing his face. He bolted out around the coffee table and rushed to the archway, gesturing for Danny to follow him.

"Down this hall, past the stairs, there's a door on the left," Robert said once they were out in the hallway. "That's where the downstairs bathroom is."

"Thank you, sir," Danny said and started to walk down the hallway.

"Please. Just call me Robert."

Danny glanced back at him. He nodded and smiled at Robert who watched him walk down the hall. Danny walked towards the stairs that led up into the darkness and then he walked past them; the steps rose higher and higher on his right the farther he walked down the hall. He saw the door tucked into the wall on his left.

He opened the bathroom door and found another room in the middle of renovation. Strips of wallpaper had been torn away, one wall completely bare. There were no doors on the cabinet that the sink sat on top of, and a few boxes of tile were piled up in the corner near the shower.

Danny hoped the plumbing worked okay.

He used the toilet and flushed it. He zipped up his pants.

And then he froze.

He heard the sound of creaking wood, like someone had taken a step right outside the bathroom door. It was a cautious and sneaky sound. Danny tried to listen, but he couldn't hear anything over the running toilet as the bowl filled back up with water.

Then silence.

Danny stood still for a long moment, listening. He couldn't even hear the sounds of Paul and the others talking in the sitting room. It wasn't that far away from the bathroom, and Danny thought he should be able to hear the sound of their voices carrying down the hallway in this drafty old house.

He finally walked over to the sink. He washed his hands in the sink and just as he turned the water off, he heard another creak of wood right outside the bathroom door. Like someone had just stepped on a loose floorboard.

Why couldn't he hear them talking in the sitting room?

A strange picture formed in Danny's mind. He saw Paul and the rest of them all huddled together outside of the bathroom door, all of them waiting for Danny to come out.

He pushed the thought away, wondering where a stupid image like that had come from. Why was he having such strange thoughts lately?

He marched to the door and yanked it open.

No one there.

He stepped out into the hall and his foot pressed down on a loose floorboard. It made the same creak he had heard inside the bathroom

Someone had been right outside this door moments ago. Had to be.

Danny looked down the hall to his right, at the front door far down at the other end of the hall. And then he looked at the archways and doorways to the sitting room, kitchen, and other rooms he hadn't seen yet. He looked back at the stairs and the wall of the stairwell in front of him. The wall rose up to the ceiling where the stairs disappeared at a landing.

He stared at the wall for a moment and then he looked left towards the other end of the hall that was shrouded in darkness. The stairwell wall was made up of large decorative wood panels that grew larger as the stairs and wall ascended to the second floor. At the far end of the wall was a door that was designed to look like one of the panels.

He walked over to the last door/panel that was tucked away next to the wall and stood in front of it. There was a latch on the door with a heavy padlock threaded through the handle.

What was this? A closet? A door to the basement? Why was it locked?

To keep people out, he thought.

Or to keep something in.

Danny again pushed this strange thought away. Where were these thoughts coming from? He had only been in this house for a few minutes and it was already getting to him.

A flash of movement out of the corner of his eye caught his attention. He turned and swore he had just seen someone dart into a doorway down the hall.

Danny hurried down the hall, moving like a cat, careful not to stomp his feet on the floor as he rushed to the doorway. He entered a room that could be another family room or a living room, but apparently right now it was being used as storage for furniture. There were stacks of chairs, a few couches, and tables piled up together in the middle of the room. Against the walls were stacks of cardboard boxes and garbage bags.

Danny stared at the objects that cluttered the large room, and then he saw someone standing in the gloom at the far side of the room.

It was a girl. He could tell that much. She might have been maybe nine or ten years old, he guessed. It was hard to make out much detail in the dark room, but he thought she wore a white raggedy dress and patent leather shoes. Her clothes looked worn and dirty. He couldn't see her face because her long dark hair covered it completely, like she was looking down at her feet.

She turned away from him, almost like she was crying and she didn't want him to see her.

"Hey," Danny called out to her. "You okay?"

No answer from the girl.

Danny took two steps towards her, and then she bolted into an archway on that side of the room.

He ran across the room, skirting around the furniture and boxes, until he came to the doorway. It led to another room that could be an office. This room was nearly empty. No furniture, not many boxes, and no closets to hide in.

The girl was gone.

"Where'd you go?" Danny asked the empty room.

He heard a commotion from behind him; it was coming from the cluttered living room he had just been in. He heard voices and running feet.

Paul entered the office first, followed by the two priests, and then by Robert and Helen.

"You okay, Danny?" Paul asked. There was concern in his dark eyes.

"You get lost, buddy?" Robert asked with a fake smile.

Danny shook his head no.

"Exploring?" Helen asked with the same smile Robert had.

"I saw a girl," Danny said. "She was like ten years old maybe." He looked at Helen. "Your daughter?"

Robert and Helen glanced at each other as the smiles slipped from their faces, and then Helen looked back at Danny. "We don't have a daughter. We've never had any children."

CHAPTER TWENTY-SEVEN

After Paul and Danny got their bags and suitcases out of the Bronco, Father Hopkins showed them to their bedrooms upstairs. These were the same bedrooms both priests had been using since they'd been staying in the house these last few weeks. Each room had a packed suitcase waiting by the door like both priests couldn't wait to leave this house.

"Figured we'd go back to town and get a motel room for a few nights since you two are going to be here," Father Hopkins said when he noticed Paul glancing down at the suitcase by the door.

"We'll be here during the day," Father Hopkins added quickly. "Every day to help with the blessings."

Paul nodded. "Thanks."

They showed Danny to his temporary bedroom which was as plain as the guest bedroom had been at Paul's house when he had first gotten there, and then they left him alone to unpack his suitcase.

He stood in the middle of the room and looked around. There was a neatly-made bed in the middle of the room with its old-fashioned brass headboard shoved tight up against the wall. Above the bed, attached to the plaster wall, was a simple crucifix. An old dresser, wounded with marks and scratches, stood against the opposite wall, directly across from the foot of the bed. There was a mirror attached to the top of the dresser and a straight-backed wooden chair next to it. There was nothing else in the room except for a small walk-in closet with the door wide open.

Danny shuddered at the sight of the open closet door, thinking of his nightmares back in Paul's house—thinking of his mother stepping out of the closet in the darkness, her water-logged bare feet squishing on the floorboards ...

He pushed the thought away and rushed over to the closet door and peered inside.

Perfectly empty ... nothing inside except fifteen or twenty wire hangers on the steel rod underneath the top shelf of the closet.

He left the door open and grabbed his suitcase and duffel bag from the floor. He laid them on the bed and opened them.

His thoughts turned to the girl he had seen downstairs.

Had he really seen her?

Paul told him that she hadn't really been there. She had been another vision.

But how could that be? She had seemed so real.

What is happening to me?

The homeless man had seemed so real, too. But so had Ricky at the basketball court with his bashed-in head.

Why was he seeing these visions? He had never seen anything like these visions before that day he walked home from school and saw that blond-haired man with the twisted half-smile and dead eyes.

What had caused him to start seeing all these visions after that? He had always had nightmares his whole life, but nothing as bad as seeing his dead mother walk out of the closet and hearing her soggy body squish while he smelled the odor of wet rot from the lake.

Danny forced the image from his mind again. He didn't want to remember his mother like that.

He felt like he was losing his mind.

A soft knock at his bedroom door startled him. He looked down at his suitcase and saw that it was open, but still fully packed. He hadn't done a thing since he had been in this room. How long had he been standing here?

The door creaked open and Paul poked his head in. "Everything all right, Danny?"

Danny nodded.

"Mind if I come in for a minute?"

"Sure."

Paul entered the bedroom and closed the door.

Danny sat down on the bed next to his suitcase.

Paul picked up the wood chair next to the dresser and brought it closer to the bed. He sat down and it creaked from his weight.

"Danny, I know this is tough for you. But you have to find your strength. You have to build your faith and use it like a shield."

"I don't understand why this is happening," Danny said and then clamped his mouth shut, afraid he was going to let out a choked cry. He didn't want to cry in front of Paul again.

"I know it's strange at first—your visions. But they are going to keep coming to you whether you want them to or not, whether you're ready or not. So you have to fight back. You must realize that the things you are seeing are visions, and they are not real."

Danny barely nodded.

"You have a gift, Danny. A gift from God. One of the Gifts of the Spirit. And you can't turn your back on a gift from God."

"I didn't ask for this gift. I don't *want* this gift."

"I know. But God doesn't give you anything you can't handle."

Danny sighed. He felt like a fool. He was sure he had embarrassed Paul when he went into a tantrum about seeing the girl in the living room and insisting that Robert and Helen Tully must have a daughter.

"Listen, Danny. I'm going to say something you might not want to hear."

Danny braced himself.

"You need to *see* these visions that come to you. They might be important. You need to pay attention to them, and to your dreams. Pay attention to what they are trying to tell you. Some of your visions may be demons in disguise, but others could be spirits with warnings for you."

Danny instantly thought of the homeless man at the gas station and his warning about avoiding this house.

"You need to decipher what you can use and what is a lie," Paul continued. "The girl you saw downstairs may be a leftover spirt from the past. She may be someone who lived here a long time ago. But now she might be stuck here. She may have important information for you. Something that could help us here in this house."

Danny only nodded.

"Come on, we're going to walk through the house. All of us together so we can bless it. Everyone needs to be there. You don't need to say the prayers we're saying if you don't want to. I know you don't know them yet."

"I feel a little embarrassed about seeing the girl. About accusing the Tullys of having a child."

"No, don't be. I've talked to Mr. and Mrs. Tully about your gift and the reason you're here. They're glad you're here. They really believe you can help."

Danny felt himself brightening up a little. Talking with Paul had really helped some. He stood up, ready to follow Paul downstairs.

"Just follow us through the house," Paul said as he stood up and put the wood chair back in its place next to the dresser. "Try to concentrate on your faith. Find your personal relationship with God. Try to reach out to Him. Try to feel His love."

†

Danny walked right behind Paul in the procession. Paul followed Father Hopkins and Father Severino, and Robert and Helen brought up the rear. They walked slowly through the house as Father Hopkins prayed in Latin.

He carried a small metal ball that dangled from a chain. There were holes in the metal ball and thick smoke and a sweet scent drifted out of it.

Danny watched Paul and saw that he was praying. His lips were moving, but Danny couldn't hear what he was saying.

They walked throughout the downstairs. They began in the mudroom, and then they walked through the kitchen. They walked out into the hall and they visited the rooms one by one: the sitting room, the dining room, the living room with the attached office where Danny had seen the girl.

Then they went upstairs and entered each bedroom and bathroom.

But they didn't go up into the attic.

And they didn't unlock the padlock on the door under the stairs that led down to the basement. As Danny walked behind Paul and listened to the monotone chanting of Father Hopkins, he wondered why they would bless all of these rooms but not enter either the basement or the attic.

As they walked, Danny took Paul's advice and tried to reach out to God. But at this moment Danny was angry with God.

God had let his mother and his sister be taken from him. He had let a group of demons come after him and his family. If he was supposedly so important to God and this war on evil, then why hadn't God protected him and his family more? He wanted to cry out to God, curse Him. Strike Him if he could.

He wasn't ready to forgive God yet.

†

Father Hopkins and Father Severino left the house after a late dinner of leftover meatloaf and mashed potatoes that Helen had heated up. Danny didn't usually like meat loaf, but this was good. Either that or he was very hungry.

After their dinner, both priests and Paul sipped whiskey.

Apparently it was okay for priests to drink. Danny didn't know. He didn't really know anything about religion. He wasn't sure if his mother had ever even believed in God or not. She never talked about it and she never made them go to church. She even criticized religion as a terrible institution that had caused more suffering and more death throughout history than all other causes combined.

After their drinks, Paul walked both priests to the gray sedan while Danny helped Helen clean up the kitchen. He saw Paul talking to the priests, and they seemed to be having a long and animated conversation out there underneath the light over the garage. Their breaths clouded up in front of their faces as they talked. It almost seemed to Danny like Paul was giving the two of them instructions, or perhaps chastising them for something. Danny wasn't sure.

All three of them glanced back at the kitchen window like they knew they were being watched.

"Thank you for your help, Danny," Helen said, tearing his attention away from the kitchen window.

"No problem," he said as he dried the last of the dishes and handed them to her so she could tuck them away into the cabinets.

Helen was a slim woman, a little shorter than Danny. She had brown hair and light brown eyes. She seemed to Danny to be the epitome of the American homemaker; if Hollywood wanted to cast someone in that role, he was sure Helen would get the job.

But there was something slightly off about Helen and her husband, something so subtle that he couldn't put his finger on it. Danny felt terrible for feeling this way, but he could tell that there was something fake about them, something a little over-the-top. A role played a little too convincingly, a little too perfectly, a cliché.

†

Danny went to bed a few hours later. The inside of the house was so dark out here in the middle of nowhere, especially underneath an overcast ceiling of clouds that promised more snow in the near future. He left the light on next to the bed, an antique lamp made from brass—maybe it was meant to match the bed frame.

He checked his IPod to make sure it was charged, and then he stuck the earbuds in his ears and lay down on the bed. He stared up at the ceiling until his eyes closed. He was exhausted from the whole day—the drive here, the new experiences, the return of his visions. He just wanted to float away into a black and dreamless sleep for one night.

But the nightmares were waiting for him.

CHAPTER TWENTY-EIGHT

Danny was submerged in the dark, churning water. He was trapped inside the sinking car with the seatbelt cinched tightly over his shoulder and chest, the deflated airbag swaying in the water in front of him.

The world around him was dark and getting darker. The only light came from the dashboard lights that gave off a flickering, greenish glow underneath the roaring water, and from the headlights at the front of the car that shined their beams out at the endless blackness of the water.

The lights were getting dimmer, maybe shorting out, but Danny still had enough light to see his own hands struggling with the seatbelt as he pushed the clinging remnants of the airbag away. He was trying desperately to get the seatbelt unclipped and free himself.

And there was still enough light to see a pale hand reach in to try to help him.

His mother's hand.

Danny looked at the driver's seat and saw his mother floating there between her seat and the deflated air bag that had shriveled in the dark water like a dead jellyfish. Her eyes were wide open, staring at him. Her mouth was wide open, letting the water flow into her mouth, but there were no bubbles coming back out. She wasn't even trying to breathe anymore.

She was already dead.

Danny got his seatbelt unhooked and wriggled out of it. He tried the button to roll down the passenger window, but nothing happened. It was shorted out.

He looked into the backseat and saw his sister pinned to the seat by a lap belt, but her arms floated free beside her, her dark hair floating around her face like a sea anemone's petals.

And her eyes were wide open.

She stared right at Danny.

A hand grabbed Danny—his mother's hand.

He looked back at her and now her face was inches away from his own, her mouth was moving like she was trying to say something to him.

Danny jumped awake in bed, sitting up and breathing hard, his heart pounding against his ribcage.

It was morning. A dull light invaded the room through the blinds of the only window. The air was chilly.

For a panicked moment Danny couldn't remember where he was. He knew he wasn't in his bed in his old house in Cleveland. No, he had gone to live with his father after his mother and sister had died in a car crash.

And the ache hit him like a sledgehammer in the heart. He had been dreaming about that car crash, the moments underneath the dark water. He had been remembering some of it—pieces of the terrible accident were beginning to come back to him.

Danny let out a sigh that sounded more like a choked sob as a shudder ran through his body. At least he had finally slept through the night. He knew that both his mind and his body needed the rest.

He could hear murmurings from somewhere downstairs, people talking quickly in hushed whispers. The conversation seemed urgent, almost heated even though the voices were low.

One of the voices was Paul's.

Danny decided to get out of bed and sneak down the hall to the stairs, get closer to the conversation so he could hear what they were saying. He was reminded of the day of his mother and sister's funeral when he had been in his grandmother's house and he had heard her and Paul talking in the living room, making their plans to send him away.

He swung his legs out from under the covers and dropped his feet down to the floor.

But his feet struck liquid and they disappeared down below ten inches of dark, murky water.

He stared down at his bedroom floor in disbelief. The whole floor was covered with the dark water.

Like lake water.

Danny stared down at his legs. His feet were submerged under the water and no longer visible. And then he realized that his feet weren't even touching the floor anymore.

How deep was this water?

He could tell that there was something moving around in the water near his feet—something large and pale.

His mother's milky white face emerged up from under the water, breaking the dark surface, sending black ripples spreading away in concentric circles from her full-moon face and dead black eyes. She opened her mouth and black water spilled out like an oil slick. Tiny fishlike and wormlike creatures wiggled out of her mouth as her head lifted up higher out of the water.

"Come down here, Danny," his mother said in a croak.

Danny realized that his mother's whispers were competing with the voices he had heard earlier from downstairs. But those voices were so much closer now. And they had changed. They weren't arguing with each other. Now they were chanting in some strange language that sounded like the same language Father Hopkins spoke when they walked in a conga line blessing this house. He recognized his own name in that strange language they were whispering. They were saying something about him, chanting something about him.

The voices were so close now—right outside his bedroom door.

His mother's arm shot up from the water, splashing the thick muck everywhere. She grabbed Danny's leg.

Her face was different now. Angry. Accusing.

"Come down here with me right now, Danny! It's so lonely down here without you!!"

Danny screamed and tried to yank his leg out of his mother's grasp, but she was too strong. She pulled on him, trying to pull him off the bed and down into the water with her.

He tried to kick at her with his free leg, but she grabbed that one with her other hand and yanked even harder.

Danny grabbed the brass headboard with one hand and a fistful of sheets and blankets with the other one. But he couldn't stop her from pulling him down deeper into the water. It was like his legs were attached to a winch that slowly and relentlessly tugged at him, pulling him down deeper into the darkness. He was already halfway off of the bed, his back bent backwards, muscles stretching, joints popping.

Then his hands slipped …

"Danny!!"

It seemed like the voices from out in the hallway were so close now—right inside his bedroom now; right beside his ear.

And this one was Paul's voice.

"Danny, wake up!

Danny opened his eyes and saw Paul's face right in front of his. His dark eyes were concerned, his mouth drawn down in a frown. He felt Paul's hand gripping his arm and he realized he was half on and half off of the bed, his back bent backwards in a painful position just like it had been in the dream.

He jumped fully awake and struggled back up onto the bed. He felt Paul helping him.

"You had a nightmare," Paul said. "You were dreaming."

Danny pushed himself up on the bed, lifting his feet off the floor. He stared down at the floor, but it was the same old wood planking—no murky black water. The bedroom door was wide open like Paul had slammed it open. There were no other people out in the dark hall huddling together, whispering and chanting.

Just Paul.

Just a nightmare.

"You okay?" Paul asked. He took a step back and stared at Danny.

Danny finally nodded. He couldn't talk for a moment. His throat was so dry. He swallowed with effort. He could feel a film of sweat all over his skin even though the room was cold. The back of his thermal shirt was soaked with sweat. His body trembled. He couldn't stop shaking.

"Danny? What did you see?"

"A … a … another nightmare. I'll be okay."

†

After a quick shower in the guest bathroom upstairs, Danny brushed his teeth and got dressed in a pair of baggy jeans, a fresh long-sleeved thermal shirt, and his sneakers. He slipped a big rugby shirt over his thermal and pushed the sleeves up to his elbows.

This bathroom, like the rest of the house, seemed to be in the middle of a massive renovation. But like all of the other rooms, it had been suddenly abandoned. It seemed to Danny like Robert and Helen had started remodeling every room at the same time instead of starting on one room or one area at a time. It seemed strange to him, but he wasn't sure why. It seemed like it was some kind of clue that was staring him in the face, but he just wasn't able to decipher it.

But what did he know? He wasn't an expert at remodeling houses. The closest he'd ever gotten to a renovation was helping his mom paint the kitchen and rearranging the furniture. Anything beyond those skills and his mom had always paid a professional to do it.

Danny was still a little shaken up from his nightmare this morning. It cloaked him and didn't want to let him go.

Like his mother's cold, wet fingers ...

He squeezed his eyes shut, pushing the image away. He opened his eyes again and stared into the mirror. He needed to get a grip here.

Paul had told him breakfast was ready downstairs. And despite the terror he'd been through, he felt his stomach growling.

Pancakes. That's what Paul told him Helen had made for breakfast. Danny thought he might even be able to smell them all the way up here.

†

Danny ate two plates of pancakes smothered in butter, jam, and syrup. He washed them down with two large glasses of ice-cold milk.

After breakfast, he helped Helen with putting the food away and doing the dishes.

Paul and Robert went to the sitting room with Father Hopkins and Father Severino who had made it to the house in time for breakfast.

"You have a beautiful house," Danny told Helen as he dried a plate and handed it to her. The woman was so quiet, especially around him, and he felt like he needed to say something to her to open up a conversation. Besides, he had a question he wanted to ask her and he wasn't sure how to ask it.

"Oh, thank you," Helen answered, taking the plate from him and setting it carefully in one of the upper cabinets over the counter.

She seemed nervous.

"It's a wreck right now," Helen said when she turned back to Danny. "But this … when this is all over and we can fix the rest of it up, it will be so much nicer."

Danny hesitated, not sure how to ask his question, but then he just blurted it out. "What kind of things have been happening here in your house? What kind of hauntings?"

Helen took another dried plate from Danny and put it away in the cabinet. She didn't answer for a full minute, her nervous smile slipping from her face. Her face had suddenly turned a darker shade of red. She looked scared. Or maybe angry.

"It's all right if you don't want to talk about it," Danny said, suddenly sure that he had offended her somehow. But it had been bothering him for a little while now. Father McFadden had sent them here because this house was supposedly haunted, possessed by an evil force. Yet he hadn't heard anyone here talk about anything that had been going on. He hadn't seen any evidence of a haunting. Unless he counted his terrifying nightmares and the ghost-girl he'd seen in the living room. But no one else had said anything about what they had seen in the house so far.

Helen nodded and seemed relieved not to re-live the terrors she'd gone through inside this house.

Danny dried a frying pan and held it up. "Where does this go?"

"The pantry. That door over there."

Danny walked across the kitchen to a small door tucked in the corner between the refrigerator and the dishwasher at the end of the counter with the sink in it. He opened the door and saw a small room with shelves lining the walls. The shelves were crammed with canned and boxed goods. On the lowest shelf were some extra pots, pans, and small kitchen appliances like mixers, food processers, and a toaster. On the floor underneath this shelf were fifty pound sacks of salt stacked on top of each other.

He set the pot on the shelf and turned and nearly walked right into Miss Helen who stood right in front of him.

"Thought you might have gotten lost in there," she said with a fake smile.

Danny smiled back and then brushed past her quickly.

†

They all gathered in the sitting room after breakfast. Two extra chairs had been brought in from the formal dining room table in the dining room across the hall. Candles were lit and bibles were stacked up on the coffee table. Both Father Hopkins and Father Severino were dressed all in black with the white squares on the front of their collars. They both had purple stoles laid over their shoulders.

Some kind of incense burned from the metal ball and chain that Danny had seen Father Hopkins carrying around the day before. He wanted to ask what the ball and incense were for, but he didn't want to sound stupid.

After fifteen minutes of whispered prayers led by Father Hopkins where he asked the Lord for strength for himself and for everyone in the room, they stood up.

It was going to be like the day before—all of them following Father Hopkins from room to room as he chanted in Latin while everyone else (except Danny) prayed silently.

But this time was a little different. Some of Father Hopkins's prayers and chants were in English rather than Latin.

"Oh God, hear our prayers and drive these demons out of this place and send them scurrying away." And then he suddenly shouted at the room they were in. "You are not welcome here, demons!! I command you in the name of Jesus to leave this place!! Go back to where you came from!!"

They had walked from the sitting room into the hallway, and then they entered the dining room, all of them following Father Hopkins as he walked slowly around the dining room table, making his way back to the archway that led back out into the wide hallway. The father's voice echoed back down from the nine foot ceiling as he read from an old prayer book clutched in his hands.

Father Severino held the metal ball that dangled from the decorative chain. A sweet scent drifted out of the metal ball and Danny walked through the mist it left behind.

As they entered the hallway again, ready to walk down to the archway to the kitchen, ready to re-walk the same route as yesterday, they all stopped in their tracks.

A sound came from upstairs—the sound of stomping feet, like someone was running around up there.

To Danny, the footsteps didn't sound heavy. They sounded quick and light. Like the sound a child's footsteps might make.

A little girl?

"I said leave this place, Unclean Spirit!!" Father Hopkins roared and rushed towards the foot of the stairs. He gripped his now-closed prayer book in one hand, his knuckles turning white. He had produced a gold crucifix from under a layer of his cassock and he held it out in front of him like it was a shield.

He hurried up the steps, the wood creaking and popping as Father Severino rushed up the steps right on his heels. Danny and Paul were right behind them. But Robert and Helen remained downstairs, watching with wide eyes from the bottom steps, huddled together.

Danny, Paul, and the two priests searched the upstairs hallway. They searched each room, starting with Danny's room, and then Paul's room. They checked under beds, peeked inside closets, checked windows. Then they checked the guest bathroom. Then the master bedroom.

Paul whispered to Danny to wait in the hall as the priests searched the master bedroom—Robert and Helen's room.

Danny waited as the three men entered the bedroom near the end of the hall. All three of them had passed right by the lone door at the end of the hall without even looking at it.

When Paul came back, walking slowly and defeated, Danny gestured towards the door.

"What about that door?"

"It goes to the attic," Paul answered. "It's always locked."

"Maybe it was unlocked. Maybe," and Danny almost said 'the girl' because he envisioned the girl he'd seen yesterday running around up here, "… maybe the spirit went through that door."

"No," Paul said a little too sharply. "It's just a demon trying to trick us. Torment us."

Danny thought about pushing more. He thought about questioning why they weren't searching the attic. Or the basement. How come when they toured the house, they didn't bless these two areas: the literal bottom and the top of the house?

But he didn't question Paul. He remembered Paul's words on the drive here: An apprentice doesn't question anything—he just performs the tasks immediately and without question or hesitation.

Father Hopkins and Father Severino came back and shook their heads slightly, indicating that they hadn't found anything.

†

They performed several more tours of the house, blessing it and praying, Father Hopkins leading the way. He either shouted at the demons to leave or he read prayers in Latin from his worn prayer book.

They stopped for a late lunch at three o'clock in the afternoon. Everyone looked spent and exhausted.

Danny had to admit that he felt drained even though all they had been doing was walking around and praying. Also, even though he had awakened from that horrible nightmare this morning, he had slept through the night for the first time in weeks. He thought he should be somewhat rested, but he wasn't.

His mind drifted back to the nightmare this morning. But then he thought of his dream before that—his first real memories of the car accident.

Were those memories coming back to him now whether he wanted them to or not?

An hour later both of the priests had left the home. Danny, Paul, Robert, and Helen were sitting at the kitchen table with cups of coffee in front of them. Outside the kitchen window, it had begun to snow again.

Danny stood up and excused himself, letting them know he was going up to his room.

Helen stared at Danny like he was crazy to be going anywhere alone in this house right now, but she didn't say anything.

Paul nodded, indicating that Danny was excused, and then Danny left the kitchen.

He walked up the stairs to the hallway. He was about to enter his room, but then he stopped and looked at the door at the end of the hallway—the door to the attic.

It looked like it was open.

CHAPTER TWENTY-NINE

Danny walked down the hallway, choosing his footsteps carefully, already learning where the loud creaks and pops were in the floorboards. Moments later he stood in front of the door to the attic.

It was open just a crack.

Danny just stared at it. He could see nothing except blackness beyond the crack in the door.

He looked back, half-expecting Paul to come rushing up the stairs. He felt like he was doing something wrong, like he was breaking some unsaid rule about going into a room that had been forbidden to him.

But no one had told him he couldn't go into the attic. Or the basement. If these rooms were forbidden, then wouldn't someone have said something to him by now?

Danny turned back to the door and pushed at it gently, like a cat hesitantly touching some new strange object found on the floor.

The door opened just a bit when he pushed on it. He had expected the door to creak open, screeching into the still and silent air, but it had opened like it was well-oiled.

He was here as an apprentice, an assistant to Paul, and maybe it was his duty to check this room. Maybe it was his duty to see what lay beyond this door that was now opened up to him.

Opened by whom? By what?

He hesitated for a moment, suddenly afraid.

But he had seen such horrible things already. How could what might lie beyond this door be any worse than what he'd already seen? And if he was ever going to learn to combat the dark forces that were after his family line, then he would need to start somewhere.

Danny pushed on the door a little more and it opened all the way. The light from the hallway spilled into the stairwell revealing twelve steps up to a landing where the stairs turned sharply to the left and then disappeared up into the darkness.

He wondered for a moment if he should go back downstairs and let Paul know that the door was open. But what if he left and then it was locked again when they came back up here to check it out? Maybe he should call down to Paul, Robert, and Helen while he waited in front of the door.

But he decided not to. He felt like he needed to face this on his own.

He noticed a light switch on the wall just inside the doorway. He flipped the switch and a light came on far up the stairs around the corner.

He wondered if he should block the door open with something, but then he made himself enter the doorway and push away his thoughts of fear. He tried to look at it like this was a mission he was on, an adventure. Like he was a treasure-seeker stepping into an unknown cavern and following clues.

Danny crept up the stairs to the landing. He made the sharp turn to the next flight of narrow steps that led up to a door.

Maybe this door would be locked.

He climbed the steps quickly and the cracked plaster walls seemed to close in on him. He got to the top landing in front of the door and twisted the old-fashioned glass door handle.

It turned easily.

Danny pushed the door open and saw the attic laid out before him. Much of the massive room was in shadows, but a series of windows along both short walls lit the large room up with the gray late afternoon daylight from outside.

The room was like another whole floor to the house. The ceiling went up to a peak high above him with bare rafters showing. There were some pieces of fiberglass insulation stuck between the rafters here and there, but much of the insulation was gone. The floor was made up of unfinished plywood panels nailed down to the floor joists. The center of the room was dominated by the brick chimney stack that went up and out of the ceiling, sealed around the top with black tar and metal flashing.

Around the perimeter of the room were more stacks and boxes of storage. There were pieces of furniture stacked on top of each other. It seemed like so much stuff up here for just two people.

One corner caught Danny's eye and he walked around the chimney to investigate it more closely. He stepped gingerly on the floorboards, testing the integrity with each step even though the floor looked solid and strong.

He stood in front of pieces of a bed. The framework of the headboard and footboard were frilly and feminine. It had been painted white a long time ago, but much of the paint was peeling off.

It was a girl's bed. And beside the pieces of the bed and mattress was a small baby carriage with a baby doll tucked down inside; the doll was swaddled up in a dirty blanket. A white dresser with an assortment of Barbie doll stickers stuck on the drawer fronts stood next to the disassembled bed. There were stuffed animals poking their heads out of a black garbage bag, their glassy black eyes staring at Danny. There was a stack of cardboard boxes labeled GAMES and another one labeled TOYS. Two suitcases stood next to a bookcase stuffed with children's books and magazines. The bookcase was painted the same shade of white as the dresser.

Why was all of this stuff up here?

Robert and Helen told him that they didn't have a daughter. They said that they'd *never* had any children.

But here was a whole bedroom set stored up in the attic behind a locked door.

And that got him wondering even more now what might be hidden down in the basement. The attic door had been merely locked, but the basement door was locked even more securely with a padlock.

Danny wondered why this door to the attic was unlocked now. Who had unlocked it? Who wanted him to see this stuff up here?

He heard a noise from behind him, like the scraping of a shoe against the gritty plywood floor.

He whirled around, his body crouched like a cat ready to bolt.

But he didn't see anyone.

Maybe it was time to go. It was already getting very dark up here now that the sun was setting low on the horizon somewhere beyond that forest of skeletal trees.

Danny hurried back to the attic door, still trying to move silently. He hurried through the doorway and spun around on the small landing to close the door. He crept down the steps to the other door that led out to the hallway. He flipped off the light switch and stepped out of the stairwell. He closed the door, but he couldn't lock the door because he needed a skeleton key.

As soon as he had closed the door, he heard the sound of footsteps rushing up the steps from downstairs.

Someone was coming upstairs.

He wasn't sure why he was panicking, but he didn't want to be caught standing in front of the attic door. He couldn't make it all the way to his bedroom, so he ducked into the hall bathroom. He closed the door and flushed the toilet and then hurried over to the sink to wash his hands.

Why was he sneaking around? What was he afraid of? He hadn't done anything wrong, had he? Shouldn't he be sharing this news with the rest of them? With Paul, at least?

He told himself that he needed time to think about this. He wasn't sure why, but he was sure that Robert and Helen were lying to him about having a daughter.

Danny stared into the mirror and saw that his face was flushed. He washed his face, cooling it off with the water. He dried off with a towel that was hung on a rack attached to the now wallpaperless wall.

He left the bathroom.

When he stepped out, Helen waited right in front of the door. She stood in front of him, smiling at him, just watching him with her brown eyes that seemed to have grown darker suddenly.

"Everything okay, Danny?"

"Yeah," he answered, nodding almost violently. "Just needed to use the bathroom," he said like he needed to explain his departure from the room. "I'm going to lie down for a few minutes. I've got a headache."

"Oh …" Helen said with what Danny was suddenly sure was fake sympathy. "Do you need some aspirins?"

"No, thanks. I'm just going to rest my eyes. I'll be okay after that."

Helen looked a little nervous as she watched Danny, and she still wasn't moving out of his way.

Danny slinked past her and walked down the hall to his bedroom, feeling Helen's eyes on him the whole time.

†

Danny jumped awake in his bed.

It was still somewhat light outside, but he could tell it was almost night.

He must have really dozed off for a few minutes. Thank God he had turned on his lamp next to the bed. He didn't want to wake up in the darkness.

For a moment he thought he had dreamt of going up into the attic and finding a girl's bedroom set. But after coming fully awake, he knew it was true, he had really been up there, he had really seen the girl's bedroom set. And then he remembered Helen standing outside the bathroom when he had come out. The way she stared at him; it was like she knew that he'd just done something wrong.

He remembered hurrying past her to his bedroom and ducking inside. He had closed the door and locked it. He had stretched out on the bed and put his earbuds in and turned on his iPod. He had closed his eyes and then he must have drifted off to sleep almost immediately.

A knocking at his door startled him.

Maybe the knocking had awakened him.

He got up and unlocked the door with the skeleton key that was sticking out of the lock as quietly as he could. He then walked softly back to his bed. He didn't want anyone knowing that he had locked himself inside his bedroom.

"Come in," Danny said, clearing his throat.

For a moment no one entered, and Danny began to wonder if he had imagined the knocking sound. Perhaps it was a remnant of a forgotten dream.

And then he wondered if it might not be a person behind that door right now. Maybe it was *something else* that had been knocking.

No ... not now ...

The door swung open and Paul stood in the doorway.

Danny sat on the edge of his bed.

"You okay?" Paul asked. "Helen said you had a headache."

"I did. Just a little one. Lack of sleep, maybe."

Paul entered the room a few steps, but he didn't close the door.

"I'm better now," Danny added. "I had a little nap."

"Sorry I woke you. Helen just served dinner and I wanted to see if you were hungry."

Danny wasn't really hungry. In fact, he still felt a little nauseous. Just hearing Helen's name brought back the memory of what he'd seen in the attic.

"Paul, can I talk to you about something?"

"Sure."

Danny still felt a little funny calling his father Paul instead of Dad, but no matter how much he tried, he couldn't say the word Dad yet. If Paul was hurt or angered by it, he didn't show it. He kept a poker face on all the time, a mask of unreadable emotions. Danny wondered if that was a result of the things he had seen and experienced during exorcisms through the years, or if he had trained himself to be this way.

Would Danny be trained to be like his father?

Part of him didn't hate the idea so much, but another part of him wasn't so sure.

Paul seemed to interpret the weight of Danny's request to talk so he turned and shut the bedroom door. He walked over to the dresser and picked up the wooden chair beside it. He brought the chair over to the bed just like he had done yesterday, like sitting down right beside him on the bed was too intimate and he needed to keep a distance between them.

"What's wrong?" Paul asked as he sat down in the chair.

Danny wasn't sure he could spit it out now that Paul was sitting right in front of him. But he took a deep breath and blurted out the words.

"Before I came up here to lie down, I noticed that the door to the attic was open."

Paul just nodded, his face still impassive, giving nothing away.

"So I went up there and checked around."

Danny braced himself for a display of anger from Paul. Or maybe even disappointment that Danny had searched a locked part of the house without permission, or at the very least without consulting him first. But Paul showed neither anger nor disappointment, just a pensive interest as he seemed to patiently wait for Danny to explain further.

"There's a lot of stuff up there," Danny said. "The attic is like another whole floor up there. And it's like there are people's … people's stuff up there. And there's a whole bedroom set that belongs to a little girl: a bed, dresser, books, games, toys, dolls."

Danny stopped talking, realizing that he had been speaking faster and faster. And a little louder.

"And you think those things could belong to the little girl you saw yesterday?"

Danny shrugged. "Is it possible that the girl I saw wasn't a vision? Could it be possible that she was real?"

Paul sighed. "A lot of things are possible. But you've seen visions before. And you have to be careful of being fooled and manipulated by evil spirits. They can be very convincing."

Paul's dark eyes seemed to say: *You've seen how convincing these spirits can be, haven't you, Danny?*

Danny wanted to tell Paul more. He wanted to tell Paul that Helen gave him the creeps, but he kept that little observation to himself for the moment.

"Robert and Helen asked us here to investigate their home," Paul said. "First, we must decide if the home is really possessed. But since Father Hopkins and Father Severino have already been here for two weeks, we can assume that they've already made that judgment. Now we must move on to the second part of why we've been invited here—to help drive the dark forces out."

"I know. I'm trying to help …"

Paul just nodded and kept his eyes on Danny the whole time like he was studying him.

"You're not upset because I went up there, are you?" Danny asked him.

Paul shook his head no and gave Danny a small smile. "No. We're here to investigate. And you said the door was unlocked. You're allowed to enter any unlocked room you want to."

Danny saw an image in his mind of the padlocked basement door and thought of asking about that. But he didn't.

"I want you to walk around the house alone if you want to," Paul continued. "I want you to explore. I want you to use the Gifts you've been blessed with. But I also want you to be careful. Remember, above all else, your faith must always be strong."

Danny nodded. He felt a little guilty because he hadn't been praying like Paul had told him to. He just couldn't make himself do it right now.

"I can talk to Helen and Robert about what you saw in the attic," Paul said. "I'm sure there's a reasonable explanation."

Paul must've seen the alarm on Danny's face because he added quickly: "Of course, I'll talk to them privately."

"Okay." Danny already felt a little better just from getting some of this off of his chest.

†

Danny went down to dinner with Paul. He really did feel better now, a little lighter. Maybe there was some rational explanation for the little girl's bedroom set being locked away in the attic with all of the other boxes and furniture up there. Maybe he had seen another vision. Talking to Paul always brought everything back into perspective, reduced everything to a single focus—their job here.

Danny was surprised that he was hungry now. They ate fish, mashed potatoes, and broccoli. Fish wasn't really one of Danny's favorites, but it tasted good, kind of salty, and he had two helpings.

He helped Helen clean up after dinner, and she seemed normal again. Not overly nervous, not any more nervous than she should be while living in a haunted house. He was beginning to feel a little silly accusing her and Robert of hiding a child in the house, and he thought about asking Paul not to say anything to them just yet.

Danny went up to his room after he was done helping Helen with the kitchen. He opened one of the books he had brought that Paul wanted him to study. But he couldn't get into it. He plugged his earbuds in and turned on his iPod.

He left the lamp on next to his bed, stretched out, and closed his eyes.

CHAPTER THIRTY

Danny was in the swirling dark waters again, trapped in his seatbelt as the car sank down deeper and deeper into the liquid blackness. The lights from the dashboard and the headlights flickered, they were about to short out and leave him alone in the suffocating darkness with his dead sister behind him and his dead mother floating in the seat next to him.

A hand brushed against his hand.

Cold, dead flesh.

A pale hand.

His mother's face floated in front of him. Her eyes were wide open in alarm, and her mouth worked frantically like she was trying to tell him something as the water flooded her throat …

†

Danny's eyes popped open and he sat up in bed.

The lamp beside the bed was off, but the room was just beginning to lighten up from the morning sun beaming in through the window.

Why was the lamp off? Why did he keep turning his lamp off in the middle of the night? He didn't think he would do something like that.

Was someone else turning it off?

He shook the stupid thought away and shivered. The room was cold. Not cold enough for him to see his breath, but cold enough to make him tremble.

He jumped out of bed, dressed only in his thermal underwear and a thick pair of socks. His pants and shirts were folded over the wooden chair that Paul had sat in when they had talked about the attic yesterday.

He checked his iPod. It was six thirty in the morning, still very early, but late enough to allow the bluish light to drift in through the window. The dark blue light reminded him of being under the water.

Underwater.

Danny shivered again.

He had been dreaming about the accident again. But he hadn't gotten much further in the dream. He hadn't learned anything new.

He walked back to his bed and wondered if maybe the electricity had gone out or the lightbulb in the lamp had burned out. He twisted the little black knob on the lamp and the bulb lit up.

Well, there went that theory. Now he was back to the fact that either he or someone (or something) else was turning the lamp off in the middle of the night after he fell asleep.

The house was silent. He listened for a moment, but he didn't hear anyone else moving around in the house. But it *felt* like someone else was awake. He didn't know why he felt that way, but it was such a certainty.

He walked over to the bedroom window just to get some blood circulating through his body and warm himself up a little. He crept across the floorboards, but none of them creaked much.

Outside the window a blanket of snow lay over the fields all around the house. Snow painted the trees in the distance, and it covered everything else in sight. The sky looked dark blue, but it was lightening up on the horizon beyond the trees, pushing the darkness back across the sky. He stared down at the snow near the house and thought he saw tracks in the snow—a set of footprints.

Small footprints.

Maybe someone had taken the garbage cans out or something.

But he knew that wasn't right, and he knew that he was just grasping at theories now and trying not to see the obvious—those footprints in the snow were made by that little girl.

Danny stared down at the footprints and then shook his head and forced himself to look away from the window and the cold panes of glass.

Maybe it was another vision. Maybe the footprints weren't really there.

He looked back out the window, expecting the footsteps to be gone—nothing left but a pristine sheet of snow.

But the footprints were still there—a track of footprints alongside the house, starting from one corner and disappearing to the other corner and out of his view. Like someone was circling the house.

He tore himself away from the window and went back to his bed. He crawled under the covers and took the shoebox out from underneath the bed. He wanted to look at the photos of his mom and sister again. He wanted to see them again like they were when they had been alive, not like they were in his dreams—dead and floating in the murky water.

The flashes of his dream hit him like a hammer again.

It seemed like he was beginning to remember some of the accident, but something was still holding him back from remembering everything. There was something else about the accident that was too terrible to remember, he felt certain about that.

Maybe he was holding back the memories himself because he still didn't want to recall the terrible moments of that day. Even though he kept seeing that part in his dreams, the part when he was trying to free himself from the seatbelt, he still had unanswered questions: there were still things he couldn't remember. Had he seen the blond-haired man before the crash? He thought he had, but he couldn't remember actually *seeing* the man. And he couldn't remember how he had gotten out of the car once it was underwater.

How had he lived when his mother and sister had died?

A pang of guilt hit him—a familiar feeling, and he pushed back the tears that threatened, and he swallowed a lump down in his throat.

He curled up on the bed, pulling the covers over him. He opened the shoebox. He looked at the photos—one after another. He looked at his mother's ring. His sister's cell phone that was dead right now and needed to be charged up.

And then his heart skipped a beat.

He rummaged through the box, sitting up quickly, the blanket falling off of his shoulders.

He made himself slow down.

It had to be here.

It was thin and dainty. It might be hiding down in a corner of the shoebox, curled up like a tiny snake.

Danny threw the covers off of him and smoothed out the sheets, creating a large space for him to work. He took out the contents of the shoebox one by one and laid them on the sheet of the bed.

And after all the contents were out and accounted for, he knew it was true. His mother's necklace with his sister's charms on it was gone.

He got off the bed and searched underneath it. He even took the lampshade off the lamp and brought it down under the bed, giving him more light to see with.

The necklace wasn't under the bed.

He put the contents back into the shoebox and tore the blankets and sheets off of the bed. He shook them out. No necklace hiding among the sheets.

He checked his suitcase and duffel bag three times. He checked the closet floor, the dresser drawers, the pockets of all of his clothes—even the ones he hadn't worn yet.

Panic set in.

He had lost the necklace. *Oh God, no. Please.*

But he couldn't have lost it. And if he had misplaced it, the only place it could be was inside this room, which he had just spent the last hour searching.

Then another thought occurred to him.

Someone had taken it.

Danny put the sheets and the blankets back on the bed, making a half-assed attempt at remaking the bed. He shoved his shoebox into his suitcase and put it away in the closet.

And then he got dressed quickly. The room was much brighter now with the sun's rays beaming in. For once it wasn't cloudy outside.

He thought about pounding on Paul's bedroom door and letting him know that there was a thief in this house. They had been invited here to help, and someone had stolen from him. They had stolen the most precious thing he owned. He felt a terrible loss about the necklace, but he also felt a fury rising inside of him.

Danny left his bedroom and stood in the hallway. He was very still, listening to the silent house for a long moment. No one else seemed to be awake yet.

He crept down the stairs to the first floor hallway. Maybe he would find Helen in the kitchen making more of her waffles on her waffle maker. If she was in there, then he would confront her. He had decided that he would ask her if she might have found a gold necklace, and then he would gauge the reaction on her face.

But Helen wasn't in the kitchen.

No one was up yet.

He went to the mudroom off of the kitchen and looked out through the glass on the back door out at the snow-covered driveway which was indistinguishable from the grass because the snow covered everything. Paul's Ford Bronco sat next to the white Dodge Durango.

A scraping noise from behind him startled him—it sounded like a shoe scuffing the floor.

He whirled around and saw Paul standing in the kitchen. He was dressed in his usual dark clothing and his black boots. He wore long sleeves that hid the array of tattooed crucifixes, religious symbols, and Scripture quotes decorating his skin. His dark hair was a little unruly and looked like it had been wetted in a sink and hastily smoothed down. His dark eyes were fixed on Danny.

"I was going to make some coffee," Paul said as if he needed a reason to be standing in the kitchen.

But he didn't make a move towards the coffee machine.

"The necklace," Danny breathed out. "My mom's necklace. It's gone."

Paul just stood there. No reaction.

"My mother's necklace," Danny said a little louder. "The one I kept after the funeral. The one with my sister's charms on it. It's gone. It was in my shoebox with all of the photos and now it's gone."

"Maybe you misplaced it …"

"No," Danny barked out. "I wouldn't have lost it. I didn't even take it out of the room."

"I could help you look for it."

"I already looked through my room three times. Every square inch of it. It's not there now. Someone had to have come in my room and taken the necklace."

"Danny …"

"Something's wrong here. There's something very wrong with this place. With these people here."

Paul nodded like that was the whole reason they were here.

Danny heard the shuffling of feet on the stairs and then in the hall. Robert and Helen entered the kitchen. They were dressed but they didn't seem fully awake.

"Morning," Robert said.

Danny burst into the kitchen from the mudroom. "My necklace is gone," he blurted out.

Robert and Helen stared at Danny, and then looked to Paul for help.

†

Paul explained everything, trying to calm Danny down. Robert and Helen nodded and cooed in all the right places. They offered to help search for the missing piece of jewelry as if it were a child's trinket that had been carelessly misplaced somewhere.

Danny searched Robert and Helen's faces as he told them about the necklace, trying to see some kind of evidence that they were guilty. But their acting jobs were flawless. He saw nothing on their faces except compassion—*fake* compassion.

They all did a quick search of the house even though Danny assured everyone again that he never brought the necklace out of his room. They came up empty. How could they find anything in this house that was a wreck with all of the remodeling supplies and tools scattered about in every room?

Helen made breakfast an hour later as Father Hopkins and Father Severino arrived.

Two more suspects, Danny thought even though he wasn't sure when they could've been up in his bedroom. Yet he still couldn't rule them out.

After Danny picked at his breakfast for twenty minutes, he told everyone that he was going to look around again.

No one protested. They all seemed to be relieved that he was leaving the kitchen.

Danny went out to the hall. He was about to check the sitting room and dining room again. Paul had suggested that maybe Danny had stuffed the necklace down in his pants pocket and hadn't remembered it. Maybe he had lost it during one of their tours of the house while they blessed and prayed.

Maybe, Danny had told him, but he didn't believe it. But what if Paul was right? Danny had been seeing nightmarish visions and he couldn't tell who was real and who wasn't real anymore. He didn't know what was true and what wasn't true anymore. He didn't know who to believe and who not to believe—not even himself. Maybe he had been turning off his lamp in the middle of the night. Maybe he had taken the necklace out of the shoebox in the middle of the night while he was asleep.

Everything was becoming so jumbled in his mind, a blur, everything spiraling out of control.

He decided that he was going to retrace every step he had taken in this house since he had gotten here. He was going to check in every corner, along every baseboard, down in every heating vent.

He had to find it.

After deciding to start his search in the sitting room near the front of the house, he walked out into the hallway. But then he stopped when a noise from the living room startled him.

Danny looked back at the archway that led into the kitchen. No one had come out. Hadn't they heard that noise from the living room?

Danny walked over to the archway of the living room. He entered the murky room with all of the boxes, bags, and furniture stacked up in the middle of the floor. If he had dropped the necklace in here, he thought he might never find it.

He stood there for a moment in the darkness, staring at the furniture stacked up in the middle of the room like it had been collected quickly for some kind of strange interior bonfire.

And that made him think of something else …

The attic.

He had forgotten about being up in the attic. Was there any way he could've had the necklace with him then? Could he have wrapped it around his wrist or stuffed it into his pants pocket without really remembering it?

Another scuffling sound from deep in the living room alerted him. It had come from the other side of the room and it sounded like a shoe scraping the wood floor. It was a light and cautious sound—a sneaky sound.

Someone was in this room with him, hiding among the furniture and boxes. Danny was sure of it.

He listened for a long moment, frozen in place, even trying to hold his breath. But he didn't hear any other sounds.

He crept around some of the boxes, making his way towards the other side of the large room towards the wall of curtained windows. He was sure that this was the area where the sound had come from.

And then he stopped.

There was someone hiding behind the wall of musty drapes that covered the bank of windows. He saw a pair of hard shoes peeking out from the bottom of the drapes; they were black patent leather shoes that were dull and scratched now, a pair of girl's shoes with a pair of girl's socks above them that were soiled with stains. One of the socks drooped down like the top had lost its elasticity.

It was her, it was the girl he had seen before, the girl with the scraggly hair that hid her face and made her look like some kind of wild animal.

He took slow, cautious steps towards the wall of drapes. The girl's feet moved a little and he could see a slight movement behind the drapes, like she was fidgeting with something in her hands. He could even hear her breathing. He swore he could see the minute movements of the drapes from her breaths.

After a few more agonizingly slow moments, and a few more footsteps closer, Danny stood only a few feet away from the drapes.

The girl behind the drapes was very still. She knew he was there in front of her now.

"I'm not going to hurt you," Danny whispered.

The girl still didn't move or make a sound. It seemed like she wasn't even breathing now.

He expected her to run, but she remained behind the drapes.

"My name is Danny," he told her.

"I know," she whispered.

She *knew* him?

"What's your name?" he asked as he risked one more careful step closer.

For a moment she didn't answer, and then:

"Melissa."

"Okay," Danny breathed out. He chanced a peek back at the archway out to the hallway but there was no one there watching him.

He looked back at the drapes in front of him. He was so close now he could nearly reach out and touch the drapes.

The girl was fidgeting again like she had something in her hands. There was a bulge in the drapes where her hands were together in front of her, clutching something.

"I'm glad to meet you, Melissa."

She didn't answer.

The small talk didn't seem to be working. Maybe he should try some more direct questions for her.

"Why are you hiding, Melissa?"

She still didn't answer, and she was fidgeting even more now.

Her hand shot out from behind the drapes and there was something in it—a folded piece of paper.

Danny stared down at the folded paper in her hand. The paper looked old, a little yellow like it had been found buried in a box or behind a wall somewhere.

She wanted him to take the paper. She was giving it to him.

"You want me to have that?" he asked, not wanting to grab it out of her hand and scare her.

No answer from Melissa.

Danny reached out with a trembling hand and took the paper from her hand as gently as he could.

He opened the folded piece of paper and read the two words that had been scrawled there in childlike handwriting, written in red crayon. He stared down in horror at those two words.

A noise from the hallway.

He turned and looked at the archway to the living room. He could hear Paul and the others hurrying from the kitchen to the living room like something had alerted them.

Danny looked back at the drapes, but the girl was gone. He hadn't even heard her leave.

Paul entered the living room, working his way through the maze of furniture and boxes.

Danny wanted to show the note to Paul. He wanted to show him proof that he had seen the girl again—he wanted to show him the physical proof he had in his hand.

But the others were following Paul and he felt suspicious of them suddenly. Something was wrong not only with this house, but with Robert and Helen. And for the first time Danny felt that he and Paul might be in some kind of danger. Maybe they had been tricked into coming here for some reason.

He folded the paper back up and stuffed it down into the pocket of his jeans as Paul came around the corner of the stacked boxes.

Danny tried to show a neutral face as he looked at Paul.

"Did you find the necklace?" Paul asked.

Danny shook his head no, afraid to speak; afraid he would somehow give away what he had just seen.

Both priests and Robert and Helen gathered behind Paul.

"We need to continue with the blessing of the house," Paul said. The others nodded. It seemed like they all had conducted a little meeting in the kitchen and had come to a decision that Danny needed to put this little hunt behind him for now and get back to the real business of this house.

"We can all look for the necklace again later," Paul said.

"Okay," Danny answered. He realized that he wasn't going to find the necklace dropped somewhere in any of these rooms. He was even more certain now that it had been stolen.

Danny followed the rest of them back to the sitting room where candles were already lit, where they would start their procession through the house again.

It felt like the folded piece of paper was burning a hole in his pocket. He was sure that Robert, Helen, and the two priests knew he had it. He was afraid the edges of the folds of the stiff paper could be seen outlined in the pocket of his jeans.

As they began their parade through the house with Father Hopkins uttering the same prayers as before, Danny had to keep touching his pocket every so often. He tried to be as inconspicuous as he could be, but he needed to keep touching it and make sure that it was really there.

He didn't need to take it out and read it again—thc words scrawled in red crayon were burned in his mind now:

HELP ME

CHAPTER THIRTY-ONE

After a late lunch, Danny, as usual, helped Helen with the dishes and helped her clean up the kitchen. He didn't want to do it, but he didn't want to seem suspicious. He kept glancing at Helen who was putting on an act of her own, making small talk, asking him about school. But Danny wasn't fooled. She was in on this, he was sure of it—both her and her husband. They were hiding their daughter in this house somewhere, pretending she didn't exist.

And Danny was going to find out why.

But he knew he needed Paul's help. And the first chance he got, he was going to talk to him about it.

†

Danny hurried upstairs after putting the last of the dishes away. He rushed down the hall and saw that the door to Paul's room was ajar. He rushed in and saw Paul sitting on the edge of his bed with his back facing the door. He had been rummaging around for something inside of his canvas duffel bag when Danny burst inside the room. Paul stuffed something down into the bag and zipped it shut. He nearly threw the bag into the closet and turned around to face Danny.

"Danny," Paul breathed out, looking surprised. "Do you know how to knock?"

"I'm sorry … the door was open."

Paul just stared at Danny. "Do you need something?"

"I need to talk to you about something," Danny said and glanced at the closet which Paul stood in front of like he was guarding it. "But if you're busy …"

"No. Please." Paul walked around the bed and gestured towards the door.

They walked across the hall to Danny's bedroom. After they were inside, Paul closed and locked the door with the skeleton key sticking out of the lock underneath the door handle.

"What's wrong?" Paul asked.

Danny paced over to the window. He glanced out through the glass, down at the snow. The footprints weren't there anymore. It bothered him for a second, but he wasn't going to let it get to him—he had physical evidence that the girl was real, and it was stuffed right down in the pocket of his jeans.

He looked back at Paul. "I saw the girl again." He continued quickly before Paul had a chance to interrupt him. "I know you're going to say that it was another one of my visions, but she was real. I know it now."

Paul said nothing. He stood very still near the foot of Danny's bed.

"When I was in the living room looking for my mom's necklace, I saw the girl hiding behind the drapes that cover all of those windows. I walked over to her slowly because I didn't want to scare her away. I asked what her name was. She told me it was Melissa. And then she handed me a note."

Danny clawed at his front pants pocket, and for a horrifying second he couldn't feel the slight bulge of the folded paper in his pocket. He stuffed his hand down and rammed his fingers against the thick paper. He pulled out the note and opened it, not too surprised that his fingers were trembling. He read the words scrawled on the paper in red crayon again just to prove to himself that they were still there.

HELP ME

He walked the five steps across the room and handed the note to Paul. He watched Paul's reaction as he read the note, but Paul gave nothing away.

Paul refolded the stiff paper and handed it back to Danny.

"See?" Danny said, trying to keep his voice low, but he couldn't help being a little excited. "She's real. She gave me this note. They're keeping her here like a prisoner in this house."

Paul walked past Danny over to the window like he needed a moment to think about this. He turned and looked at Danny.

"I've talked to Robert and Helen again," Paul said. "They swear they don't have a daughter. They swear they've never had a daughter or any other children."

"They're lying," Danny nearly shouted, and then his eyes flashed over to the bedroom door.

"Danny …" Paul said in a disappointed tone.

"What about the attic?" Danny had tried to go back up to the attic earlier to look for the necklace, but the door was locked again. "Have you been up there? Did you go up to the attic and take a look at the girl's bedroom furniture?"

"I asked Robert and Helen about it," Paul answered. "They told me that when they bought this house, the attic was already full of other people's possessions. It was like many families had lived here over the years and then had suddenly left their possessions behind. Almost like people had left the house in the middle of the night and only grabbed the things they could carry, the things that were most precious to them."

Danny took a breath and looked at Paul who still stood in front of the window. "I think we might be in danger here. I think there might be something wrong with Robert and Helen. Maybe even the two priests. I think this could be some kind of trap."

"Trap for what?" Paul asked. His voice was still reasonable, he was still patient with Danny.

"I don't know. But a lot of things don't make sense. Have you seen any signs of hauntings in this house besides my supposed visions of this little girl?"

Paul waited a moment, and then he shook his head slightly. "It may take some time for these demons to reveal themselves. I told you that before we came here."

"But you haven't experienced anything yet," Danny pressed.

Paul didn't answer. He didn't have to.

Danny was ready to reveal everything he had seen in this house now—no holding back now. "Why is the door to the basement locked? There's a big padlock on it."

Paul didn't answer.

"How come we never go up into the attic or down into the basement when we walk around this house, blessing it?"

Paul looked away, glancing out the window. It seemed like he might really be giving Danny's questions some thought. Or was that only Danny's imagination?

"And the remodeling of this house. How come every single room is in some stage of remodeling? I'm not an expert, I admit that, but wouldn't you start in one room or area at a time? And I don't see many tools or supplies. I see wallpaper torn down, floors ripped up, walls half-painted, wood trim in the middle of scraping and sanding, but not too many tools anywhere or new materials for the house like flooring, cans of paint, carpeting, or drywall. The garage is practically empty."

Paul didn't answer.

"Maybe the tools and supplies are in the basement," Danny said sarcastically.

"Danny, these are good questions," Paul said like a teacher talking to a slow child. "But you have to at least open yourself up to the possibility that the girl you've seen is not real."

Danny held up the note. "This is real."

Paul looked anguished for a moment, and Danny was sure Paul was going to wonder aloud if Danny couldn't have possibly written that note himself. But he didn't. It was a thought that had crossed Danny's own mind, a thought he had pushed away as soon as it had surfaced because he knew it wasn't true.

"You need to be careful," Paul told Danny. "There's also the possibility that a demon is taking the form of this little girl and visiting you."

Danny sighed. He could see that Paul wasn't going to believe him. And in a way he couldn't blame him since he had been seeing people who weren't there lately.

But this was different, Danny was sure of that. She had given him something tangible, a piece of paper that he still held in his hands.

He decided that he needed more proof. That was the only thing Paul was going to believe.

"I know this is frustrating," Paul said in a gentle voice as he approached him. "I know this is all new to you. And you're handling it well. Maybe you need some more rest."

Danny nodded in agreement. But he knew that rest was the last thing he needed right now. What he needed to do was to find that girl again.

CHAPTER THIRTY-TWO

Later in the afternoon, Danny set out exploring the house again—the rooms that were unlocked anyway. He brought his iPod with him, hoping to take a photo of the girl if he saw her again.

He crept downstairs and stood in the wide first floor hallway with the stairs, guest bathroom, and the padlocked door to the basement behind him and the front door of the house at the other end of the hallway.

He walked past the kitchen and saw Helen preparing dinner. He walked past the sitting room and saw that Father Severino and Robert were huddled together on a couch. They spoke to each other in whispers, talking quickly, their shoulders hunched. And then they glanced up at Danny as he passed. He saw the nervousness in their eyes, the suspicion. And then Danny was past the sitting room.

After grabbing his heavy coat from the front closet, he opened the front door and stepped out onto the front porch. He closed the front door and walked to the peeling wood railing. He needed some time by himself. He needed some time to think. He needed some fresh air after being cooped up in that old house for nearly three days now.

The cold air was a shock to his lungs, but after five or six breaths he was already used to it.

The front porch ran the length of the front of the house, and it looked out onto the front field and the stand of woods beyond it. The narrow trail they had driven through to get to this house cut right through the middle of the trees.

To Danny's right was the garage wall where it jutted out from the house like it had been added on at the last minute. But the vehicles were out of his view, parked on the other side of the garage where the big overhead door was.

There wasn't too much on the front porch: a few wooden chairs, a frozen welcome mat, and an untrustworthy, rickety porch swing that was chained to the ceiling closer to the garage wall.

Danny shuffled down the front steps to the snow, letting his shoes sink into the snow as he walked. He walked the length of the raised front porch, looking down at the lattice covering the space underneath it. He bent down and peered inside the lattice, but he only saw frozen dirt and darkness. Some of the snow was piled up almost to the floorboards on the far side of the porch.

He started feeling a little better just being outside. The air was cold, and for once the sky wasn't overcast—it was deep blue with hardly any clouds.

As he got closer to the garage wall, he heard voices.

Two people were talking—two men.

He had just seen Helen, Robert, and Father Severino inside the house, so he had to assume it was Paul and Father Hopkins outside by the garage door talking to each other.

And it seemed to be a heated discussion.

Maybe Paul was telling Father Hopkins about the girl Danny had been seeing.

Danny moved cautiously down the side of the garage until he was near the corner, as close as he dared to get. He could hear them clearly now.

"Does he know what's going on yet?" That was definitely Father Hopkins's voice.

"I don't think so," Paul answered. "Not yet."

"When are you going to let him know?"

"Soon. When it's the right time."

What the hell are they talking about?

"We can't wait too much longer," Father Hopkins snapped.

Paul didn't answer and there was a brief, tense silence, and then the sound of a sharp inhalation of cigarette smoke from Father Hopkins.

"What we're doing is incredibly dangerous," Father Hopkins growled. "The most dangerous thing. We're messing with things we shouldn't be messing with."

Paul said: "Remember the oath you took."

"We should get back inside," the priest told Paul, and then Danny heard their crunching footsteps in the snow as they walked away.

For a horrifying moment Danny thought they were walking his way and they were going to turn the corner of the garage and see him standing there, eavesdropping. But then he realized it was a trick of the sound bouncing off the snow and now the footsteps were definitely fading away.

Danny stood there in shock for a moment.

What had they been talking about? Were they talking about him?

Of course they were talking about him.

What was Paul supposed to tell him? And why was he keeping it a secret so far? Was it something they were keeping secret from Robert and Helen, or were they in on this too? Did all of this have something to do with Melissa, the girl he had seen in the house?

It must have something to do with her.

Danny's mind raced. He realized that he had been standing in the same spot next to the garage wall for at least four or five minutes now. The cold was beginning to seep into his bones and no matter how much he would rather stay outside where he felt safer, he knew he needed to get back inside where it was warmer.

He hurried back through the snow to the front porch steps. His legs were getting stiff from the cold but he climbed the steps quickly and clomped across the floorboards to the front door.

Just as he was about to grab the door handle, the front door swung open and Father Hopkins stood there in the doorway, dressed all in black, the white square on his collar practically gleaming in the sunlight. He seemed surprised to see Danny on the front porch, but he also seemed to have suspected it.

"Danny? What are you doing out here?"

"Just getting some fresh air."

Father Hopkins nodded like he understood that—just a slight nod of his head. "You coming inside now?"

"Yeah. Too cold out here."

For a moment Father Hopkins stared at Danny like he knew he had been eavesdropping on his and Paul's conversation.

Danny looked at the priest in a new light now. He was keeping secrets. And Paul was keeping secrets. Why? What was really going on here? Why were they really at this house?

He wanted to go find Paul and ask him these questions, but he didn't dare do that right now. He felt like he needed to wait, he needed to watch more, listen carefully, and find more clues. He needed more information. He needed to know who he could trust. Including his own father.

Danny kicked his shoes against the doorframe, knocking the snow off of them and then he entered the house. Father Hopkins closed and locked the door behind him.

"I'm gonna go upstairs and lay down," Danny said.

"Another headache?" Father Hopkins asked with suspicion in his voice. "Helen told me you had one yesterday."

Danny nodded. "Yeah. Not too bad, though."

Danny hurried down the hallway to the stairs. He climbed the steps and walked to his bedroom. He entered and closed the door. And for the second time since he had been staying in this house, he locked the door with the skeleton key and left it poking out of the lock.

He went to his bed and plopped down on it, stretching out. His mind still reeled, questions bouncing around in his mind over and over again.

Then he froze.

He heard a noise coming from his closet.

The door creaked open as a pale hand pushed at it from the inside.

There was someone inside his closet.

†

After Father Hopkins went back inside the house, Paul walked to his Bronco and popped the hood. He raised the hood and looked down at the engine for a moment. Then he went to the back of his Bronco and opened the hatch; he grabbed a small toolbox.

He went back to the engine and he used an adjustable wrench and a screwdriver to unhook the battery cables. And then he lifted the untethered battery out of the truck.

This was it. It was going to happen very soon now, he was sure of it, and they all needed to be ready. There was no turning back now. There would be no running away. They had made a commitment to this. They had made an oath, a pact, and they were going through with it no matter what happened.

Paul carried the battery to the garage. He walked to the far corner of the nearly empty garage and hid the battery on a cracked wooden pallet underneath an old tarp.

He walked back out to the sedan the priests had driven here in and he removed the battery from their car. And after he was finished with the sedan, he would take the battery out of the Dodge Durango that Robert and Helen owned.

†

After Paul was done removing the batteries, he went back inside. He stood inside the mudroom as snow dripped off of his black boots. His fingers were numb with cold and he stood there for a moment letting the heat from the house slowly bring him back to life.

Father Hopkins rushed up to Paul from the kitchen.

"I found Danny coming inside from the front porch about fifteen minutes ago."

Paul didn't say anything.

"He might have heard what we were talking about out there. He might have even seen you taking the batteries out of the vehicles."

Paul just nodded.

"We have to start this now," Father Hopkins said. "We can't wait any longer."

CHAPTER THIRTY-THREE

Danny was frozen with fear on his bed for a moment as he watched the closet door creak open. And then it stopped halfway, still hiding the person inside the closet.

But Danny wasn't ready to bolt out of his room just yet.

He had seen the pale hand on the door, pushing it open. He could tell that the hand was small—a child's hand.

It was the girl … it was Melissa. She had been hiding in his closet.

Waiting for him? Seeing if he had delivered her note, perhaps?

Danny jumped off the bed, careful not to make too much noise. He crept across the wood floor to the closet until he was in front of the open door, only six feet away.

"Melissa," he whispered.

She hadn't come out of the closet yet. The door was still halfway open. She dropped her hand down from the door handle and she stood in the darkness. But he could make out her ghostly white dress, her pale arms and legs, her black patent leather shoes and droopy socks. The dark blob of her head hung down, her scraggly hair hiding her face like she was looking down at her feet.

"It's okay," Danny whispered. "It's just me in the room."

She didn't move a muscle.

"I've got the bedroom door locked," he added. "No one can get in here. You're safe."

Melissa didn't seem convinced. She waited in the darkness of the closet. Danny's suitcase was beside her feet and a few of his clothes hung on hangers right beside her.

"My parents hate me," Melissa whispered.

"Robert and Helen?" Danny asked. He wanted to take a step closer, but he didn't want to frighten her.

It seemed like Melissa nodded yes to his question, but the movement was so slight he couldn't tell for sure.

"They keep me locked in the basement."

Danny had suspected that.

"They chain me to a wall sometimes," Melissa whispered, hesitating a moment before continuing, like what she had to say was too awful to be uttered. "Sometimes they strap me down to a wooden chair in the basement."

Danny realized that her voice sounded a little muffled. She still hadn't raised her head to look at him yet. He could see glimpses of her face underneath the scraggily hair—her face seemed pale like her skin, but it was different; it was rough and bumpy.

"They use brown leather cuffs and straps," Melissa whispered.

"Why do they do that?" he asked, trying to keep her talking. "Why do they hate you so much?"

It took a moment for Melissa to answer. "They're afraid of me. I can see things. Visions. Sometimes I just seem to know things. They say I'm possessed by a demon. They say that I need an exorcism."

Danny's heart skipped a beat. Was that why they were really here? To perform an exorcism on this poor little girl? Obviously Robert and Helen had been trying the exorcism on their own, that's why they kept her strapped to a chair in the basement, but now they needed expert help.

Like Paul's help.

No, he wasn't doing that. He refused to help Paul exorcise a demon out of this poor girl.

"I got out of the basement," Melissa whispered. "A few days ago. I've been hiding and they've been looking for me."

Danny thought about Robert and Helen's nervous smiles, their frightened eyes. He thought about the constant touring and blessing of the house. Were they really just looking for Melissa when they walked around, going from room to room looking for signs of where she might be hiding?

He thought of the footprints in the snow that he had seen this morning, small footprints—a little girl's footprints. Were they her footprints that she had made as she kept on the move, finding new hiding spots?

But then the footprints weren't there when he'd looked out the window again. But he didn't want to think about that. Maybe the snow had blown over the footprints. Or maybe someone had covered the footprints over with more snow. Who knew? It didn't matter now anyway. The girl was real—she was right here inside his room.

"I want to help you," Danny said. "Come out of the closet."

"You're in danger, too," Melissa hissed, and it seemed like something was partially covering her mouth when she spoke. That's why her voice sound a little muffled.

"Come on out here," Danny said. "Please, Melissa. Let me see your face."

She didn't move, but she raised her head slightly and Danny saw something rough and gray all over her face now.

"I can see things," she said. "Things I don't want to see. And I know you can see things, too."

Danny didn't answer that.

"The car accident," Melissa continued in a whisper. "The one that killed your mother and sister … it was no accident. They were murdered."

For a moment Danny's heart stopped and he couldn't draw a breath in.

Melissa stepped out of the shadows of the closet, pushing the door all the way open. Danny could see her better now. He saw the bruises and marks on the skin of her bare arms and legs. He saw the fading yellowish bruises around her wrists where cuffs had been cinched down tight.

And when she lifted her head up to look at him, he saw that her face was covered with old, gray bandages held in place with strips of faded adhesive tape. There were holes in the bandages for her eyes, the tip of her nose, and a line between the strips of cloth for her mouth. The bandages disappeared up into her hairline, and the dark hair cascading down both sides of her head to her shoulders hid the edges of the bandages at the sides of her face. The tape and bandages tucked down under her chin and a few went down her neck into her dress.

Danny felt sick to his stomach as he stood in front of her. What had these monsters done to her?

"I'm going to get help," Danny said, not really sure yet what he was going to do or who was going to help him. Paul? If he was in on this the whole time, then he wasn't going to help.

Melissa shook her head slightly. "You have to run. It's the only thing you can do. You can't let them get you. You can't let them take you down to the basement."

Danny felt helpless tears threatening.

Could that happen? Would they take him down to the basement? Would they think he was possessed? Was that the reason he was here?

Oh God, no.

"Go check your father's room," Melissa whispered.

"What?" Danny took a step back from the girl, shaking his head. His world felt off-kilter, like everything was sliding just a bit and he needed to hold on.

But he knew that he needed to help this girl, and he needed more information. He needed more proof.

What was in Paul's bedroom?

"His bag," Melissa whispered like she had read his mind. "It's in there."

"What's in there?"

"What you've been looking for."

Danny knew he needed to go and look.

"Wait here," he told Melissa. "I'm going to check his bedroom and then I'm coming right back for you. And then I'm going to get you out of here. Okay?"

Melissa shook her head no again, so slightly it hardly disturbed her hair or the bandages. "Don't worry about me. I'll just slow you down. Go and get help. Bring help back to me."

The idea made sense to Danny, but he couldn't leave her here. She didn't have any heavy clothes on, but he could give her one of his jackets, a pair of his sweat pants, a hat, and a pair of gloves. He could get the keys to Paul's Bronco and then come back and get Melissa. They could get down to the truck and drive away. He wasn't an expert driver yet—he only had his learner's permit from Ohio—but he had driven his mom's car enough that he was sure he could drive Paul's Bronco to the nearest town and get some help.

Taking Melissa with him might slow him down—but he wouldn't leave her here with these people.

What would they do if they caught her again? Would they drag her down to the chair in the basement and strap her to it? Would they do worse things this time?

What would they do to him if they caught him trying to help her escape? Would he finally see what was locked behind the basement door?

Paul and Father Hopkins's words that he had overheard earlier by the garage echoed in his mind. *Does he know anything yet? Does he have any idea what's going on here? What we're doing here is dangerous. The most dangerous thing.*

"Wait here," Danny told Melissa. "Please. Just stay right here while I'm gone."

Melissa didn't say anything, and he took that as a sign of confirmation.

He turned and hurried to the bedroom door and unlocked it with the skeleton key that he had left sticking out of the lock. He slipped the key into his pants pocket in case he might need it to open Paul's door. He wasn't sure if one skeleton key opened all similar locks, but he would have one with him if he needed it.

He glanced back at Melissa one last time before he left.

She stood in the same spot, watching him through the ragged eyeholes in the dirty bandages. His stomach dropped and his heart ached. He felt more flashes of anger building up inside of him. She was only a nine or ten year old girl. Who could do something like this to a little girl?

Danny slipped out into the hall after looking both ways and listened for a moment. He didn't hear anyone coming up the stairs. He didn't hear any voices or noises up here or downstairs. He didn't hear anything at all—the house was totally silent.

He crept down the hall towards the attic, and he stopped in front of Paul's bedroom door across the hall. He inhaled a deep breath and let it out slowly, realizing he was breathing quickly and trembling. He needed to get his nerves under control. He *had* to do this.

After another quick glance around, he knocked lightly on Paul's door.

Then he waited, counting down from twenty in his mind. He could imagine Paul opening the door, looming there in his dark clothing, his muscles bulging underneath the fabric, his dark eyes pinning Danny there in the doorway.

What would he tell Paul he wanted? Would he bring Paul to his bedroom and show him Melissa, show him proof of what Helen and Robert had been doing? But what if Paul already knew and he was in on this?

But then Danny thought that if Paul knew that they had come to perform an exorcism on Melissa and not the house itself, then why wouldn't he have told him? Why would he have kept that a secret? Maybe Paul didn't think he was really ready for an exorcism yet.

But even if that was true, then maybe Paul didn't know or realize yet the conditions that Robert and Helen had been keeping their daughter in. Maybe Paul was still innocent to some degree here.

At least Danny hoped so.

He knocked again, a little louder, and made himself wait another ten seconds, ticking off each second in his mind. It seemed to be stretching out forever.

Danny gripped the old-fashioned, cut-glass door handle and turned.

The door was unlocked. He wouldn't need the skeleton key in his pocket after all.

He pushed the door open, praying that it wouldn't creak or let out a squeal in the silence.

It didn't.

He ducked inside the room and pushed the door almost all the way shut behind him.

"Paul," he whispered even though he could clearly see that his father wasn't in the bedroom.

This bedroom was much like the bedroom he had been using, almost the same size, one window, one door to a small walk-in closet. There was a bed with a crucifix over the headboard, an end table next to the bed with a lamp on it, a dresser against the wall with an extra wood chair beside it. No TV or radio—just like his room, like there was no outside contact allowed with the world in this house. Either these rooms hadn't been remodeled yet or this was the way Robert and Helen wanted them.

The bed was neatly-made of course, just like Paul made his own bed at home.

Danny didn't see any of Paul's personal items on the end table next to the bed or on top of the dresser. He didn't see a wallet, money, a comb, or more importantly the keys to his Bronco.

His heart sank a little. Paul must have the keys on him.

Of course he does.

Getting out of here might not be as easy as he thought. But he wasn't going to give up.

Melissa had told him to check his father's canvas bag. He didn't know how she knew about his bag, but she did. There was something in there that she wanted him to see.

Danny glanced back at the bedroom door and then he hurried over to the closet. He opened the door and saw Paul's long dark coat hanging from the rod along with a few dark pairs of pants and sweaters. His hat was on the top shelf by itself. On the floor was the small suitcase Paul had carried his clothes in and it sat right next to the dark canvas bag. There was nothing else inside the closet.

He grabbed the bag and pulled it, dragging it until it was completely out of the closet. His heart thundered in his chest as he unzipped the bag. His mouth was going dry and it felt like he had tunnel vision, everything in his peripheral vision was going dark around the edges.

Danny had asked Paul about the canvas bag before and Paul had told him that it was the bag he took with him to exorcisms and hauntings. He told Danny what he kept inside the bag and when Danny unzipped the bag he saw the items Paul had told him about: metal containers with screw-on lids that contained salt and iron fillings; an old bible and prayer book handed down to him from his father; several crucifixes, some of them big and heavy and made of silver; a copper chafing dish that had scorch marks in it where something had been burned; one of the small wood boxes that Paul made in his garage woodshop. The box was painted black and had those strange symbols carved into it. Paul had told him before what the symbols meant—*The names of God.*

But there were other things inside the canvas bag that Paul had not told him about. Leather straps and cuffs with buckles. They seemed like the ones Melissa had described, the ones used to strap her down to the chair in the basement. And there were lengths of rope connected to these cuffs and straps.

Why were they in his bag? Who was Paul going to use these on?

Was that what Melissa had wanted him to see?

He was about to zip the bag back up, but a winking of light from a dark corner of the bag caught his eye. He dug down deeper, pushing items out of the way.

And then he saw it. He picked it up carefully with two fingers and held it up in front of him. He felt his breath leave him for a moment. It was his mom's necklace with his sister's charms on it. The one that had been taken from his shoebox, the one he had been looking for; the one Paul had seemed so concerned about and helped Danny look for. Paul had the necklace with him the whole time.

CHAPTER THIRTY-FOUR

Danny shoved the necklace down into the front pocket of his jeans where the skeleton key was.

His mind reeled and he felt a little dizzy.

Paul had stolen the necklace.

His own father. Why? And then he had lied about where it was the whole time.

Danny zipped the canvas bag back up and shoved it into the closet.

He was sure that the necklace was what Melissa had wanted him to find, proof that his father was not on his side here, not to be trusted. But Danny still needed to find something else—the keys to the Bronco.

He took the suitcase out of the closet and laid it down flat on the floor. It felt heavy like Paul still had a lot of clothes in there. He opened it and saw neatly packed clothes, mostly black or dark blue. But the object on top of the clothes stopped him in his tracks. It was a large manila envelope just like the one Paul had handed to Father McFadden at St. Mathews that contained his report. Except this envelope didn't have a wax seal and the family crest sealing it shut. This one wasn't sealed at all.

Danny turned the envelope over and read the two words written in Father McFadden's scrawling handwriting: *Paul Lambert.*

It was the same manila envelope that Father McFadden had given Paul before they left Boston to come to this house.

The same envelope that Danny had asked Paul to see. The same envelope that Paul refused to let him see.

With shaking fingers, Danny pried the envelope apart and pulled out a few sheets of crisp paper and some color and black and white photographs. The photos were big and glossy. Some were a little grainy and out of focus, but Danny could see what was going on. These were photos of the accident that had killed his mother and his sister.

It was no accident … Melissa's words echoed in his mind.

In one of the photos, Danny saw himself sitting in the back of the squad car, the door wide open, his legs drawn up to him, his head down. Officer Booker talked to him as the paramedics waited in the background, keeping a watchful eye on him.

Another photo showed his mother's car being pulled up out of the water by a tow truck, police lights shining on the scene. A diver was still in the water, several feet away from the car, watching and signaling to the tow truck driver. Water poured out of the car, out of the doors, the windows, the trunk.

Danny couldn't hold back the tears as he saw the metal tomb his mom and sister had died inside of.

And for a brief moment, he saw a flash of memory from that night. It was something so fleeting yet so profound, a key to everything.

But then it was gone as quickly as it had come, and he couldn't get it back.

There was something very important about that night that he had forgotten; there was something he didn't *want* to remember. But what was it?

The other papers looked like copies of an official police report. How did Father McFadden have these? How had he gotten them from the police? Did the police give these out to family members if they asked for them? Had Father McFadden gotten them for Paul? Did the Church have friends inside the police? How deep did this whole thing go?

And another thought occurred to Danny; Paul had told him that the contents of this envelope contained instructions to the haunting of this house, their assignment. But that wasn't true. The only thing this envelope contained was the accident report and the photos from it.

Paul had lied to him.

Danny was wasting too much time—he could ponder these questions later. Right now he needed to hurry. He needed to get Melissa and himself out of this house.

But he still hadn't found the keys to the Bronco yet, and he was getting more and more certain that Paul must have them on him shoved down in one of his pants pockets. He would need to think of a way to get them away from Paul.

He slid the photos and accident report back into the manila folder and laid it back down on the clothes. He shut and latched the suitcase and shoved it back into the closet. He was about to shut the closet door when the dark coat caught his attention.

It was the same coat Paul had worn when they drove here.

Maybe the keys were still in the pockets.

He checked the pockets and found a set of keys. He pulled them out and held them in his hand, hardly able to believe that he had found them.

All he needed to do now was get Melissa dressed in warmer clothes, get her downstairs somehow without being seen, and get her out to the Bronco. And then they would be home free. Maybe he should grab a kitchen knife and slash the tires of the other two vehicles before he left, slow them down a little so they couldn't follow him.

He would decide that when he got down to the kitchen.

Danny slid the keys down into his other front pocket and shut the closet door. He hurried across the room to the bedroom door, still as silent as a cat burglar.

He inched the bedroom door open and peeked out into the hallway, glancing in both directions several times.

No one was in the hallway and there were still no voices from downstairs. No sounds from anywhere. It was eerily quiet, like they were all hiding in the shadows and waiting for him.

He left Paul's room and closed the door as quietly as he could. He darted across the hall to his bedroom and slipped inside.

Melissa wasn't in the room. He ran over to the closet and opened the door all the way, but she wasn't in there. He checked under the bed—no Melissa. He checked the window, but it was still locked.

He should've locked the door when he'd left the room, and he cussed himself for that mistake. Now she was gone, tucked away in one of her shadowy hiding spots again, and he would waste too much time trying to find her. But that was the way she wanted it—he supposed that she thought she would just slow him down. He was sure she wanted him to go without her and bring back help.

And that's what he would do.

He thought about slipping a coat on over his sweater, but he was afraid it would make too much of a rustling noise as he snuck through the house out to the Bronco. And if they saw him with the coat on, they might question him about it.

Of course he could say that he was going outside for some fresh air.

But then Father Hopkins might say that Danny had just been outside not even an hour ago.

Danny shook his head, realizing he was paralyzing himself with possible scenarios. He needed to move, and whatever happened was just going to have to happen. He was going to have to wing it. He grabbed his wool hat and shoved it on his head. He grabbed a pair of gloves and stuffed them down into the back pocket of his jeans.

If they saw him downstairs, he would just have to act naturally, try to pretend that he hadn't just had a conversation with a girl who had escaped from the basement, a girl with bandages on her face covering God knew what kind of wounds.

Hopefully Paul was still ignorant of the atrocities that had gone on here, but Danny now knew that he must have something to do with all of this. Paul had stolen his mother's necklace from him and he had a copy of the accident report in his suitcase. No, he couldn't risk confiding in Paul right now. He just needed to get out of here, get some help, and then he could sort it out with Paul later. He had tried to talk to Paul several times already and he had gotten nowhere. He couldn't waste any more time with that.

Danny took a deep breath and then left his bedroom. He hated leaving the shoebox full of photos and memories behind under his bed, but he couldn't take them with him right now. At least he had the necklace.

He would be back with the cops, and then he could get his shoebox back.

He left the bedroom and walked towards the steps that led downstairs. He had decided not to creep around, afraid that he would draw more attention to himself if he did. Father Hopkins and the others still believed that he didn't know anything about what was going on here, so as long as he acted naturally they shouldn't think he was trying to escape.

Danny shuffled down the steps to the first floor hallway, his heart thudding in his chest from all of the noise he was making.

Nobody in the hallway.

He paused for a moment, listening. He still couldn't hear any voices or movement in the house. He walked to the sitting room, but no one was in there. He checked the formal dining room across the hall. It was empty.

Danny hurried down the hall to the archway that led into the kitchen. Surely someone would be in there. At least Miss Helen—she was like a permanent fixture in the kitchen these days, always preparing something or cleaning something or putting something away.

But the kitchen was empty. No food preparations on the counters, nothing laid out for dinner.

The house was still so eerily silent.

Danny could see into the mudroom, and no one was in there, either.

Where were they?

His heart skipped a beat. Were they outside waiting for him? Were they already aware of what he was doing? One step ahead of him?

Danny didn't take time to think about that, he forced his legs forward and practically jogged to the door that led outside to the parking area in front of the garage.

The vehicles sat in the same spots in the snow. The cold hit him right away as he shut the door to the mudroom and shuffled down the steps. He wanted to put his gloves on, but he decided not to because he wanted to be able to feel the keys with his fingers.

The sky was still deep blue with a few wispy clouds high up in the sky. It seemed even colder now than when it had been snowing yesterday.

There was no one out here anywhere.

He couldn't believe his luck.

Maybe they were having a meeting somewhere inside the house.

Maybe down in the basement.

Oh God, maybe they had found Melissa and they had taken her back down to the basement.

Maybe he should go and check the door to the basement, see if the padlock was still in place.

He was torn for a moment—so close to getting away, yet wanting to make sure Melissa was safe.

But he couldn't risk it. If they had Melissa, then they could get him too. He needed to get away and get help for Melissa. That needed to be his priority no matter how guilty he might feel.

Danny forced himself not to think about it anymore. He walked through the snow to the Bronco. He got to the driver's door and looked around before he opened it. No one was at the kitchen window or at the door to the mudroom, watching him through the glass. No one was at the side door of the garage.

He couldn't believe it. He was going to make it.

He thought of the kitchen knife and wished he had grabbed one to puncture the tires of the sedan and the Durango. But it was too late to go back now, and he wasn't even sure if he would be able to stab through the frozen rubber of the tires anyway.

The driver's door was unlocked. He yanked it open and hopped inside the truck. He pulled the door almost all the way shut, not wanting to slam it closed and have the sound echo across the quiet fields that stretched way off to the trees. He stuck the key into the ignition and it slid in smoothly. He turned the key, expecting to hear the roar of the motor firing up.

But there was nothing.

He turned the key again and again.

Still nothing.

Was the battery dead? There wasn't even a ticking sound. No lights lit up on the dashboard when he turned the key.

Danny looked out the windshield and saw Paul standing in the open doorway of the mudroom that led back inside the house. The same doorway Danny had just come out of only minutes ago.

His heart skipped a beat as he watched Paul casually shuffle down the concrete steps and step down into the snow-covered parking area. He started walking right towards the Bronco.

Paul didn't seem angry—if anything, he seemed confused.

Danny took out the keys and shoved them into his pocket.

Paul was closer to the truck now, close enough that Danny could hear his voice clearly. "What are you doing, Danny?"

CHAPTER THIRTY-FIVE

Danny tried to think of a lie as Paul stood in the snow only ten feet away from the truck.

"I … I … just wanted to sit in your truck."

Paul stared at him for a long moment, standing very still in the snow, his breath barely pluming in front of his face. "I know you might be getting a little bored here, but you have to stay focused. We still have a lot of work to do in this house."

Yeah, what kind of work is that?

Danny swallowed hard.

"Come on," Paul said and gestured with a nod of his head back at the house behind him. "Let's get back inside. The others are waiting for us."

"Why?" Danny croaked out. He wanted to stay inside the Bronco. And for a moment he couldn't make his legs work. He felt like if he got out of this truck he might be about to willingly walk to his own execution.

"I told you," Paul said. "We have some work to do. They're all waiting for us."

Danny got out of the truck and stood up on numb legs.

Paul turned and began to walk back to the house like he expected Danny to follow him.

And Danny did. He could've started running. But where? There was nothing but square miles of open fields and the winter woods in every direction. How far would he get before Paul (or some of the others) ran him down in the snow and dragged him back to the house. To the basement.

Paul walked up the steps to the door of the mudroom.

As Danny followed Paul, he wondered if he should tell Paul about Melissa, tell him that she had told him to look in his room, in his bag. Maybe he should question Paul about the necklace he had stolen from him. Question him about the police report and photos in his suitcase.

Paul opened the door to the mudroom.

Danny stopped in the snow, right in front of the concrete steps.

Paul turned around in the doorway and stared down at Danny. He still didn't look angry, there didn't seem to be any kind of emotion on his face. He was giving nothing away.

"Paul."

Paul waited in the doorway, frozen there for a moment.

"I saw Melissa again."

Paul didn't respond.

"She was in my room. She was hiding from Robert and Helen. They've been keeping her in the basement, strapped down to a chair. There are these … these kind of bandages all over her face."

"Danny … you're seeing visions again …"

"She's not a vision!" Danny yelled at Paul, surprising himself from his outburst.

Paul glanced into the house like he was seeing if anyone else was close by and listening. And for just a moment Danny saw a strange expression on Paul's face. Was it a moment of doubt? Was Paul possibly beginning to believe Danny's story, maybe just a little?

Danny realized that this could be his only chance. He wasn't going to be able to get away from this house without Paul's help—he was certain of that now.

Paul walked through doorway into the mudroom. He turned and went into the kitchen without a word or a glance back at Danny.

Danny rushed up the steps and followed Paul into the mudroom. He slammed the door shut on the cold air, and he didn't even bother kicking the snow off of his sneakers or wiping them on the mat.

Paul was already inside the kitchen, walking across the floor to the archway at the other side of the room that led out to the hallway.

Danny wanted to call out to Paul, he wanted to beg him to stop walking and just listen to him for a minute. He wanted to call him Dad, but for some reason he couldn't even seem to utter the word, like his throat froze up every time he tried to say that word.

Instead, he croaked out the word: "Paul!" He shouted it louder than he had meant to.

Paul stopped in the kitchen, only steps away from the archway that led out to the hallway. Little by little, he seemed to be leading Danny deeper into the house.

Danny didn't see anyone in the hallway beyond Paul. Where was everyone else? In the basement?

This is your last chance to run, Danny told himself. *They want to strap you down to the chair in the basement, the one that's probably bolted to the floor. They want to hurt you.*

Danny tried to push the voice away, but it didn't even sound like his own voice in his mind anymore.

It sounded like Melissa's voice for a moment in his mind, Melissa's voice whispering to him. But then it seemed to be more than just her voice. It was a cacophony of voices, a collection of whispers that buzzed in his mind like tiny insects, and the voices no longer formed intelligible words or sentences anymore, just white noise now.

"Paul, wait!" Danny yelled. "Just ... just wait a minute."

Paul waited near the archway.

Danny stumbled farther into the kitchen, and then he leaned against the counter. He suddenly felt weak and he needed the support to help hold himself up. The noise in his mind sounded like static from a radio between the stations. But in that static, he could still hear voices whispering to him and it was getting harder and harder to think.

"I want to know what's going on here," Danny demanded, his voice growing louder as he fought to hear himself over the white noise in his mind. "What's really going on here?"

"I think you're beginning to see what it is," Paul said in a calm and even tone. His face was grim, his mouth a slit. But there was compassion in his dark eyes and those eyes were just beginning to glisten with tears.

"They're keeping that girl down in the basement," Danny said. "They think she's possessed. They've been trying to exorcise this supposed demon from her, but they've been torturing her! Cutting pieces of her face off! Piece by piece!"

Paul shook his head no with a sad look in his eyes. "There is no Melissa, Danny. You have to see that by now."

"We have to run ..." Again, Danny tried to say the word Dad, but he couldn't form the word. "Paul ... we have to get out of here before it's too late."

"No, we're not running," Paul answered. "It's time to face the truth now."

Danny felt a sudden surge of strength, and he wasn't sure where it had come from. He pushed down on the edge of the countertop and snapped a small section off in his hands like it had been Styrofoam. He let the pieces drop down to the linoleum floor and looked at his hands like he couldn't believe he'd actually just done that. There was an energy coursing through his body that he could barely control, that he could barely stand. He spun towards the wood block of kitchen knives on the counter. He plucked the biggest knife out and turned back to Paul, gripping the handle of the knife, pointing the blade at him.

"I saw the necklace in your bag!" Danny shouted.

Paul didn't say anything.

"I've got it in my pants pocket!" Danny pulled out the keys to the Bronco and threw them on the busted countertop. Then he pulled out his mother's necklace that was intertwined around the skeleton key now.

"You stole it from me!" Danny shouted, and his voice sounded so much deeper to his own ears. "I saw the accident report in your suitcase! I saw the photos of my mom's car!"

"Yes," Paul said. "I had to leave them there for you to find. I had to make you see things on your own. You've been resisting so hard … I had to make you *see*."

Paul walked out of the kitchen and into the hallway, out of Danny's view.

"Don't walk away from me!" Danny roared and raced after Paul. "Don't walk away from me, Paul Lambert!"

Danny ran out into the wide hallway and saw Paul a few feet away, closer to the front door. But then Danny heard a noise from behind him, from down the hall where the stairs went up to the second floor, and where the door to the basement was.

Turning towards the stairs, Danny saw Melissa standing down the hall near the foot of the steps. She was only twenty feet away from him. She still wore the same dirty white dress and droopy socks and scuffed black shoes. Her pale arms and legs still showed bruises. And the gray and grimy bandages still covered her face underneath her long scraggily hair.

"See?" Danny said, his face flushing, tears stinging his eyes. He looked back at Paul. "See? She's real. There she is."

"No," Paul said. "That's a demon disguised as a person. They want you to run from this house. They're trying to convince you to run. They want to trick you. They don't want you to see the truth."

For a moment Danny's world seemed to stop and he saw everything in a brief moment of clarity.

The night of the accident came back to him in a sudden moment of vivid memory.

Oh God, how could he have forgotten this?

"You back away, you unclean and foul spirit!!" Paul roared at Melissa as he took a step closer to Danny. He had pulled out his silver crucifix from underneath the neck of his black sweater and he held it in front of him. His face was a mask of rage, his eyes burning dark embers of fury. "In the name of Jesus Christ, I command you to leave this boy alone!!"

"No," Danny said weakly, still trying to cling to the belief. "No, Paul. It's only … it's only Melissa."

"It's not Melissa," Paul said, taking another step closer to Danny. "It's a demon disguised to look like your sister."

"My … my sister?"

"Lisa," Paul said, and a tear slipped from his eye.

Danny looked back at the girl and saw her in a new light now.

"When she was a baby," Paul continued, "and you were only three years old, you used to call her your Lisa. You would say, 'My Lisa,' but it would come out as Melissa."

"No …" Danny breathed out. This wasn't right. He was trying to concentrate, but the whispering voices and chirping of insects was louder in his mind now. The white noise of static was becoming deafening.

He looked back at Melissa who was peeling the dirty bandages away from her face. The bandages fell away in one large piece like a paper mask and it landed on the floor with the crackling sound of a dry husk of corn.

Or the husk of an insect.

Underneath the bandages was the face of his sister Lisa, blue and bloated. It was the face of a drowned girl. And then the bloated dead thing smiled with dark blue lips. The smile was a twisted half-smile and her eyes turned as black as two chunks of coal.

Then the entire apparition turned to murky water and collapsed down onto the floor in a puddle of dark water.

Danny turned back to Paul who was crying now and shaking his head no.

"Dad …" Danny said, suddenly able to say the word, suddenly able to remember everything.

"Son," Paul said and took another step closer.

"I remember now, Dad. I remember that night. I remember what I did. I … I killed them."

PART FOUR

CHAPTER THIRTY-SIX

Danny was suddenly in his mother's car that night. His mother drove down the dark road, the marshy lake laid out before them at the bottom of the hill where the road made a sharp curve. The reflectors on the guardrail shined back at them, bouncing the car's headlights back to them.

There were some bags packed. They were in the trunk. There had been some arguing before they left. Rachael told them that they needed to leave town for a few weeks. Danny and Lisa didn't want to go, and he remembered that his mother wasn't giving them a very good explanation about why they were leaving.

They were still arguing as they drove.

As they headed down the decline towards the lake, Danny saw the blond-haired man standing on the side of the road—the same man he'd seen on the way home from school, the same man who had tried to break into the basement door.

What was he doing out here in the middle of nowhere?

He stood at the side of the road, close to where the trees began, his feet invisible among the weeds and grasses.

The man just watched them as they approached, smiling that twisted smile of his.

And then the man raised his arms like he was gripping his own invisible steering wheel, and then he yanked it suddenly.

Danny saw himself trying to grab the steering wheel his mother was suddenly fighting to control.

"The steering wheel!" she screamed. "It's locked! I can't move it!"

Danny tried to help her move the steering wheel.

Or did he? Was that how it really happened? Or was he the one holding onto the steering wheel, keeping their car straight as they raced towards the guardrail.

Screams from the backseat. Lisa, screaming.

There was the sound of the car crashing through the guardrail, the impact, the screeching of metal.

The crash of the airbags.

Then the rush of water.

The darkness.

The cold.

Mom struggling for air, fighting with her seatbelt, gulping in mouthfuls of water, gurgling and screaming. Lisa was knocked out from the crash, already unconscious and inhaling water.

Danny held his breath, fumbling with his seatbelt.

He had to get free …

†

Danny was back in the hallway again. He stared at Paul through his tears. "I killed them."

"No," Paul said. He had to get his son to see the truth. "The demons killed them. They got inside of you. They did it, not you."

"I have a … a demon inside of me?"

"You're possessed," Paul said. "It's called perfect possession. It's when a demon has buried itself so deeply inside of you that you don't even know it's there. It messes with your mind, tries to convince you that you see things. It lies to you. Tries to confuse you."

Paul saw Robert, Helen, and both priests coming out of the sitting room. They were watching. They were waiting.

"Put the knife down," Paul said in a gentle voice. "Please, Danny."

Danny looked down at the knife like he just realized he still had it in his hand.

"Danny," Paul said again, and took a step closer. "We don't have a lot of time. You need to come with us. We need to exorcise the demons from you while you're still able to help us."

Danny just stood there.

"Danny, please. We don't have much time. I need your help, son. I need you to fight your way back. You can do this."

Danny nodded and dropped the knife on the floor. "I want them out," he whispered.

Paul glanced back at the others and they hurried past Paul and escorted Danny towards the stairs, all of them cautious and nervous with Danny, constantly whispering reassurances to him the whole time, praying with him—praying *for* him.

As they walked Danny past the foot of the stairs towards the door in the panel that led down to the basement, Paul hurried up the stairs to his room.

He was going to need his canvas bag now.

†

Danny allowed himself to be led to the basement door. He watched as Father Hopkins unlocked the padlock. He entered the darkness of the basement and walked carefully down the steps.

He drifted off into blackness for a moment, escaping into a cocoon of safety from this madness, from the unbelievable reality he was living right now.

He came to his senses once his wrists were strapped down to the flat arms of the wooden chair that was bolted to the concrete floor in the basement. The leather cuffs were attached to the arms of the chair; they were thick and they were buckled around his wrists. He tried to move his arms, but he could only move them an inch or two up from the arm of the chair. His bonds were too strong to break. He was helpless now. He was their prisoner.

They're going to do the same thing to you that they did to Melissa, a voice whispered at him, like someone was standing right behind him in his mind.

Danny felt panic building up inside of him, and he struggled a little harder.

You let them strap you down, and now they're going to cut little pieces of your face off until you tell them that your demons are gone. They're going to wrap your face in old dirty bandages while your wounds fester and rot. They're going to keep you down here until you die in this chair!

Down at Danny's feet, both priests worked frantically to buckle the cuffs to his ankles and strap them to the legs of the chair.

Father Severino, who was in front of Danny's right leg, let out a scream. He toppled backwards and jumped to his feet. He stared down at his hands as smoke drifted up from his fingertips where blisters had suddenly formed.

"Holy water!" Father Hopkins called out. "Quickly!"

Robert dashed out from the darkness of the basement into their circle of light with a glass bottle in his hand. He sprinkled the blessed water on Father Severino's fingers.

Father Hopkins crouched down at Danny's right foot and he pulled on the straps, grunting with effort, pinning Danny's leg to the chair. Danny tried to extend his leg, but it was too late. Father Hopkins had his leg secured already.

And then the old priest scrambled away from the chair and got up to his feet.

"What's going on?" Danny tried to say, but his mouth was too dry. It felt like he had swallowed a quart of beach sand. His tongue felt swollen and rough.

Nobody answered him.

"No, I'm not possessed," Danny said, but his own voice sounded so far away from his ears.

They're going to slice off pieces of your face, Danneeee!

No! Melissa's not real. She was never real. I saw my sister's face under those bandages.

Lisa. Melissa. Lisa. Melissa. LisaMelissaLisaMelissa…

Danny had to fight, he knew that, but it felt like some unimaginably strong force was trying to push his mind down into the darkness. He could feel himself shrinking back, further and further away from his body.

I saw Melissa turn to water, Danny wanted to scream, but he couldn't find his voice anymore. He couldn't make it work now.

And then he felt himself being pulled away into the darkness again, and now he couldn't stop it. He was so tired now. He didn't want to fight anymore.

Before he was lost in the darkness, Danny heard his own voice giggling. He could hear words coming from his own mouth, but they weren't *his* words, and his voice didn't sound like *his* voice anymore.

He slipped away …

†

"We're losing him," Father Hopkins said as he watched Danny. He held a crucifix in his hand and kept his distance even though Danny was securely strapped down to the chair.

"You think that crucifix, that worthless piece of metal, is going to do anything to me?" Danny growled at Father Hopkins.

The priest didn't answer; he knew better than to converse with a demon—it was a never-win situation. Instead, he prayed.

"That trinket?" Danny continued taunting the priest in a guttural voice. "You think that trinket is going to do anything to me?"

Danny didn't thrash in the chair. He didn't test his bonds. He just sat very still like a powerful animal watching and biding his time, waiting for the perfect time to strike, waiting for everyone's guard to be down.

"Your faith must be strong for that trinket to work," Danny growled and then he chuckled. A plume of mist drifted out of Danny's mouth as the chilly basement grew even colder.

Father Hopkins continued praying. He whispered the same prayers over and over again in Latin. He knew his faith had to be strong, and it was. But he could feel doubts trying to creep their way into his mind. He wasn't sure if he was prepared for what was coming and he hoped his faith wouldn't falter.

Father Severino's faith hadn't been strong enough—that's why his flesh had burned when he had touched Danny's ankle. It was a quick and brutal lesson to all of them. Their faith must be strong because none of them, except for Paul, had seen anything like this before. Of course they were all experienced in the ritual of exorcisms—that's what this house was for. But they had never seen a perfect possession before. And they had never dealt with a demon this strong before.

†

Paul was on his knees in a corner of the basement, praying, preparing himself for the exorcism.

The basement was vast, the size of the floor plan of the whole downstairs of the house. And this basement was dug down deeper into the earth than most basements—the ceiling was nearly ten feet high. Little slits of windows were set high in the block walls, but all of the windows were blacked out with paint and plastic.

The center of the basement was a wide open space, the size of a large living room. And that's where the chair Danny sat on was bolted to the floor. Twenty feet in front of Danny's chair was a small table. Collected on the table were two burning candles set in fancy candlesticks. Between the two candles were ancient bibles and prayer books, their leather covers cracked with age. There were also bottles of holy water, crucifixes, rosary beads, a small statue of the Virgin Mary and Christ on the cross.

And next to the table on the floor was Paul's canvas bag—a mixture of the holy and the pagan. But all of it worked, Paul knew that. And none of it worked. Both at the same time. The faith in God was the key.

God drove demons out of people—not man.

The perimeter of the basement was taken up with more storage: boxes, crates, bags, machines, all of this stuff stored here by churches in a hundred mile radius. The edges of the basement lay in shadows, the only light came from light bulbs overhead and the burning candles on the table in front of Danny.

It was in these shadows that Paul kneeled and prayed and prepared himself.

He got to his feet, suddenly determined. He needed to be focused, his faith strong. He could not fail tonight. He had to exorcise this demon from his son's body, and he had to free his son's soul.

He felt terrible bringing Danny to this house. He felt terrible tricking him into believing he had been in training, that he was on his first assignment. But Paul needed to resort to tricks to fool the demon that was imbedded inside of Danny. It was a taste of the demon's own medicine.

But he still needed Danny's help with this exorcism. He needed Danny to be strong and fight his way back. He needed Danny to fight for his soul.

And the only way Danny could do that was if he understood what had happened, that he understood he was perfectly possessed, that many of his memories and visions were lies told to him by the foul spirit that embodied him.

Perfect possession was very rare. A person who was possessed so deeply could go about their daily lives and seem normal to everyone around them while the demons waited in hiding, waiting for the right time to strike. A perfectly possessed person could touch religious objects. They could take communion. They could speak the Lord's name.

All of this is my fault, Paul thought. *These demons attacked Danny and killed Lisa and Rachael just to get to me. And now he realized that they'd done it to get to Danny.*

He should have been there for them. He should have protected them.

Tears slipped from Paul's eyes and he let them come. He clenched his fists and his body shook with both sadness and rage. He needed to cry. He needed to grieve for Lisa and Rachael. But he couldn't grieve for Danny yet. Danny wasn't gone yet and Paul was going to do everything he could to bring his son back.

The first thing Paul needed to do was push his grief and sadness for Lisa and Rachael away. He needed to push all of the guilt out of his mind because the demon would use that against him. There would be plenty of time for grieving later.

If there was a later.

The second thing Paul needed to do was expunge from his mind any doubts. He could not lose this fight for his son. He would die trying if he needed to.

Paul took a deep breath and exhaled slowly. He wiped at his tears with his hands, and his face was set in stone again.

He looked up to the basement ceiling of exposed floor joists, wiring, plumbing, and duct work.

"Lord God, Father. Please give me the strength I need to help my son. Please, I beg of You, help me drive this wretched demon out of his body and send it back to Hell where it belongs. Help me end my son's torment, and free his body, mind, and soul. Help me be strong, the strongest I've ever been. Help me to be brave, the bravest I've ever been. Help me to be pure, the purist I've ever been. God, I ask this of You in the name of Jesus Christ Our Savior."

Paul crossed himself slowly.

"Amen."

He walked out of the shadows and into the sphere of light created from the bare light bulbs hanging from the floor joists over Danny's chair and the two burning candles on the table where Robert, Helen, and the two priests were gathered.

He was ready to begin.

CHAPTER THIRTY-SEVEN

"Is the door locked?" Paul asked as he walked out of the darkness of the basement and into the light.

"Yes," Father Hopkins answered. He waited near the table along with Robert, Helen, and Father Severino who cradled his injured right hand in his left. The four of them stood very still, their eyes on Paul as he approached.

"Keys," Paul said and held out his hand to Father Hopkins.

Paul was dressed all in black: black boots, black pants, and a long-sleeved black shirt, and he seemed to have emerged from the shadows themselves. His crucifix of pure silver hung from his neck, gleaming in the light from the candles.

Father Hopkins, dressed in a long black cossack and white collar, just like Father Severino, hesitated.

"Keys," Paul said again.

"This is not the usual protocol during an exorcism," Father Hopkins said. "Locking ourselves inside a basement."

"This is not a usual exorcism," Paul answered and glanced at Father Severino and his injured hand. "We all took an oath. We all vowed to fight this evil that has now willingly showed itself to us through Danny. We vowed to fight to the death in the name of God. We vowed never to flee."

Father Hopkins sighed and dug the keys out of his pocket. He plopped then down into Paul's palm while the others stared at him like the hope had drained out of them. Paul closed his fingers around the keys and shoved them down into his pants pocket.

"We need salt," Paul said.

Father Hopkins nodded at Robert who hurried over to the edge of the darkness where three fifty pound bags of salt were stacked up. He carried one of the bags back and laid it down on the floor. He dug a finger into the plastic of the bag and tore it open (none of them were allowed to have knives or any other weapons on them during the exorcism). He picked up the bag, struggling with it a little, and poured a thick and uneven line of salt around Danny's chair, creating a circle that was fifteen feet in diameter.

Paul crouched down beside his canvas bag and unzipped it. He found the large container of tiny iron fillings. He unscrewed the cap and poured out the iron fillings in a thinner line right inside the circle of salt.

Paul prayed the entire time.

He completed the circle where he had begun—right in front of Danny.

"Paul ..."

Paul looked up at Danny who stared at him with wide, terrified eyes.

"Please, Paul. Help me."

"I'm going to help you. God is going to drive this unclean spirit festering inside of your body and send it back to Hell."

"But ... wait. I'm not possessed. I feel fine. I'm okay. Just untie me and take me home."

"I can't do that."

"Please, Paul," Danny said and began to cry. Tears slipped down his cheeks which were suddenly shiny in the flickering candlelight. "Don't you love me? Why are you trying to hurt me?"

Paul stood up and stared at Danny. He held the half-empty canister of iron fillings in his hand. "I'm going to help you."

"Please ... you don't understand. I'm sick. I've got some kind of mental problems. Mom never told you about them. There aren't any demons inside of me. I just need some medicine. I haven't been taking my medicine ... that's why I've been seeing things."

Paul didn't say anything for a long moment as he stared at Danny.

"Call me Dad," Paul finally told Danny.

"What?" Danny spat out, suddenly angry. He struggled in his chair, pulling at his wrist cuffs. "What the fuck's wrong with you? Let me out of here!!"

"Call me Dad," Paul said again with patience. "Or father. Or Pops. I don't care. Tell me that you love me."

"Why should I do that?" Danny asked. "You've got me strapped down to a fucking chair in the basement!"

"Because if you were really Danny, you would be able to call me Dad. You would be able to say the word."

"Of course I'm Danny! You're the one who's sick! All of you! Child abusers! Torturers!!"

"Who am I speaking to?" Paul asked, his voice still steady and calm. "Name yourself, demon."

"Untie me right now, you sick fuck!" Danny struggled even harder against his bonds. The leather creaked, the wood of the chair popped in the silent basement.

"Name yourself, demon!" Paul yelled and took a step closer.

Father Hopkins hurried up beside Paul, his crucifix still gripped in his hand, a purple stole draped over his shoulders.

"Behold the cross of the Lord!" Father Hopkins yelled at Danny, thrusting his crucifix forward. "Depart, enemies! God, the father of Lord Jesus Christ, I invoke your Holy Name and suppliantly request you to give me strength against this and every other unclean spirit which is tormenting this creature of yours."

Danny stopped struggling in the chair. He became perfectly still, his face emotionless except for the twisted half-smile frozen on his face. His head was cocked at a crooked angle, and his eyes had turned completely black. His skin was pale and small plumes of frost drifted out of his nostrils with each breath.

"I think I've heard that one before," Danny growled at Father Hopkins through his twisted smile.

"Drive this demon out, Oh Lord!" Father Hopkins yelled.

Robert, Helen, and Father Severino crowded around the table with the two burning candles on it; all three of them were praying as they gripped their crucifixes and rosary beads. They trembled and shook as they watched Danny change.

†

Father Hopkins rushed inside the circle of salt and iron. He draped the end of his purple stole on Danny's neck and he touched the end of his two fingers of his other hand (blessed with holy water) on Danny's forehead.

Steam hissed up from Danny's skin as the priest touched him.

"I exorcise you, unclean spirit, in the name of Jesus Christ! I expel you from this boy in the name of ALMIGHTY GOD!!!"

Danny's perfectly black eyeballs shifted to Father Hopkins, but he hadn't moved his head or any muscle in his body yet.

"Careful, priest," Danny whispered in a guttural voice.

Father Hopkins kept his fingers on Danny's forehead as long as he could, but his fingers were beginning to burn.

"Leave this boy, foul demon!!"

Father Hopkins couldn't stand it anymore; he pulled his burning fingers away from Danny's forehead and he backed up two steps away from the side of the chair.

Danny still watched Father Hopkins with his coal-black eyes, the half-smile still frozen on his face. "Who is Molly?" he asked.

Father Hopkins froze.

CHAPTER THIRTY-EIGHT

"Yessss," Danny said. "Molly."

Father Hopkins backed away another step from Danny's chair, closer to the circle of salt and iron.

"Get out of the circle," Paul told Father Hopkins.

"Molly, your little dolly …" Danny sang out in his guttural voice, and it sounded like four voices all speaking at the same time.

Father Hopkins whispered prayers in Latin, his lips moving rapidly, his eyes nearly closed.

Danny repeated Father Hopkins' phrases in Latin, making a mockery of the words, creating an abomination of the prayers Father Hopkins recited. More whispers joined in with Danny's voice until it seemed like there were dozens of voices in the basement surrounding all of them.

"Father Hopkins …" Paul said as he took a step closer to him.

"Molly was a little dolly," Danny sang out in a suddenly high-pitched and screechy voice as the whispers continued from all around them like they were coming out of the shadows at the edges of the basement. "She was a girl you *wanted* so baaaddd …"

Father Hopkins kept his eyes squeezed shut, whispering his prayers faster and faster.

"Did you hurt your little dolly?" Danny asked as he contorted his head, his smile widening, his eyes impossibly dark, his face twisted and older now.

"LIES!!" Father Hopkins screamed as he finally opened his eyes and broke his string of prayers. He lashed out at Danny. "ALL FILTHY LIES!!"

Paul was prepared, already anticipating that this would happen. He was across the floor in a flash and inside the circle of salt and iron. He grabbed Father Hopkins and pulled the older priest out of the circle easily, guiding him away from Danny.

Father Hopkins seemed to come to his senses suddenly, his eyes clearing. He stared in horror at Paul. "What did I almost do?"

"You can't let them bait you," Paul said in a whisper. "They want you to hurt Danny and you can't do that. Danny's still inside there somewhere."

Paul walked Father Hopkins back to the table, joining the others.

"This is too dangerous," Robert stammered out. The other two looked at Paul as if they had made this decision to speak out together with Robert.

"This is an exorcism," Paul told them.

Robert shook his head and glanced at Helen. "No, this isn't a normal exorcism. We've been assistants at many exorcisms, but this ... this is ... we need help here."

"We only need God."

"Let us out of this basement," Robert begged. "I'll go and get us some help. More priests."

"Remember your oath," Paul growled. "We stay in this basement until these demons are gone from my son."

Paul pointed at some of the stacks of supplies in the gloomy reaches of the basement. "We have stores of food down here. Gallons and gallons of water. A bathroom area and cots to sleep on. We can survive down here for days. Weeks, even. We stay until my son is free from these creatures!"

Robert glanced again at Helen and Father Severino who barely nodded at him. He turned back to Paul; obviously he was the spokesman for their group. He was about to object, but then his words froze on his lips.

They all heard the creaking of the leather cuffs and straps that held Danny to the wooden chair. They looked at Danny who seemed to be stretching his arms and legs as much as the restraints would allow. His torso rose up off of the seat of the chair. His muscles stretched, his joints popped. The leather straps and cuffs pulled tight. The wood of the chair crackled and groaned.

"Oh, Lord God," Helen said. "He's going to get out of that chair."

Danny's body fell back down to the chair with a thump. His body suddenly went limp, his face frozen, the half-smile still on his face, his eyes seemingly depthless black holes. Clouds of frosty mist blew out of his nostrils, and he looked like a bull ready to charge.

Paul crouched down beside his black canvas bag. He pulled out the wooden black box with the names of God carved into it. And then he pulled out the roll of iron wire to wrap it in once the demon was trapped inside. He stood up with the box and wire in his hands. He marched towards Danny and entered the circle of salt and iron. He set the box down on the concrete floor just inside the circle and then he looked at his son.

"Danny!" Paul yelled. He pulled out his wallet from his back pocket and walked towards the chair. He opened his wallet to a photo of Danny he always carried with him. Danny was fifteen years old in the photo, and he was smiling. He needed Danny, who was trapped inside his body somewhere, to see this photo. He needed Danny to see himself and know who he still was.

"I know you're in there somewhere," Paul told Danny. "If you can hear me, come to the surface. Come out of the darkness. Fight your way out! Please, Danny!!"

No reaction from Danny—just the smile. "He's not here anymore," Danny told Paul.

"Danny, Listen to me," Paul said as he took a step closer, ignoring the voice of the demon. "Pull yourself out. Keep pulling. Keep coming towards my voice. You have to fight this!"

"You let them get murdered!" Danny said in his own voice which dripped with accusation. Danny's eyes were clear again, with tears threatening. His half-smile was gone and his lips trembled.

"Danny," Paul said.

"You let my mother and my sister get killed. You let me get possessed. What kind of exorcist are you? You don't have any power. You're not even a priest."

It wasn't Danny, Paul had to keep telling himself. No matter how much this voice sounded like Danny, it wasn't him talking. It wasn't his son—the demons were using his son like a puppet, manipulating his facial expressions, mimicking his voice.

"You're right," Paul told Danny, knowing he might be treading dangerous ground for a moment by opening up his guilt to these demons, giving them more ammo for their weapons. But if Danny was down there and he could still hear Paul's words, then he wanted him to know how sorry he was.

"I should've seen it," Paul said. "I should've been there. As soon as I realized these foul creatures might be after my family, I should've gotten on a plane at that moment and came to protect you and Lisa and Rachael."

"You failed," Danny said. "You failed me. You failed your daughter. You failed everybody. You don't deserve to preach to anyone. You should just kill yourself before you let anyone else get killed."

"Danny … I know you can hear me." Paul felt the tears streaming out of his eyes. "I'm sorry. So very sorry. I did fail, I know that. But I'm not going to let it happen again. I won't let these things take another child away from me … my only child now."

Danny began crying, his face twisted in misery. "I just want this to be over with."

Paul took another step closer to Danny as the tears flowed down his cheeks. He reached out, almost touching Danny. "I'm going to save you, Danny."

Danny nodded. "Yes. Please take these cuffs off."

Tears flowed from Paul's eyes and he shook his head slowly. "I can't release you yet," he whispered. "Not yet. Not until these demons are gone from your body."

Danny's face changed again. His skin grew pale and his eyes turned pure black again. The half-smile was back. A vein throbbed in his neck as he cocked his head violently to the side, cracking vertebrae in his neck like he was popping his knuckles.

"We'll take him from you, Paul," a dark symphony of voices sang out through Danny's mouth. "We'll take everyone in here from you. We'll take everyone else away that you touch. Your bloodline ends here!"

"I know you're afraid of my bloodline," Paul said. "And I know you're afraid of me. But now I know that you're afraid of Danny. You're afraid of the Gift he has, a Gift you haven't seen in a long, long time."

Danny chuckled.

"And you *should* be afraid," Paul said as he lifted the silver crucifix from his necklace and yanked the chain free. He laid the cross and necklace on Danny's chest and Danny thrashed, screaming the cries of a hundred voices.

Paul pulled the cross away from Danny and backed up to the edge of the circle of salt and iron where he had laid his black box down. He picked up the wooden box from the floor. He unwound the iron wire binding the box and opened it. The scent of filth drifted out from inside the box. Paul pulled out a piece of parchment and a piece of charcoal sharpened to a point from inside the box.

"I summon you, demon," Paul called out, holding the piece of charcoal and parchment in his hands, ready to write down the demon's name. "I conjure thee, you Terror By Night, and I am strengthened by the power of Almighty God. Appear and show thyself without delay. I summon thee by your real name given to thee by God to whom you owe obedience, and by the name of the Prince who rules over thee. I command thee in the name of Adonai, King of kings and Master and Lord. I command thee in the name of Yahweh, of El, of Elohim, of Eloah, of Elohai, of El Shaddai, of Tzevenot, and all the names of God."

Danny began convulsing, his black eyes rolling back up into his head, showing only the whites. He trembled in the chair, convulsing, thrashing against his bonds. He dry-heaved, his throat bulging as he vomited up hordes of black beetles and roaches caught in a thick slimy dark liquid.

He leaned his head forward, choking and gurgling as the liquid of squirming bugs flowed out of his mouth, down the front of his shirt and down into his lap. The mass of living bugs dripped down from the sides of the wood chair, pooling on the concrete floor underneath Danny.

And then the liquid moved out from under the chair, crawling away towards the darkness beyond Danny's chair.

Paul stared in horror at the mass of insects that moved as one. Then he looked up at Danny's face.

The twisted half-smile was back, his lips rimmed in the dark liquid he had just vomited up. "You want to know my name?"

Paul didn't answer; he waited inside the circle of salt and iron near Danny's chair with the piece of sharpened charcoal gripped in his fingers, the tip of the charcoal poised above the ancient piece of parchment. He was ready to write the name down.

"I am Astaroth!!" Danny screamed. "But there's nothing you can do now!!"

Before Paul could write the name down on the parchment, before he could even react, Danny pulled his arms up in a quick and violent motion, snapping the leather straps that his cuffs were attached to like they were strips of paper. He kicked his legs forward and snapped the leather straps attached to his ankle cuffs just as easily, breaking one of the chair legs apart in the process.

Danny was free.

That's when the light bulbs in the ceiling exploded and went out. That's when the candles blew out. That's when the basement was plunged into darkness.

CHAPTER THIRTY-NINE

Paul felt something strike his chest—Danny's fist—and he was thrown back in the darkness. He landed with a thud on the concrete floor, and he knew he was lying on the line of salt and iron, half inside the circle and half outside the circle. And he knew he had lost the parchment and the piece of charcoal. He groped around his body in the darkness and felt his fingers disrupting the lines of salt and iron.

Danny was free from his bonds, free from the chair.

Paul heard Danny moving around in the darkness. Getting closer.

The paper and charcoal. If he could just get the name written down and trap it inside the box … but he couldn't find the parchment; he couldn't even find the box.

And then he realized he didn't even have his silver crucifix anymore—he had lost it!

Paul groped in the darkness, his fingers frantically searching the concrete floor for the silver cross he had torn from the chain around his neck. It had been his father's crucifix, and his father's before him.

From somewhere behind him in the pitch-black darkness, Paul heard the commotion of Robert, Helen, and the two priests. Helen was still screaming and it sounded like one of them, Robert most likely, was running to the set of wooden steps that led up to the locked basement door, trying to get out. But the door was too strong; no one was going to get out of here.

The light bulbs had exploded. Paul knew they had extras among their store of supplies—the basement had been well-stocked before they got there—and light bulbs, candles, lighters, flashlights and batteries were as necessary as the food and water. It might take too long to find the light bulbs in the darkness, but they could at least get the candles re-lit.

The others were panicking, but Paul hoped that at least he could still count on Father Hopkins to stay strong.

"Father Hopkins!" Paul yelled. "Get the candles lit again!"

Father Hopkins didn't answer Paul.

A sound of sneakers scuffing on concrete sounded in front of Paul. Someone was near him and moving closer and closer by the second.

From behind him, Paul heard the flicking of a lighter. Father Hopkins had probably not answered Paul either because he didn't want to waste the energy and pour all of his efforts into getting light back into the basement, or he didn't want to reveal his position to Danny.

There was another sound very close to Paul in the darkness—it was the sound of metal scraping across the concrete floor, like Danny might be pushing the crucifix across the floor with the bottom of his sneaker.

"Looking for something?" a voice growled in the darkness.

Even though it had come from Danny's throat, it wasn't Danny. Paul had to keep reminding himself of that.

"In the name of Father God—" Paul began, but he never finished the words because he felt a kick to his chin that knocked him backwards flat on his back. For a moment he saw bright motes of light dancing in front of his eyes in the darkness. He felt consciousness wanting to slip away from him, but he held on to the pain in his jaw and the back of his head which had collided with the concrete floor after the kick from Danny. He was lucky he hadn't bitten his tongue off in mid-sentence, but a few of his bottom teeth felt loose and blood was dribbling out of his mouth.

Then Paul heard the unmistakable sound of Danny kicking the black wooden box across the room like he was kicking a soccer ball. The box landed somewhere in the distance, and Paul wasn't sure if Danny had broken the box apart or not.

A flickering of light appeared from behind Paul. Then more light.

Father Hopkins had the candles lit, and it was amazing how much light they put out in this area of the basement.

Paul sat up on the floor, his hands up and ready to defend himself from another kick from Danny.

But Danny wasn't there.

Paul hopped up to his feet. He stood in a crouch with his hands still up in front of him, ready to fend off punches and kicks. His eyes darted back and forth, searching as far as the flickering candlelight would allow.

"Danny," Paul called out. "Where'd you go?"

No answer from Danny.

Paul could see the empty wood chair in the darkness. He could make out the torn leather straps hanging off the arms and legs of the chair like pieces of broken strings.

And then a gleam on the floor caught his eye—his crucifix. He ran forward and plucked it up from the floor. It was bent and slightly mangled, but he gripped it in his hand anyway.

The dancing shadows created by the candlelight moved around the edges of the light, and each trembling shadow could be Danny.

Paul backed up towards the table where Father Hopkins waited. The father gripped his own crucifix in his hands. He looked scared, but still strong.

"Where are the others?"

"Father Severino found a flashlight," Father Hopkins whispered. "He's looking for more light."

"Robert and Helen?"

"I think they ran for the door."

"They don't have an extra key, do they? Please don't tell me that one of you kept an extra one."

"No. You have the only key."

Paul nodded, his eyes still constantly scanning the vast basement. "We can't let Danny leave this room no matter what happens."

Father Hopkins didn't bother answering; he just gave a curt nod.

"If Danny gets out, the demons may jump to others," Paul said. *Or to one of us*, Paul thought, but he didn't want to utter those words aloud. He was sure the others knew the dangers they faced down here.

A scraping noise sounded from somewhere deep in the darkness.

Father Severino hurried up to the table from the darkness with an armful of flashlights. He had scratches across his face that had welted up. A few of them dripped blood. His eyes were orbs of terror, but he wasn't running away yet.

"I found some flashlights," Father Severino whispered.

Paul was proud of the young priest's fortitude, but he didn't want to waste time with words right now. He took the offered flashlight and turned it on.

"What happened to you?" Paul asked Father Severino. "Did Danny do that to you?"

Father Severino handed a flashlight to Father Hopkins and then set the other two flashlights down on the table next to the candles. He looked at Paul and shook his head no. "It was someone else. A woman I'd never seen before."

Rachael.

"Did you see Danny anywhere?"

Father Severino shook his head no.

"I want you two to stay by this table for now," Paul told the two priests. "Keep together and keep praying. Don't stop praying. I need to find the black box and the parchment."

Paul left the priests and the candlelight. He walked towards the chair that Danny had been strapped to, and he clutched the slightly bent crucifix in one hand and the flashlight in his other, which lit his way through the darkness. He walked past the chair and then he moved towards the stacks of crates, boxes, and furniture in the gloomy distance.

There were hundreds of places to hide and Paul's mind flashed back to Julia Whittier's exorcism and seeing Father James holed up on top of the refrigerator like a spider waiting to jump out of its nest, his long arms and legs somehow impossibly folded up underneath him in the small space, his large pale face and black eyes staring out at him.

He could imagine Danny packed into some small hiding place, waiting to attack. Normally, Paul would be stronger than Danny, but not now that Danny was in this possessed state.

Paul ventured deeper into the basement, moving past stacks and stacks of boxes, crates, furniture, shelves. The flashlight only illuminated a small part of the basement, the rest was hidden in pitch-black darkness.

He heard a sloshing sound and shined the light down at his feet. He was walking in a few inches of murky water. He panned the flashlight from his feet towards the block wall of the basement in the distance and saw that the whole floor was covered in the dark water.

This isn't real, Paul kept whispering in his mind.

He saw something long and serpentine swimming quickly just underneath the surface of the water, and then it was gone.

"Paul …" a woman's voice whispered to him from the darkness, her voice gurgling with water.

And then he heard her footsteps sloshing through the thick and murky water, getting closer to him.

"Paul … why didn't you help me? Why weren't you there for me? Why weren't you there for Lisa?"

"I tried," Paul called out.

He had to stop himself. He couldn't let himself converse with the demons, he couldn't let them pull the strings of his guilt and use it against him.

He saw her.

Rachael stepped out from behind a stack of boxes. She wore a thin, white dress that clung to her wet and bloated body. Her flesh was bluish-gray. Her dark hair was matted to the sides of her bloated face. Her lips were so dark they looked like they had black lipstick on them. Some of her skin hung in loose folds from her elbows and knees, like her flesh was sloughing away from her bones.

Yet she walked … she stumbled towards him in the beam of light from his flashlight.

"I'm so sorry," Paul whispered.

"Come down here with me, Paul," Rachael said and lifted her arms up, reaching out for him like a lover. "Come down here under the water with me. I'm so lonely. I want you back. Lisa's down here, too. We can be a family again."

For a split second the thought struck him. It had always been his fantasy to reunite with Rachael and his children again. To be a family again.

Paul snapped out of it and brought his crucifix up in front of him like a shield. "Back away, demons!"

Rachael attacked. She moved with a sudden and blinding speed. She knocked him back into a stack of cardboard boxes that crumbled when he crashed down into them. He dropped both his crucifix and his flashlight down into the water.

He felt cold and wet hands grab his throat.

He looked up, expecting to see Rachael's bloated face inches away from his. He expected to smell the rotting lake-bottom smell coming from her open mouth.

But it was Danny's face in front of him, it was Danny's hands gripping his throat and squeezing the breath from him. Danny's face was twisted into a mask of rage and hatred.

"Die!!" Danny growled.

CHAPTER FORTY

Paul grabbed Danny's wrists and tried to break his grip on his throat. Paul could still breathe, but he could feel Danny's fingers tightening and his own strength beginning to fade.

"Danny," Paul croaked out. "Danny, I know you're still in there somewhere. I know you can hear me …"

Danny's grip tightened.

"Danny, fight it. Fight this evil. It's your only chance. Our only chance. You can control these demons. They're afraid of you."

Danny growled, and he mounted Paul. The crushed cardboard boxes underneath Paul flattened even more under their combined weight. Something sharp poked at the back of Paul's leg, but not enough to pierce his flesh yet.

"Danny … this isn't your fault … you didn't kill your mother and sister …"

Paul felt Danny's fingers tightening even more, and his words were choked off. He could barely utter any other words. But there was something he had to say, something he needed to say.

"Danny … I … I love you … son …"

†

Danny floated in a black void. It seemed like he had been in this darkness forever, but at the same time it only felt like mere moments. He saw a light far away in the distance, a flickering light. He realized he was underwater. He pulled himself towards the light and he was suddenly …

… in his mother's car again.

They drove down the dark road towards the lake down in the valley. Danny saw the blond man on the side of the road. He saw the man raise his hands and pretend he was gripping an imaginary steering wheel. And then the man gave it a sharp turn with his dark eyes on Danny and that half-smile pasted on his face.

His mother screamed.

She couldn't control the steering wheel, and she couldn't move her leg, her foot stomped down on the gas pedal.

Danny tried to help her, he tried to move her arms and legs, but they were rock-solid; they felt like stone.

"I can't move!" his mother screamed. "Danny, hold on!"

They crashed through the guardrail …

… down the embankment …

… crashed into the water. The nose of the car plunged down into darkness. The headlights barely cut through the muck.

Lisa's screams were cut short as she slammed into the back of his seat, knocked out immediately.

Mom was dazed as the car sank deeper into the water. Blood floated out from a gash in her forehead, mixing in with the dark water. The exploded airbag deflated and sank down to her lap.

Danny's airbag was now a wasted white thing floating in front of him. He pushed it away and looked down at his lap and the seatbelt still holding him in place. He struggled to hold his breath.

So cold.

So dark.

Danny fought with the seatbelt clasp. It was stuck.

The dashboard lights and headlights flickered, beginning to short out.

Danny held his breath, and his lungs were beginning to burn. The entire car was under the water now, sinking down to the muck-covered lake bottom, hitting it with a muffled thump.

He looked down at his seatbelt in the fading light, trying to unclick it.

And then he saw his mother's pale hand. She laid her hand over his, calming him down instantly.

She unclicked his seatbelt and freed him.

He looked at her. Her eyes and mouth were open. She was dead, but somehow she had helped him.

She had helped him.

The passenger window burst open and Danny turned to see the blond-haired man with the twisted smile reaching in for him. He touched Danny's arm, grabbing at him.

And then Danny blacked out. He felt a slimy creature slithering inside of his mind, swirling down into his soul ... taking it over.

And that was the last thing he remembered before he came back to consciousness in the back of the police car with Officer Booker standing over him.

Now Danny floated outside of his mother's car underneath the lake. He watched it in the darkness; the car was just a black mass at the bottom of the lake with its dimming headlights shining into the black void. But Danny knew he wasn't really there at the bottom of the lake ... he was just remembering it.

And he remembered now. He remembered everything.

He *hadn't* killed his mother and sister. The blond-haired man had done it—the demon inside the blond-haired man had done it. And then that demon had jumped from the blond-haired man and into him.

And now that same demon was inside of him now.

But it was more than one demon—it was a legion of demons led by one very powerful demon.

Danny felt himself floating away from the car, further into the darkness.

No ... he couldn't let himself float away again. He had to fight.

He swam in the water, dog-paddling frantically like he was fighting a strong underwater current.

He looked up into the darkness above him and saw a light. This light was much brighter than the headlights of the submerged car; this light was so warm as it shined down on him through the water.

This light was calling to him.

As Danny tried to swim up to the light, he felt something grab his ankle from the darkness below. He looked down and saw a monster from his worst nightmares, a constantly changing form of evil reaching a muscular arm out to grab him. One of the creature's clawed hands gripped his ankle. And swirling around this demon were other smaller demonic forms that circled it like small feeder fish around a shark.

You will stay down here with us, the demon growled. But Danny heard the creature's voice in his mind.

Danny tried to pull out of the thing's grasp, but it was too strong. He looked back up at the light and for some reason he knew the light was God. He wanted to go to God, to swim up to God.

"Help me, God," Danny whispered in the dark water and then he pulled his leg up as hard as he could in one quick jerk.

And he was free.

He swam and swam up through the water as hard as he could, knowing the demon and his minions would be swimming after him, rushing up through the water like a torpedo. The monstrous demon was reaching for him again, about to grab on to his ankle again, and this time Danny was sure that he wouldn't be able to tear his leg out of the thing's grasp.

But it was also just a memory. At the same time Danny knew that this monster, this demon, was already *inside* of him. It was already at home inside of Danny, like a rat tucked away in a burrow, like a parasite inside a host. But now everything felt different. He *knew* that the demon was there, and he knew that he could control this demon if he wanted to, hold on to it, use its power, and use its strength if he wanted to.

He stopped swimming in the dark water. He looked down below him into the depths, but the monsters were gone.

Because they're inside of you now ...

Danny heard a voice. It sounded both far away and so close at the same time.

"Danny ... it's not your fault ... you didn't kill your mother and sister ..."

It was Paul's voice.

"Danny ... I ... I love you ... son ..."

It was his father's voice.

Danny screamed in rage and in one explosive moment he was ...

†

... strangling Paul on top of a collapsed stack of cardboard boxes.

He pulled his hands away from his father's throat.

What was he doing to him?

Paul looked barely conscious, but he inhaled a wheezy breath as soon as Danny let him go.

"Dad," Danny whispered and he felt tears slipping from his eyes, dripping down his checks.

"You're back," Paul whispered.

Danny helped Paul up and Paul found his crucifix in the water. He clutched it and hugged Danny.

"Pray with me."

Danny closed his eyes as more tears squeezed out. "I didn't kill them, Dad. It wasn't me."

"I know you didn't. I always knew."

"It was Astaroth."

"I know," Paul answered.

Paul prayed. He felt more hands on him from the darkness. Father Hopkins. Father Severino. He heard two more people sloshing around in the water, bringing more flashlights—Robert and Helen. They laid their hands on them.

And then one of them forced the wooden black box into his hands.

With a shaking hand, and with the help of a flashlight beam from Father Severino, Paul scribbled the demon's name down on the parchment and folded it in half. He stuffed the parchment down into the box. But he didn't close it yet.

They all joined together, their voices separate whispers of words, but all becoming one voice.

A mist escaped from Danny's mouth and nostrils as he backed away from their group. He stood there in the shallow dark water, his body trembling as more mist began to rise up from him; it seemed to come out from every pore in his skin.

The misty fog collected above Danny, growing bigger and denser, swirling around and around. It felt like they were in the middle of a funnel cloud with the fog racing past them.

A moment later, hundreds of wailing demonic voices cried out from this spinning black mist.

Creatures formed from the mist as it swirled around them faster and faster. A face with a yawning mouth full of sharp teeth lunged out at them …

But they kept praying. Paul pulled Danny back into their group and held on to him. They kept their hands on each other and kept praying.

The monstrous face melted back into the fog. And then giant spider legs unfolded from the mist, reaching out to touch the six of them with poisonous tips, but then the legs folded back in on themselves and became part of the swirling mist again. The spinning wall of fog looked more and more like the inside walls of a silent tornado.

More creatures formed: snake-like creatures, insect-like creatures, demonic faces of rage, tormented faces. But then they all melted back into the fog.

Danny looked back at the tornado of fog all around them. These creatures were the same ones he had seen swirling around the main demon under the water. "I know who you are now, Astaroth!" he screamed.

Paul lifted up the box with its lid open. "We command you, Astaroth, into this prison in the name of Almighty God!!" Paul screamed, still clutching his son with his other hand, all of them still clutching each other.

The others joined in, shouting at the spinning fog and the forming and re-forming creatures that wailed in misery. They shouted the demon's name and commanded him and his minions back to Hell in the Almighty name of God.

The mist rose up into the air above them like a storm cloud, and then with one last desperate cacophony of wails and moans, all of the mist and creatures were sucked down into the black box.

Paul struggled to hold on to the box. He closed the lid and latched it shut.

"The wire!"

Paul felt the roll of wire thrust into his hands, but he wasn't sure who had given it to him, and he didn't care right now. He wrapped the wire around until all of it bound the box completely.

And then everything was silent.

They all opened their eyes and looked around. Their flashlights lit up their surroundings a little, enough to see that the fog and the dark water on the floor were gone.

Paul looked at Danny. "I'm so sorry."

"You saved me," Danny said.

"No," Paul answered him. "God saved you. And you saved yourself. You fought your way back."

CHAPTER FORTY-ONE

Hours later the snow-covered parking area in front of the garage was filled with vehicles: Paul's Ford Bronco, the two priests' sedan, Robert and Helen's Dodge Durango, two sheriffs' cruisers and an ambulance.

Danny had some bruising around his wrists and ankles that a paramedic looked over, but his injuries weren't too serious.

Paul had bruises around his neck from Danny's hands. He also had a slight concussion, a swollen jaw, a cut lip, and a few loose teeth.

Father Hopkins, Robert, and Helen were okay physically, but still shaken by the things they had seen.

Father Severino had the worst injuries out of all of them. His right fingers were blistered and he had some deep lacerations on his face. But he would recover over time and the scarring from the scratches wouldn't be too bad.

The police officers talked to Father Hopkins. They had been called there by the priest—it was protocol once an exorcism was over. The officers and paramedics were members of Father Hopkins' congregation and they were always advised in advance when an exorcism would be performed in the house.

Father Hopkins watched Danny and Paul as they talked quietly together. This had been the most extreme exorcism he had ever been involved with. He had seen things he would never be able to get out of his mind, images that would haunt his dreams, things he couldn't even believe. But in the end they had won, they had defeated the demons, and now a powerful demon was trapped inside that black, iron-wrapped box that Paul held on to.

Father Hopkins wondered what Paul was going to do with the box. Was he going to destroy it? Bury it? Save it?

He wasn't so sure he wanted to know the answer.

At least they were safe for now.

But Father Hopkins knew the demons would be back, infecting someone else, trying to worm their way into someone's life little by little. They never gave up.

And he wouldn't give up. And he was certain that Paul and his son would never give up, either.

†

Later, after wounds were treated and statements were recorded, the paramedics and the police left.

Paul and Danny packed their bags. Everyone else had their bags packed, all of them eager to leave this house locked up and alone until another venue for an extreme exorcism was needed.

They all gathered in front of the garage once their bags were stowed away in their vehicles. The house was dark in the early evening light—the night coming so quickly this time of year. None of them wanted to drag out the good-byes longer than necessary, but they all felt like they needed some closure.

There were hugs and handshakes all around, there were good wishes given, promises to stay in touch and to keep up the Good Fight.

"Thank you for all of your help," Paul told them as he held his arm around Danny's shoulders.

They nodded, some feeling guilty that they hadn't helped as much as they could have, but no one was made to feel that way by Paul.

They left the house.

CHAPTER FORTY-TWO

Paul and Danny drove the highway back towards Boston under the cover of darkness.

Danny had slept a little on the way, but now he was awake, watching the front of the Bronco eat up the road under the glare of its headlights. He didn't know what to feel right now. He could remember bits of pieces of the ordeal, but not everything. He was sure he would ask his dad about everything that had happened, but maybe not right away. Maybe not for a while.

He felt terrible, still aching from the loss of his mother and sister. But he also felt better because he knew the truth now. He remembered the accident, and it hadn't been his fault. And he knew it hadn't been his mother and sister who had been haunting him. They couldn't haunt him because they were in a better place now. They were with God.

Danny didn't know how the demons had entered him so easily from the blond-haired man. But Paul had explained a little of it, telling Danny that somehow he had pulled the demon into his own body without being aware of it, trapping the demon and his minions inside of him, holding them there.

"Some members of our family line have been blessed with the Gifts of the Spirit," Paul told Danny as he drove. "These gifts have been passed down from father to child through the centuries. I've been able to summon demons, able to draw them into the wooden boxes. But you, you can draw the demons into yourself and hold them there and use their power. But it's so important for your faith to be strong so that the demon doesn't overtake you."

"Can you do what I can do?" Danny asked Paul. "Can you keep the demons inside your body and control them?"

"No," he answered simply. "I've never known anyone who could do what you can do. There have been rumors of it throughout history …"

Paul let his words trail off.

"What about the black box?" Danny asked. "What are you going to do with it? Destroy it?"

"I'll store it for a while. Keep them trapped."

"Why not destroy it?"

"Because they will just get back out and start over again."

"Then bury it."

"Someone might find it in the future." Paul paused for a moment. "Besides, we might need the demons again. If you needed one to enter you again … if you needed their powers and strength …"

"You mean I could just let them back inside me and use their powers? What? Like a superhero or something?"

Paul smiled. "Sort of. But you would do that only if you needed to, and only after you've completed your training and you were a lot stronger. Only after your faith was stronger."

Danny didn't say anything, and they were quiet for a long moment as Paul drove.

"They're afraid of us," Paul finally told Danny. "They've always been afraid of us. And they will never stop trying to attack us and anyone close to us."

"How far does our family line go back?" Danny asked as he watched the road.

"A long way."

Danny had an idea of how far it went back to. He had a quick vision of knights in front of a temple in the desert. But he didn't say anything.

"The dark forces will never stop," Paul warned Danny again. "They'll keep on trying over and over again to attack anyone you love, anyone you care about, anyone you know."

"But we can stop them, can't we?"

"With God we can," Paul said and nodded.

Danny was silent for a long moment as they drove down the highway. The illuminated skyscrapers of Boston were just visible on the dark horizon.

"I want to help you with your investigations," Danny finally said. "I want to begin training as an apprentice. For real, this time."

Paul looked at him, studying him for a moment before returning his eyes to the road.

"You're sure about that?" Paul asked. "God gave us free will, and it's always our choice."

"Yes, I'm sure," Danny answered. "I want to learn."

And Paul could tell that Danny was certain. And he was proud of his son.

"We'll start training immediately," Paul told Danny. "I know it won't be long before Father McFadden has an assignment for us."

AUTHOR'S NOTE

Thank you so much for purchasing my book, and I hope you enjoyed it. I would really appreciate any feedback you might have. Please feel free to leave a review on Amazon and Goodreads. I read all reviews, and they are more helpful to me and other readers than you might realize.

I have novels that I'm writing at this moment and they should be available very soon. They include: The Superhuman Gene and Devil's Island. I hope you'll keep an eye out for them.

I would love to hear from you. You can contact me at marklukensbooks@yahoo.com You can also reach out to me on Facebook at MarkLukensBooks. And on Twitter @marklukensbooks. My website is www.marklukensbooks.com

Thanks again for reading my book!

ABOUT THE AUTHOR

Mark Lukens has been writing since the second grade when his teacher called his parents in for a conference because the ghost story he'd written had her a little concerned.

Since that time he has had several stories published in magazines. He has also had four screenplays optioned by producers in Hollywood, with one screenplay in development to be a feature film. He is the author of Ancient Enemy, Descendants of Magic, The Summoning, Night Terrors, Devil's Island, Sightings, The Exorcist's Apprentice, The Changing Stone: Book One, What Lies Below, Devil's Island, Ghost Town: a novella, and A Dark Collection: 12 Scary Stories, most of which are available on Amazon/Kindle. He is also a proud member of The Horror Writers Association.

He grew up in Daytona Beach, Florida. But after many travels and adventures, he settled back down in Florida, near Tampa, where he lives with his wonderful wife and son, and a stray cat they adopted.

Please feel free to comment or ask any questions at MarkLukensBooks@yahoo.com and you can find Mark on Facebook at MarkLukensBooks and on Twitter @marklukensbooks, and on his website: MarkLukensBooks.com
He would love to hear from you!!

PLEASE FEEL FREE TO CHECK OUT ANCIENT ENEMY

Ancient Enemy – it's been asleep for centuries and now it's awake. It wants things … and you have to give it what it wants …

www.amazon.com/dp/B00FD4SP8M

AND IF YOU LIKE SHORT STORIES …

… you might like A Dark Collection of twelve horror stories, one for each month of the year.

www.amazon.com/dp/B00JENAGLC

And if you want a supernatural mystery to solve … you could try my book THE SUMMONING.

www.amazon.com/dp/B00HNEOHKU

IF YOU'RE IN THE MOOD FOR A PARANORMAL THRILLER …

… you might want to check out NIGHT TERRORS.

www.amazon.com/dp/B00M66IU3U

AND IF YOU LIKE A SCIENCE FICTION/HORROR BLEND …

… then SIGHTINGS might be for you.

www.amazon.com/dp/B00VAI31KW